Frie...
The Opposite Sex . . .

"IS A BOOK OF VALUE. . . . Davidson has made us care deeply about her characters. . . . I have yet to read a writer who better captures . . . the singles dilemma."

—*Chicago Sun-Times*

"Davidson . . . is a fine observer and convincing writer whose prose has its own momentum. . . ."

—*People*

"She [Davidson] is the liveliest historian of her generation."

—Malcolm Cowley

"AN ENTERTAINING, RELEVANT READ . . . with believable characters and situations and plenty of witty observations on the singles world."

—*Publishers Weekly*

"Filled with wonderfully wry touches. . . . A love story . . . exquisitely attuned to the human condition as we experience it in the 1980's."

—*Palm Beach Life*

Books by Sara Davidson

Friends of the Opposite Sex
Loose Change
Real Property

Published by POCKET BOOKS / WASHINGTON SQUARE PRESS

Friends Of The Opposite Sex

Sara Davidson

PUBLISHED BY POCKET BOOKS NEW YORK

Distributed in Canada by PaperJacks Ltd., a Licensee
of the trademarks of Simon & Schuster, Inc.

Grateful acknowledgment is made for permission to quote from the following material:

The Condor Passes, by Shirley Ann Grau, Copyright © 1971 by Shirley Ann Grau. Reprinted by permission of Alfred A. Knopf, Inc.
''One—Two—Three,'' by Hannah Senesh. Reprinted by permission of Schocken Books Inc. from *Hannah Senesh: Her Life and Diary*, Copyright © 1966 by Hakibbutz Hameuchad Publishing House Ltd., English edition copyright © 1971 by Nigel Marsh, Introduction copyright © 1972 by Schocken Books Inc.

POCKET BOOKS, a division of Simon & Schuster, Inc.
1230 Avenue of the Americas, New York, N.Y. 10020
In Canada distributed by PaperJacks Ltd.,
330 Steelcase Road, Markham, Ontario

FOR GLEN
AND FOR ANDREW

Contents

Acknowledgments

I want to thank Rob Cohen, who read and discussed the manuscript with me and saw me through every roadblock. Without his counsel, this book might not have come to be.

I'm also grateful to Kate Medina for her encouragement and faith.

Prologue
April 1979

Shortly after sunrise, a Cessna 402 was flying to Santa Katarina in the Sinai Mountains. The mountains were most impressive at this hour, rising from the desert floor, red and stark, empty and silent in the pale gold sky. The mountains contained no roads, and appeared to contain no trees, but in a high valley, hidden between two ridges, was an oasis toward which the Cessna 402 was beating.

"You see," said Uzi, the pilot, "it's Garden of Eden."

The plane made a low pass over the valley, offering a sudden view of palm trees and pools. The plane rolled up over the ridge, circled and flew back down.

"Aren't we awfully low?" Lucy said. She was sitting in front, trying to clear her ears from the drop in altitude.

"No worries." Uzi circled and made another low pass.

Joe, the other passenger, seated behind Lucy, leaned toward the window. They were coming to the cliff. Uzi advanced the throttles and raised the nose of the plane but as they were about to cross the ridge, an air current took hold of them like a hand and pushed them down. They cleared the ridge, but the plane began to shake all at once. Every surface was buzzing and vibrating—dashboard, seats, windows.

3

Lucy's hands flew out, trying to grab hold of something. "What's happening!"

"Propeller strike," Uzi shouted. "It's okay." He reduced the power and the vibrating lessened. "I think I can make it to Santa Katarina."

"What do you mean you think!" Joe said.

Uzi shut down the right engine. Lucy saw the propeller blades slow down and stop in air. Sweat ran down the center of her chest. It was 120 degrees.

"Shit."

"What!" Lucy said.

"Losing oil."

No, it can't be. She saw a chunk of the propeller blade break off.

Uzi cupped his mouth so the sound would be directed. "I'm going to take _her_ down in the wadi. I can land in the sand easy, no problems. I want you to lean forward, hold your ankles and put your head in your lap. Stay like that until the plane stops. Try to relax."

No.

Joe was saying in her ear, "Get out of that seat and come in back."

The ground was slanting up fast; there were cracks in the earth, boulders.

Bad, it's going to be bad. No, there has to be a way out!

"Get in back, away from the windshield. Undo your seat belt," Joe yelled.

Lucy's fingers fluttered helplessly. She began reciting the _Shema._

Joe stood up, leaned over and struggled with her belt.

"Stay put," Uzi cried, "don't move around."

Joe was pulling Lucy—yanking her—between the front seats into the back, buckling her in. "Now lean forward." Why? She had read somewhere about the crouch position. Joe pushed her head down.

Shema Yisrael Adonai Elohenu . . .

4

The plane hit the sand, knocking the wind out of her. The plane bounced again and again—like a series of belly flops from a high board. She bit through her tongue and blood ran out her mouth.

She was hurled sideways, her head smacked against the cabin as the plane skidded wildly over the rocks. There was the sound of metal crunching, glass breaking. Her leg was caught, it was burning, twisting, and her mouth, her eyes . . . The plane rammed into something hard and stopped.

This has happened. She could not go back and start again, play it over, make it come out better. *This has happened.* When she opened her eyes, she saw double. Joe was moaning but no sound came from the front. She leaned forward . . . she screamed. Uzi's neck had been snapped, his head was hanging slack like the head of a puppet. She smelled gas; straining ahead, she saw a fire sputtering in the engine.

She pushed open the left rear door. She tugged at Joe's arm, but he would not move. "Joe, we have to get out!" She was dizzy, everything was swirling. She slapped his face, tried to lift him but he was too heavy. Black smoke seeped into the cabin and at last, with her help, Joe rose and stumbled out the door.

Holding each other, the two survivors struggled toward a cliff at the side of the wadi. A large rock threw shadows on the sand, and as they reached it and sank down, the plane went up in a ball of fire.

Hours passed; the temperature rose to 140. Joe lost consciousness and lay sprawled on his back. High above, an Israeli jet fighter flew over, breaking the sound barrier, disappearing with a trail of white vapor. No, don't hope. *I gambled on what mattered most.* She laughed ruefully. No one will come. There are no telephones at Santa Katarina. When we don't show up, they'll assume we've changed our plans. They'll think we're in Jerusalem and people in Jerusalem will think we're in Santa Katarina.

We have to walk out. She began to shiver and perspire at the same time. Later, when it's cooler. Her lips and tongue were parched and cracking. She was feverish, she wanted to sleep, but she thought, if I do, I won't get up. Dear Lord, have you brought me all this way just to stop? Why, why, was I allowed to search so long, to come so near?

The blurring in her eye was becoming worse.

All the back and forth with Joe . . .

Her head drooped over her knees and she went out.

I The Beach

June 1977

1

It was like falling through a chute: they sped down and around past darkened houses and moist night lawns with sprinklers running until they came out on the Pacific Coast Highway, the beach. The sand was gray and damp, the parking lots closed up. Joe shifted gears impatiently when they hit the light at Sunset Boulevard. There was tension in the car, the accelerating tension of sexual possibility, and the sweet scent of Thai grass. Lucy guided him along the foggy streets that led to her house. He put on the hand brake, opened the door of the Porsche and helped her out.

They had the house to themselves. Pam was staying with Henry and would not be back until Sunday. Lucy poured amaretto into glasses and told Joe to pick out an album. She heard familiar chords, then Mick Jagger. "You can't always get what you want."

Wonderful party, Lucy thought. Her pockets were crammed with phone numbers written on scraps of paper and matchbook covers. Elated at the appearance of so many prospects after a dry few months, she slipped out of her shoes and sat down on the rug, facing Joe.

They knew little about each other. He was from Los Angeles, she from New York. Both had made films for television and had been married.

"How long have you been separated?" Joe asked.

"Two years."

"What was he like?"

"Want to see a picture?"

"Sure." He lit another joint.

She went into her study and brought back a photo she had always liked. Her former husband's face was split by shadow, so that the right half appeared sunlit and ingenuous, the left half withdrawn and dark.

Joe studied it, then frowned. "I don't like him. I'm sorry."

Lucy took the picture back. "No one feels neutral about Jerry."

"How long were you married?"

"Seven years. And you?"

He stretched his arms over his head. "Ten months. I'm afraid it wasn't serious."

"What's the longest you've been with someone?"

"Few years." He smiled, dimples coming to his cheeks. He was tall, athletic, with dark blond hair and a beard that, together with his close-set eyes, gave his face a soulful cast. "Can I help it if all the women in America are screwed up?"

"Funny, they only say wonderful things about you."

He laughed, as if to say, your point. They talked some more and listened to music and it was 3 A.M.

"Want to go upstairs?" Lucy said.

He shook his head no.

Pity.

"Not yet."

"Hmm?"

In a casual tone, Joe said, "I think we should prolong this through the evening. I'm going to arouse you one small step at a time."

"What are you talking about."

He moved closer, picking up the amaretto bottle. "The rest of the evening is in my hands. You don't have to do anything. You're not going to do anything."

Something prickled in her.

"I know it won't be easy, you're the kind of woman who likes taking charge." He tilted his chin, as if to say, come on, I dare you.

Who do you think you are . . .

"I bet if you're with four people trying to decide on a restaurant, you can never just sit back and go along."

"That's true."

He set down his drink, moved toward her and kissed her. She was aroused, he was aroused, she thought they were going to lie right back on the floor but he broke away, leaving her beached and breathless.

"I don't like this," she said.

"Too bad." He smiled.

She threw a shoe at him. She could feel that crazy, instant intimacy—the almost palpable sense of closeness—induced by the Thai grass. He turned over the record. "I wish you had some David Bowie."

"David Bowie. Is he the one who pretends to shoot himself on stage?"

"Not lately. He's the only guy around still saying something. Course, the reason I like the Stones is that they don't want to say anything, except fuck me."

"They've had some good lyrics."

"It's all fuck me. Fifteen years of Rolling Stones music is one lyric."

" 'Jumping Jack Flash.' "

"I can shake it good, fuck me."

" 'Brown Sugar,' no, that's obvious."

"Fuck me black woman."

" 'Street Fighting Man.' That was about something."

"Yeah, I'm a street fighting man. When I get home from the riot, fuck me."

Lucy laughed. There had to be one. "What about that song . . . oh, what was it called. It was on 'Between the Buttons.' "

" 'Ruby Tuesday'?"

"No, that's not on 'Between the Buttons.' "

"Sure it is."

"No it's not."

"You're wrong."

"I have the album, I'm positive."

"So am I."

"What do you want to bet?"

"Let's make it juicy."

"Okay."

She lay down on her back to think. He slid over, lifted her blouse and moved his lips slowly across the smooth, taut hollow of her stomach. She sighed, and reached up to run her hand along his back, but he took the hand off and set it on the floor.

"I can't touch you?"

"Nope. You can't do anything." He went to the record cabinet to look for "Between the Buttons."

"This is stupid."

"You'll come around."

"What shall we bet?" Lucy said. His arrogance was galling.

"Dinner at the restaurant of one's choice."

"In Paris."

"It's not here," Joe said.

"Might be upstairs."

He got to his feet, she started up after him but he turned, pointing at her. "Sit down." She did. He walked behind her, lifted the long dark hair and kissed the nape of her neck. "Nice try."

"I'm not going to throw this."

12

He began unbuttoning her blouse. "You hold still."

She did.

He set her blouse on a table and sat about six feet from her. "You look better with your clothes off."

"You're blowing this, you know. When you want to, I'll have cooled."

"I'm not worried." He sipped his drink. He was wearing a blue shirt with the cuffs rolled up, and she could not help staring at his arms. They were tan, smooth, with muscles rippling under the skin and a covering of fine blond hair. She felt a shock of desire so strong it was like pain.

"Lucy, it's an act of almost superhuman control for me not to jump on you right now, but I'm not going to. Because delaying it will make the pleasure even more intense."

"No!" She twisted in frustration. "You're playing with me and I don't like it."

"I'm not."

"Yes you are and I want you to stop."

He crawled across the floor and put his face up to hers. "Can you tell me exactly what you want me to stop?"

She considered how to phrase it.

"No."

They laughed. Joe rolled with her to the floor, kissing her again and again in the crook of her bare neck, but then he stopped himself.

"Let's decide what the bet will be," he said, returning to his chair.

"The loser has to be the other's slave. See how you like it."

"For how long?"

"Twenty-four hours."

"Okay, if you want to prolong the agony. Where's the album?" He started for the stairs.

"Not up there."

He turned.

"In the bookcase. Bottom shelf."

13

When Joe found the album, a smile came to his face.

"I'm right, aren't I," she said.

He slid the record out of the jacket, cued it on the turntable and paused. "Still want that bet? I'm willing to let you off now, because I'm such a nice guy."

He was bluffing. "Play it."

Lucy's hands flew in the air, she was certain she had won, but at the first chord she was slumped in defeat. "Good-bye, Ruby Tuesday." How could this be? She had believed with all her soul that she was right, and she wasn't. She walked to the window.

"Here are the terms. Tonight doesn't count. You'll be my slave on any day I choose."

"You really want to humiliate me, don't you."

He came up, took her by the shoulders with a gentleness that surprised her and kissed her, a kiss like those she had dreamed of at thirteen: walking down a dappled lane in a faraway place with a strange new boy. When Joe pulled away, she burst into tears. "I'm scared."

She saw a look of alarm. He walked closer and when his face was next to hers, the pouting, hurt look in her eyes turned to merriment. He grabbed her. "You're fantastic." Then he put one arm under her legs, the other under her arms and, hoisting her sideways, headed for the stairs.

For the next several hours, she was not permitted to move a hand, she could not tell him where or when to touch her but he knew.

She was not fighting anymore, she was nearly out of her mind with pleasure. It was every fantasy she had ever daydreamed. Foreplay that had no end. Lovemaking that had no objective but to tantalize and please. This was going to last all night—nights and nights and nights—and it was all being done *to* her.

She was on her back and Joe was above her, balanced on his arms. "I want you to be my slave now. Tell me I'm better than everyone."

"You think you're better than me?"

"I'm not saying that. Tell me I'm better than everyone."

"You ain't better than me."

He slid out. "You're my slave, you have to." He began to stroke her with his finger.

"I can't say something I don't . . ."

"Is that right?"

". . . believe, and have it be . . . credible."

She loved what he was doing, she loved him, she wanted it to last forever. The finger stopped.

Looking at him earnestly, she said, "You're better than *everyone.*"

The finger resumed. "Big deal." He burst out laughing. He slid down between her legs, homing in with the same instinctive accuracy he had shown all night. She could feel the climax now, swishing its tail like a fish. He was pulling it up and out of her. Up and up it came, big, this fish was going to set records, they were going to weigh it, they would pose beside it for photographs. You could see its powerful form rising up through the water, navy blue.

"Let me now, Joe," she said, "please, let me . . ."

It broke the surface, shooting into the air with spray.

She was jelly, she could not stop laughing. He plunged into her as she lay, arms flopped above her head. "Move a little," he said. "Okay, stop now." She lay still, the way she had always, secretly, wanted to lie. It felt good, oh it was good like this, she loved lying back passively with her arms flung up, but as he went on, she began to move, involuntarily at first. Her small rump began to bounce, then she was matching his movements, pulling on him, squeezing.

"Oh sweetheart."

"Give it to me . . ."

"Yes."

"Now."

"So fucking good!"

* * *

It was seven in the morning. They had been making love for almost four hours. She had not kissed him or touched him with her hands and he had been hard the entire time.

"Have you done this before?" she said.

"No."

They stared at each other, awed and a little scared, until the room became a bubble of heightened feeling and the world outside—the people in their apartments, sleeping, eating corn flakes, turning on the television—seemed to exist on another plane that was shallow and dull.

They tried to sleep, but kept thinking of things they wanted to say and arousing each other unwittingly as they tossed.

"We've got to sleep," Joe said. "I wish I had a Valium."

She went to the bathroom and returned with two yellow pills.

Joe swallowed his, took a swig from the amaretto bottle and kissed her, sweetness on his lips.

2

"Edna."

Lucy heard it as if from the bottom of a swimming pool.

"Edna, the beer."

Her mind tried to shake itself out. Everything was rippling.

"Don't forget the beer!"

"Shaddddup!"

Her eyes blinked open and turned, by reflex, to the digital clock: 11:53. Night? Black on the dial meant night and it was not black, it must be day. She lay still and tried to fix things. She was at home, in her bedroom, on Sea Shell Avenue. Edna and Gino were at it next door, and she could hear the muffled thwacks of a volleyball game on the beach at the end of the lane.

She worked back: Saturday night, the party, Joe . . . she tensed. He was behind her, but she did not feel his waking presence yet.

Carefully, she lifted herself and turned to look at him in daylight. He was curled on his side away from her, feet sticking outside the quilt. He had large feet. She studied the back of his head. She could see through the hair to the scalp:

17

pink. She shivered. There was a silver chain around his neck she had not noticed the night before. What was on it? He twitched, jackknifing his legs. She held her breath. He seemed to drop back asleep. Good.

She sat up quietly, stepped out of bed and went to the closet. Slipping on a white terry-cloth robe, she tiptoed out of the room and down the stairs.

She found Pam standing in the middle of the living room, holding Joe's jacket. "Who is he?" Pam whispered. She was wearing shorts and a halter and, with her bare, lightly suntanned limbs, reminded Lucy of girls on the cover of *American Girl,* a magazine Lucy had read with devotion while growing up. The girls on the cover wore faded jeans and large straw hats, sat on levees and dangled their legs while butterflies swarmed in the air.

Pam had long, wheat-colored hair, hazel eyes and a mouth that expressed innocence and romantic longing. She also had the body *Playboy* looks for: the body of a girl who developed late, acquiring oversized breasts that remain high and firm into her twenties.

"His name is Joe Sachs."

"I checked out his car," Pam said. "I liked it. I was about to go through his wallet." She slipped her hand inside the pocket of the jacket.

"Pam, you shouldn't." Lucy looked at the stairs, then walked over and took it from her. "Let me."

Pam laughed. "Where did you meet him?"

"A party."

"Whose?"

"A guy at CBS." Lucy counted the money in the wallet. Forty-seven dollars. Three credit cards.

"I thought you were working late."

"I quit at ten. I probably shouldn't have, I'm way behind and the deadline is next Friday."

"You'll make it." Pam was squinting at the driver's license. "Six-two, a hundred and ninety pounds."

Lucy looked at the photograph. "He has a beard now."

"What does he do?"

"Makes documentaries. He did that special, *Heroes of the Airwaves.*"

"That was excellent."

"I know."

Whispering, huddled over the wallet, they filed through a stack of membership cards:

> Santa Monica Athletic Club
> Los Angeles County Museum
> Academy of Television Arts and Sciences
> N.A.U.I. Licensed Scuba Diver

Lucy held up the next card: "Member, Beverly Hills Tanning Salon."

"What's that?" Pam said.

"One of those places where you put on goggles and lie naked under sunlamps." She shook her head. "That's suspicious."

"Yeah, he might have skin cancer."

Laughing softly, Lucy slid the cards back in the wallet. "Where's Henry?"

"Out getting lox and bagels."

"How're you doing?"

Pam shrugged.

"What's the latest?"

Pam sighed. "Luke called me at Henry's last night, and now both of them are mad at me." Lucy sighed in sympathy. The phone rang. "Luke," Pam said. She answered the phone and, nodding at Lucy, carried it into her bedroom at the back of the house.

* * *

Lucy walked outside to pick up the newspaper. To her surprise, the garden was awash in sunlight. The beach had been socked in with fog for weeks, fog so heavy and oppressive that the horizon had disappeared and there had been a continuous blanket of gray from sand to sea to sky. She had not seen blue above, green on the earth, for a month, but on this Sunday, the gray was breaking up like ice on a thawing lake. She looked down the lane toward the oceanfront and saw people in bathing suits floating by on bicycles and roller skates. Across the lane, two men of about twenty were setting up their stereo on the balcony. One yelled down to Lucy, telling her they were planning a big party for the fourth of July and of course you two ladies are invited.

Lucy waved. She and Pam were having a party on the fourth of July, and now there would be a third-rate bar band across the street and drunken kids crashing into the wrong house. She turned to go back inside. She noticed a gardenia blossom on the bush by the fence, bent down to pick it and carried it upstairs.

Joe was awake, sitting on the edge of the bed, wearing a pair of maroon briefs. His eyes were puffy. "Good morning," he said, and they began speaking with an artificial politeness.

"How'd you sleep?"

"All right, how about you?"

"The sun's out," Lucy said.

"Good, now I don't have to kill myself."

Lucy laughed. "When the sun disappears here, people go insane."

"With good cause."

"They get depressed, they commit more crimes. After a week, it's dangerous to drive on the freeway . . ."

"Come here," he said. She walked toward him and set the gardenia on the nightstand. He pulled her to the bed, un-

20

loosening her robe as he did. She wrapped her hands around his neck and felt his chest against hers.

"Gardenias are my favorite flower," he said.

"I know."

"Are you casting a spell?" He slipped the robe off and rolled over with her and almost before she knew it, he was inside her. "Sweetheart," he murmured into her shoulder.

When they came downstairs, Henry had returned and was lying on the sofa, reading the Sunday New York *Times*. Henry glanced at Joe, and did a double take.

"Haven't I seen you at the club?"

"Think so," Joe said. "You play racquetball?"

"Right."

Joe seemed ill at ease, wearing his clothes from the night before. Henry was wearing a bathing suit. And Pam—Lucy had to bite her lips not to laugh. Pam had changed into a sloppy shirt and baggy pants. She had pulled her hair into two ponytails and removed her contact lenses and put on thick gray glasses.

The four of them sat down at the oak table and began passing platters of bagels, lox, cream cheese, scrambled eggs. Joe asked if there was coffee. Lucy stood up to fix it. "Nobody here drinks coffee?"

"It makes me nervous," Lucy said.

"I don't like the taste," Pam said.

Joe was watching Lucy. "Where were your grandparents from? Hungary?"

"Romania."

"I knew it."

"Oh?"

"A lot of Romanian Jews have dark hair and blue eyes. You come from Gypsies, people who danced around wagons. You don't need coffee. I come from Russian peasants. They were more stolid, trudging behind the plow."

"Me too," Henry said. He beat a rhythm on the table with his fist. "My grandfather was a grain miller in Russia."

"My great-grandparents were peasants," Pam said.

"In Scotland," Henry said, "that's a different kind of peasant."

"Who let her in?" Joe said.

"Be nice to her, we love her," Lucy said.

Pam sat up, feigning protest. "I'm surrounded by Jews. What hope is there for me? I come from Lovington, Illinois. Have you ever even heard of it?"

"Can't say that I have," Joe said.

"In Lovington, the biggest 'cultural event' is the corn pageant at the high school. Jews have Mozart played to them in their cradles. Jews make lists. At Henry's house, all the plants get watered because they're on the list. It doesn't matter whether he feels like it, if the thing is on the list, it *gets done.*"

"Something wrong with that?" Henry said.

"It's just that sometimes, you wish that . . ."

"Wish what, sweetie?" The word "sweetie" was icy.

She looked at her plate.

Lucy told them about the party being planned across the street. "Maybe we should cancel ours."

"No, we can't do that," Pam said. She turned to Joe. "Are you coming?"

"I don't know."

"You've got to come," Pam said. "The fourth of July is the best night of the year here. People from all over bring their fireworks to the beach, and there are shows on the Venice and Santa Monica piers."

"I may be going to San Francisco."

Lucy looked at her watch. "My God, it's two o'clock. I should get in to work."

The conversation moved on, Lucy smiled, and ate, and

talked, but she was less and less present, and as soon as the plates were cleared, she said to Joe, "Let me walk you to your car."

In the sunlight, he looked paler and was sweating through his long-sleeved shirt. Lucy was barefoot, trying to avoid stepping on glass.

"I'll give you a call," Joe said.

"Okay." She turned.

"Lucy?"

"Yes?"

"What's the best way out of here?"

She told him. He thanked her, opened the door of the Porsche and, by the time she was in the gate, he had pulled away.

Lucy stood with her back against the gate. What had happened? It was like the fable about the sun and the moon, the brother and sister who unite in the darkness and, when the light comes, flee from each other. She heard a burglar alarm going off nearby.

"You should see the way he was looking at you," Pam said, walking out of the house.

"What do you mean?"

"Every time you said something, he was so . . . taken. He barely listened to anyone else. When the two of you walked out, I told Henry, 'Something special just happened. This one's going to be around.' "

"Come on, Pam," Lucy said with a laugh. "He's the kind of guy who was popular in high school. He has a brother who's a year older. They used to go surfing all weekend and take out cheerleaders."

"Please, Lucy, go easy on this one."

Lucy hooked her arm through Pam's as they walked inside. "You can undo the ponytails now. I appreciate that, by the way."

Pam nodded. "I love you."

"Besides," Lucy said, "he's thirty-three and the longest he's been with someone was ten months. He must have problems."

Pam looked defeated. "Henry wants to go to the beach. Just leave all the dishes . . ."

"Don't worry."

Lucy put on Jimmy Buffet, and while he sang about wasting away in Margaritaville, she set about restoring order. She felt better with every ashtray emptied, every record put back in its jacket. After straightening the kitchen, she went upstairs, gathered glasses, put away clothes and was making the bed when Joe called.

He said he had left his belt. Lucy had not seen a belt, but as they talked, she caught sight of a buckle under the bed. Did he need it?

"No, I'll pick it up later. Listen, did I say something . . . you seemed unhappy when I left."

"No."

He waited.

"I have trouble letting people close to me." She had learned to use such bluntness to advantage.

"I've been accused of the same thing."

"I'm sorry if I behaved badly."

"I thought you were great."

"You did?"

"I'm really happy about the way things worked out."

There was a softening in her voice. "I'm glad I went to that party."

"I'm glad I went too. But I had an instinct . . ."

"You always follow your instincts?"

"Try to," he said. "They're not always right."

"That's distressing."

"The percentages are pretty good." Joe said he would

24

call her, this time adding, "as soon as I get back from San Francisco."

When Lucy hung up, she had a sick, doomed feeling in her chest. She recognized the symptom: a new person was invading her boundaries and she was recoiling. He was blond, alien; all the men in her life had been dark. He was provincial, he had no timbre, he had never lived outside of California. It would not work. A wave of nausea came over her. She tried to breathe calmly, normally. She placed her hands on the center of her chest and told herself to relax, it would pass.

3

The kitchen was pale green, with large windows looking out on the oleander trees with their flowers like plump pink stars. In the center of the kitchen, dividing it, was a shiny butcher-block counter at which the two women were standing, making fruit pies.

Lucy was showing Pam how to roll the dough. She rolled the pin over the dough once, twice, and she had a flat sheet. Pam took the pin but when she rolled, some of the dough came up on the pin and the rest split off in ragged pieces. "Maybe I should stick to peeling fruit."

"Don't give up."

The phone rang. Pam answered, wiping flour from her hands, and walked into her room. When she came back, Lucy was spearing peaches with a fork, dipping them in boiling water and pulling off their skins. The kitchen was steamy with the scent of peaches. "Trouble?"

"Luke's angry that he can't come to the party. Everyone else from our acting class is invited."

"Mmm."

Pam began cutting a green apple. "I woke up this morning and I thought, I'm a woman in trouble."

"You'll always have a home here."

Pam started another apple.

Lucy said she had had a bad morning also. Dreams of being burned alive had left her with dread and the shakes, like a hangover.

"Lucy, we'll get a baby. Okay? Baby food, everything." Pam raised her chin in small, squirrel-like jerks, a gesture that always made Lucy laugh. Between them, a baby had come to stand for a state of serenity and grace. A room with white organdy curtains. A gently rocking cradle. Stuffed toys. Happy mobiles. Peaceful sleep.

"What about Joe?"

Lucy shook her head. "Not the father type."

"You're impossible."

"Realistic."

The desire to have children had come fairly recently to Lucy, surprising her with its urgency. All through her twenties, all the years she had been married to Jerry Rosser, she had not wanted a baby. She had looked upon infants as blobs who made irritating noises, and the idea of being at home with them was not attractive. What she had hungered for was success, recognition, freedom to do the work she wanted, and any maternal instinct had been so buried as not to be felt.

Then, as she was crossing the gate to thirty, her feelings had boomeranged. She had found recognition and the freedom to do what she wanted and she felt an emptiness. Missing a child, she thought she was missing a crucial element in life's pattern. It became almost a pure physical longing: she must have a baby. This was her "next year in Jerusalem," the prayer she repeated, the wish she made when blowing out candles or finding an eyelash on her cheek.

Unfortunately, it was proving more elusive than success in television. She was no longer married, and she was thirty-one. As each year passed she grew more concerned. Doctors kept extending the age of safe childbearing—to thirty-five, then to forty. What if she couldn't find a mate before the sand ran out? Would she have the courage to have a baby on her own, and if so, who would be the father?

The phone rang—another call from Luke. Lucy could hear Pam in her bedroom. "I told you, I have to help Lucy. No, we can't do it another night."

One more call, Lucy thought, and Pam will give in. The women had been living together for a year and could predict each other's moods. Lucy had grown as close to Pam as she had ever been to a woman, and yet, the arrangement had been made for economic reasons.

Lucy had met Pam at a party. Pam was younger, twenty-five, and the six years had seemed a considerable gap, but they had made each other laugh and exchanged phone numbers with the customary "Let's have lunch." Lucy had found that in Los Angeles, such exchanges were often made and rarely pursued, but Pam had called and they had arranged a date.

The following weekend, Pam had arrived at Lucy's apartment two hours late, wearing a yellow T-shirt that fit snugly over her large breasts and carrying the classified section of the Santa Monica *Evening Outlook.*

"I've been jilted."

"What do you mean?"

Pam dropped into a chair. "Henry doesn't want to live together. He's changed his mind, after I gave notice on my apartment and they rerented it." Her face looked drained, as from a long cry. "He says he needs more time to get settled in his job." She pushed the wheat-colored hair behind her ears. Spreading the classified on the floor, she asked if she could use the phone to check out one more place.

The sight of her on the floor with the papers—a waif, determined to go on—stirred something in Lucy. "I've just bought a house by the beach. It has three bedrooms, and I don't know if you'd want to do this, but you could have one of the bedrooms and pay me rent . . ."

"Are you serious?"

Lucy nodded. What was she doing?

"I'd love to!" Pam stood up, extended her hand like a kid on the playground and Lucy took it.

The house Lucy had purchased was a pink stucco bungalow built during World War II. There were water stains outside and peeling paint and cracked tile inside, but the house had "potential," and the front yard was planted with the most romantic flowers: birds of paradise, gardenias, Hawaiian snow. The address was 22 Sea Shell Avenue.

Sea Shell was one of a dozen little streets, one block long, that ran between Pacific Avenue and the beach. The houses were a jumble of styles: Victorian gothics, Spanish haciendas, new condominiums and dilapidated shacks. They were crowded together on narrow lots, and every house had a garden. Cactus gardens stood alongside English primrose gardens, next to vegetable gardens with unruly corn and fat zucchini. To Lucy, Sea Shell was a fairy-tale lane: foghorns blew at night, cats scampered across rooftops, people walked barefoot wearing white drawstring pants and gathered on the beach in the hour before sunset for a game of volleyball.

Lucy and Pam divided the pink bungalow into two suites. Lucy took the upstairs rooms, which looked out on a palm tree, and Pam took the downstairs bedroom and bath and sun porch. If they wanted, they could go for days without seeing each other. Pam made a nest in her bedroom for Henry so he would come and burrow in. She installed an armchair in front of the television, put up a rack for his bicycle and made sure there were plenty of lemons and tequila and Pepperidge Farm cookies in the kitchen. She was with Henry every night, and Lucy worked long hours, but the women began to call each other through the day to keep in touch.

Lucy looked on Pam as a happy sprite, who laughed, sang and tapdanced through the house. The romantic gesture filled Pam's head. Feeling was all! If feeling was there, anything was permissible. Her favorite movie was *Picnic,* which she had first seen at the Rialto (pronounced rye-alto) in Lovington. She liked to imitate Kim Novak, swinging her breasts as she danced up to William Holden. She would put her hands on her hips and say to Lucy, "I'm so tired of just being told I'm pretty." She told Lucy how, in the movie, William Holden said to Kim Novak after one night together, "I've got to claim what's mine. . . . You love me, you know it!" He ran to hop a freight train for Tulsa, and as the whistle blew, Kim Novak packed her bag. She would leave her mother and sister, leave her boy friend, leave her job at the dime store and catch the next bus for Tulsa. As the film ended, the bus and train could be seen speeding across the countryside, heading in the same direction, toward destiny. Pam had been waiting to be called to get on a bus for Tulsa.

She had a capacity to be vague and irresponsible that amazed Lucy. Keys being lost, laundry shrinking in the machine, checks bouncing, cars getting stuck in the sand—incidents that would have ruined a day for Lucy were to Pam nothing more than bad weather. It was muzzy? Okay, she would put up her umbrella and wade out, singing, "I like to walk in the rain."

If Lucy admired Pam's buoyancy, she knew Pam was envious of her efficiency and skill. Like a younger sister, Pam wanted to follow her. If Lucy bought a new Danish schoolbag, Pam wanted to have the same one. She went to Lucy's doctor, and bank, and hair stylist, and learned to cook the way Lucy did. She thought Lucy possessed the tools for accomplishment she had been deprived of, growing up in Lovington.

Pam watched as Lucy rolled out the dough for the top crust. All eight pie shells had been filled with fruit and sprinkled with brown sugar and butter. When the dough was even, Lucy flipped it onto the first pie, cut off the overhanging edges and pressed a fork around the rim of the pie pan to make a fluted edge.

"Want to try the next?" Lucy said, but the phone rang. "I can't handle another call."

Lucy picked up the phone. "Hi, Luke."

"I just ran over my dog."

"What?"

"I was so fucking mad at Pam, I backed the truck out fast and hit Riggs while he was trying to jump in."

"Just a minute." Lucy put her hand over the receiver. "You better go out there."

When Pam had left, Lucy rolled out the remaining seven crusts, wrapped the assembled pies in aluminum foil and stacked them in the freezer. She would bake them on the day of the party.

She felt bad for Luke, and Pam, and Henry, none of them was happy. She was addicted to this drama, following it with the eagerness of people who follow a daytime soap opera. At first, Lucy had been on Henry's side. They were both from New York and looked enough alike to be brother and sister. She had thought Luke crude, a loser, but as she had grown to know him, she had come to see his saintly qualities and now she did not know what she would have done in Pam's place.

"Do you think I'm terrible?" Pam would say.

"No."

"What do you think I should do?"

"Whatever will make you happy," Lucy said.

The drama had begun in December. Henry had left his old firm to become an associate at one of the most prestigious corporate law firms in the city. The competition at the new firm was so fierce that he had to work nights and weekends. When he came home, he wanted Pam to rub his shoulders and bring him food, and he was too anxiety-ridden to make love.

Pam had no work to do. She had been a music major in college, but had quit her first teaching job before the year was out. She had worked as a photographer's assistant, taken classes in ceramics, written half of a film script, applied for a license to sell real estate and presently, she was collecting unemployment and receiving brochures almost daily: applications for nursing school, acting school, courses in landscape architecture.

In December, she had enrolled in an acting class led by a teacher from New York. They began each class with a "repeat exercise." Two people would sit on the stage and repeat a phrase to each other, such as:

"I'm wearing a red shirt."

"You're wearing a red shirt."

"I'm wearing a red shirt."

If it was a good exercise, other messages would begin to be relayed through the words, and an encounter would take place.

Pam was asked to do this with a man who looked about thirty-five. He had a head of curly hair, green eyes and a great, booming, operatic voice. As they walked on stage, he pumped her arm. "I'm Luke Goodfellow."

"Pamela White."

They sat down in metal folding chairs and stared at each other. Luke spoke first. "I'm wearing blue pants."

"You're wearing blue pants," Pam said. As she would

tell Lucy later, they found that they could speak to each other perfectly.

"I'm wearing blue pants," Luke said. How do you like the class?

"You're wearing blue pants." I don't know yet. It seems more like group therapy than acting.

All acting is like group therapy.

What about technique? "You're wearing blue pants."

They went on, trying different roles, until they fell into playing the parts of a couple who were fighting.

"I'm wearing blue pants," Luke said. You do this to me *all the time.*

Do what?

I can't breathe without you criticizing me.

Pam, falsely sweet, "You're wearing blue pants."

"I'm wearing blue pants." Don't speak in that patronizing voice.

Now who's criticizing.

Look, can we drop this hostility?

It wasn't my idea.

Tell me, just tell me, what do you want me to do?

"You're wearing blue pants!" she yelled.

He slapped her face.

She slapped him back.

He lunged forward and kissed her, pushing his tongue back in her mouth, squeezing her breast and running his hand up her thigh and into her crotch.

"Thank you," the instructor said. As they walked back to their seats, the instructor said they had done "good work," but Pam did not hear, it might as well have been "I'm wearing blue pants."

When class was over, Luke asked if she wanted to have a drink.

"My boy friend is picking me up."

He put his hands on her shoulders. "I want you to know I

think you're wonderful." She looked at him, her chin raised.

"I'm going to find a way," he said.

Luke was out of work, so he could call Pam and keep her on the phone for hours in the afternoon, when she felt most alone and lacking purpose. He persuaded her to drive out to his house in Topanga Canyon. It was a primitive cabin with slanting floors, but the windows looked out on a pine forest in which deer wandered.

His approach to Pam was the same as William Holden's had been to Kim Novak: he was claiming what was his. The minute she walked in the door, he grabbed her in what she came to call a "bone-crushing hug." When Pam left his cabin, she drove straight to the television station to find Lucy and make her take a break.

"He said my cunt was like a flower. Nobody ever said my cunt was like a flower."

Lucy smiled, but she felt old.

Pam went to Frederick's of Hollywood and bought a black corset and trick underwear. She put on the corset and called Luke. "Listen to the sound the zipper makes . . ." She showed Lucy pictures that Luke had taken of her face while she was coming. Lucy stared at the grainy images. Pam seized the pictures. "It's my youth, let me have it."

After two weeks of chasing out to Topanga and back to the beach, Pam decided to tell Henry about Luke. He responded, as Lucy could have predicted, by asking her to marry him. He would see a psychiatrist, take est, have sex therapy. For three years, Pam had been wanting nothing but to marry Henry Wexler, and now, when she was with him, she missed Luke. She could not leave Henry and she could not stop seeing Luke.

Each of the men tried to break off with her. When Luke

said he was finished playing games, she took her bags up to his cabin and moved in. They wandered around the hills, singing, watching clouds, making love, but after two days Pam grew nervous: she would drift with him to oblivion. She packed her things and drove straight to Henry's law firm, reassured to see people working.

She told Henry she was ready to get married. For a week they went out with real estate brokers, looking at homes, but the prices were ridiculous and before long, Pam was going crazy missing Luke.

It was almost 10 p.m. when Lucy finished cleaning up the kitchen. She heard the gate open. Henry. He walked through the house, his eyes darting. "Where is she?"

Lucy lowered her head.

"She was supposed to be helping you bake pies."

"She left a half hour ago."

He sank to the couch.

Lucy sat down beside him. "She still talks about marrying you."

He shook his head miserably. "Remember, I wouldn't live with her when she wanted to, that's what started all this. I feel like I caused it in some way."

"You didn't cause it."

He walked into the kitchen. Lucy noticed the way he moved about the room unself-consciously—taking out ice, pouring tequila, cutting a slice of lemon and wrapping it in Saran Wrap, as if he were at home.

"I've tried going out with other people," he said.

"I know. I've been trying for two years."

Henry returned to the couch, took a joint from his pocket and lit it. "I went to a bar and I found, if I sat at a table and looked sad, girls would come talk to me. If I made the right noises, I could take them home."

"Wasn't it depressing?"

35

He exhaled. "Disaster." He handed the joint to Lucy, moving closer. His face was flushed, he had been playing racquetball all evening.

"What's going on with you?" He touched her shoulder.

"The show is almost finished, and it's good, maybe the best thing I've done. But I've been lonely."

"Mmm."

"Sex is not the problem, it's intimacy."

"Lucy, you're a very special person. There aren't going to be that many people with whom you *should* have a deep connection. You can't just pair up with any old schmuck."

She laughed.

"What about Joe Sachs?"

"What do you know about him?"

"Not much. He's a good ballplayer."

Lucy took another hit. "We had a great time, and after he left, I threw up."

"Uh oh, this may be serious."

She wanted to lean her head against his shoulder. He looked unusually handsome, wearing a pink shirt with the top three buttons open. She turned her face, and he made a move, subliminally, toward her but checked himself, not seeing a clear sign.

Strange, all these months they had been sleeping in the same house, sharing bathrooms, fixing meals, and no hint of sexual feeling had passed between them. If she had met him independently of Pam . . .

"What are you thinking?" he said.

She looked down. "I'm embarrassed."

He nodded. "It will be our mutual embarrassment."

They sat together, as if they had been watching television a long time and could not move. Lucy reached for his hand

and pulled him to his feet. "Let me walk you out. Or are you going to wait up for Pam?"

He shook his head. The saying of the name had broken the spell.

At the door, hugging him, Lucy thought she felt him crying. She kissed his neck. "Good night, Henry."

4

With the arrival of Monday, Lucy had five days left to work on her film. She drove to the station early Monday, knowing she would not go home, except to sleep, until Friday. She did not want to see or talk to anyone not involved with the film. She put off errands, phone calls, visits. She ordered all her meals in. The world outside became a pale interruption from the world she was bringing to life on screen.

When she entered this period, which she called "the trance," her face changed. The furrows of care and anxiety disappeared. No matter how preoccupied she might have been with personal matters, when she sat down at the flatbed, she was at peace.

As was true with many of her contemporaries, Lucy gained from her work the fulfillment and continuity which her personal life could not supply. She had been with Jerry, then she had been alone, now with Pam, but always, she had had her work. Closed in a small room with no windows, she drew comfort from the sense of being up while the city was alseep. After nine or ten at night, there would be no interruptions. The phone would not ring. Her light was often the only light in the building: a soothing image, the light of creation, staving off the dark.

When she drove home at 3 A.M., the streets were calm and night-slick. She dreamed about the film and, on her way back to work, pulled off the freeway to jot some notes. She was eager to discuss them with her assistant, Gordy Gelfand, but when she walked into the cutting room, she found Gordy and one of the secretaries, Betsy Ching, playing Boggle.

"What's going on?" she said.

"We have a lit-tle problem," Gordy said, handing her a letter on floral stationery.

Dear Mrs. Rosser,

I hereby take back my permission for you to put my daughter, Angela, in any film or on t.v. On thinking things over, I believe it will only harm Angela to show her suffering to millions of strangers we do not know. In God's name, I ask you to leave her be.

Yours truly,

(Mrs.) Coreen Marinetti

"Oh, brother," Lucy sighed. "Let me see the scene."

The film was called *Carey's Children*. It was about a young doctor, Carey Winter, a specialist in pediatric rheumatology, who treated children with lupus, a fatal disease in which the body literally eats itself up: the joints and bones, then the muscles and vital organs are attacked from within and disintegrate.

Carey was one of the few doctors in the country able to help such children, but he was on strained terms with his own daughter, Jennifer, who was nine. Because of his absorption in work, he had rarely been alone with the child. Then, after a divorce, he was awarded joint custody. He saw little girls in his practice all day and they brought him cookies and their artwork from school, but he was shy with Jennifer.

When Lucy decided to make him the subject of her film, Carey was just beginning to live with Jennifer three days a week. Lucy would follow Carey around the hospital, then go home with him to his daughter. She brought a cameraman, who appeared to be shooting but had no film in the camera. Lucy had found that after a few weeks, people would grow tired of posing and censoring themselves, at which point she would start using film.

At the end of the first day with Carey, she felt as if she were emerging from hell. The hospital was noisy, with bells ringing, voices squawking over intercoms, babies crying. Carey had to see forty children—one every five or ten minutes—each of whom was terribly sick and had no more than a 50 percent chance of living. Lucy began to develop headaches and stomach aches—symptoms the patients complained of. Carey said most doctors know little about lupus and are frightened of it. "That's what makes this field so exciting," he said, "there's a chance to make a real difference."

"Here we are," Gordy said, cuing the film on the flatbed. He turned off the overhead light, and the three of them watched the scene.

In it, Carey was examining a sixteen-year-old girl, Angela Marinetti. She appeared as her name, angelic, with fair skin, a blue vein visible at the temple, and ringlets of fine brown hair. She was sitting up in bed, painting on a tablet with watercolors. Other paintings of hers were hanging about the room: horses and birds, waterfalls and trees, in haunting, pallid colors.

Carey walked in wearing not a white uniform but, as was his custom, jeans, boots and a blue denim shirt with a stethoscope in the pocket. "Hello, Angela," he said.

"Hi, Carey."

"How are you feeling?"

"Not great."

He looked over her shoulder at the painting — a chicken with a blue-gray body. "That's nice, can I have one for my office?"

"I don't know. I'm still mad at you."

"Okay, lay it on me."

"The pains don't go away. Nothing helps."

"We talked about that, remember? How you're into a period where you're going to have pains, especially in your joints and your stomach."

"Just how long do these cute little pains last?"

"I can't say for sure. The average is from four to eight weeks."

"Eight weeks!"

"Sweetheart, you're doing great. I keep trying to remind you where we were three weeks ago. You were in a coma, you had no liver functions."

Angela threw the brush on the floor. "I still feel like you're playing games with pills and don't know what the shit you're doing!"

He fingered the stethoscope. "You're reaching the age where you realize we don't have all the answers. Lawyers, doctors, teachers, aren't perfect at what they do."

"Lawyers don't play with people's lives, and you have controls over mine."

"Are you a perfect artist?"

"I have a feeling I'm doing a lot better at art than you are at rheumatology."

He sat down on her bed. "What do you want me to do?"

41

"Make me better, and fast." She clutched her stomach. Tears sprang to her eyes. "It hurts so bad."

A nurse came in, saying there was a phone call for Dr. Winter, an emergency at home. "I'll be right back, hold on," he said to Angela, squeezing her shoulder, and told the nurse to give her Mylanta. He walked to a phone in the corridor, and learned from his housekeeper that Jennifer had been suspended from school for talking in French class. She was crying inconsolably. "Put her on," he said.

"Sweetheart, it's okay. I was suspended from school once, it happens to everybody. I know you feel bad, but it's not that serious. We'll straighten it out."

He continued trying, without success, to comfort her when the nurse came up. "Dr. Winter, Angela is vomiting blood."

"I'll be right there." Into the phone: "Jennifer, I have to go, there's a girl here who's in great danger of dying if I don't help her. You're going to grow up and become a beautiful woman and you'll laugh at this one day . . . Sweetheart, I'll be home as soon as I can . . . please . . ."

He dropped the phone. His daughter had hung up. Bells began to ring in the corridor. He put his head down and clapped his hands over his ears.

Gordy stopped the film. "Seen enough?"

"They really do forget about the camera," Betsy said. "It's amazing."

Lucy folded her arms. "We can't lose it."

"I sort of see the woman's point," Betsy said. "Her daughter is dying. How can you press her about this?"

"Look, this wasn't done hastily. We all discussed it— Angela, her mother, the doctor. The film has something important to say about medicine, ethics, families, the preciousness of life. If we lose that scene we'll lose the heart of the film and nobody will benefit.''

''What about having the thing with Angela happen off-screen,'' Gordy said. ''Reshoot some scenes with Jennifer to explain it . . .''

''No, it won't be as poignant. We have to see Angela as a real person who could live or die with every second Carey stays on the phone with his daughter.''

Lucy tried to call the station's attorney. His secretary said he was in conference and would call back. Ten minutes later, when the button on her phone lit up, she assumed it was the attorney.

''Hi,'' a male voice said.

''Who is this?''

''Joe Sachs.''

She was disoriented. ''Joe, I thought you were in San Francisco.''

''Couldn't get away. Listen, I want to see you, can we get together?''

''Not right now. I'm working round the clock.''

''When do you finish?''

''It should be in the can Friday, but it may be academic because I may not have a film.''

''What do you mean?''

She told him, briefly, what had happened that morning, and Joe said, ''You can't take out the scene. Obviously.''

''You know what the network will say if we don't have releases.''

''Throw the letter out. Is it registered?''

''No, but I wouldn't feel right.''

''Then go down and talk to the woman.''

''I'm thinking about that.'' Lucy took a breath. ''I'm not looking forward to it.''

''You've got to do it, if I have to drive you to her house myself.''

"Would you do that?"

"If you want."

"No, that's okay, I'll crank myself up."

Gordy signaled to her—the attorney was on the other line. "I've got to run," Lucy said.

"Let me know what happens."

Joe was gone from her mind five minutes after she had hung up. The attorney advised her the letter would "leave us exposed." She called Mrs. Marinetti and arranged to go to her house at four. She told Gordy to continue working, on the assumption that everything would be okay. She was showing him how she wanted two scenes recut when her private line rang. It was Luke Goodfellow. Lord, what now.

Luke wanted to chat. He said he was starting a job with a friend, selling condominiums in Beverly Hills. "It's a chance to make some fast bucks, but I'll be working seven days a week. I feel frustrated, like I'm going off into the woods and people will be telling me what I'm missing."

"I've been in the woods so long, I don't know anything else," Lucy said, running film through the viewer.

"You're in the Rockies."

"That's right, I come to town every three years with my furs. Get drunk, have a spree and go back."

"You like it though."

"I do. Listen, I'm in the middle of something . . ."

"Have you heard from Pam?"

"Not today. Why?"

"She left here this morning in a car that has bad brakes. She shouldn't be driving it. She said she was going home, but that was five hours ago, and she's not at your place."

"Maybe she stopped somewhere."

"I'm worried, it's an unsafe car."

"Have you thought . . ."

"She said she wasn't going to see him."

"Let's give her a few more hours before we panic. If I hear anything, I'll call you."

Lucy dialed Henry's number and Pam answered. "Hey, Luke's looking for you. What's going on?"

"I don't want to talk about it, Lucy."

"Okay." Lucy's voice became cool. "Anything wrong?"

"Sometimes I think you'd step over my dead body if you wanted something."

"What on earth are you saying?"

"I hear you and Henry had a little scene the other night."

Lucy was startled. "We had a nice talk."

"Henry said there was 'a definite current' between you."

Lucy clicked her tongue. "Pam, nothing happened. You know I would never do anything like that."

There was crackling on the line.

"We have to be for each other," Pam said.

"I agree. Henry and I were stoned and he was drunk and there was a warm feeling, but that was it. I don't know why he said that to you."

"Well, it worked."

Lucy laughed, nervously. "When are you going to get your brakes fixed?"

"Tomorrow, probably."

"That's good. You better call Luke, or do you want me to?"

"I'll call him."

"I love you," Lucy said. She felt a lag, as if a line were being played out.

"I know."

"I can't stand it when there's bad feeling between us."

"Neither can I," Pam said.

* * *

Coreen Marinetti lived in a small, square tract house in Culver City. Her husband had died many years before and she had three children, two of them married. Angela was her youngest.

Lucy recognized Angela's paintings of flowers and animals on the walls. Mrs. Marinetti offered her a soda. She accepted a 7-Up. They talked about the neighborhood. Mrs. Marinetti said the property values were finally going up, her house was worth something now, but if she sold it, where would she go? Lucy steered the conversation to the film.

"Angela is very excited about the movie. She wants to see herself on television, she wants her friends to see her. She keeps asking me when it will be on. It's giving her something to aim for."

"She's not in her right mind."

"I think she is. I saw her two days ago . . ."

"Why would she want people to see her so sick like that, and feel sorry for her."

"She wants people to know what it's like to go through an illness like this. It's a very human desire, to want to share your story. And I don't think people will feel sorry for her. They'll admire her spirit, and her paintings. They'll be inspired, they'll feel . . . with her."

"How do you know what people will feel? You don't know what I feel, do you? No, you don't."

"You're right. I haven't had to suffer what you have."

The woman began to cry. Lucy put her arm around her, tentatively. "Mrs. Marinetti, if you tell me the film is causing this, I'll drop it. I won't ask again. But I don't think it is the film, is it?"

The woman blew her nose. "I'm afraid, if the film goes out . . . Angela will die." She began to sob. Lucy hugged her and the woman collapsed, like a float losing air. After a time, she rose and walked to the bathroom, came back and sat in a rocking chair. "I'll be all right."

"Have you been to the hospital today? How's she doing?"

"A little better. She may be able to come home next week."

"That's wonderful."

"I don't know. She's been in and out so much."

"If she's coming home, that must be a positive sign."

"Dr. Winter says she's strong."

"She is."

Mrs. Marinetti rocked, and there was the rhythmic creaking of the chair. At length, she turned her hopeless eyes to Lucy. "All right, Mrs. Rosser. If Angela wants it, I won't go against her."

5

It was a perfect beach day, the kind that made everyone feel happy and optimistic. Blue sky, bright sun that turned the water into a sheaf of twinkling lights, fluffy clouds and sailboats coming out of the channel like a swarm of white butterflies. It was a storybook day, the kind the Beach Boys sang about, the kind of day that people who lived there expected as their due. It was the kind of day that had led Lucy to conclude, shortly after her arrival, that if she was to live in California, the point was to live at the beach.

She liked the sound of the waves, the smell of the air, the changing colors of the ocean and the letting down of inhibitions that came from having sand outside your door. What she had not counted on was the ethos of the place. Until she had lived on Sea Shell for a time, she had not realized that the beach was a holding pen for the unattached: people of all ages, living by themselves in a state of arrested adolescence.

On this perfect day in July, though, Lucy did not mind that she could see the vacant underside, she was taken by the beauty. She felt not just cheerful, not just optimistic, but euphoric. *Carey's Children* was in the can, and it was good. After ten months of work, all the uncertainty of the shooting period, the six months being shut up in the cutting room, she was sprung! She wanted to sleep, cry, eat chocolate cake and ice cream, have a gang bang, burn a palm tree.

"I know what you're feeling," Joe said. They were sitting on her patio, drinking piña coladas. "It's the greatest high there is, and it's not that easy to get. Then, of course, there's the letdown, the loneliness, when all those people in the film have gone away. Do you feel that?"

"No, not at all. But . . ."

"There's still hope?" Joe said.

Her shoulders shook with mirth. She enjoyed it when he made her laugh at herself. Lucy told him she felt guilty about the way she had handled the matter with Mrs. Marinetti. "Everything I said to her was true, but it was manipulative. My first concern was for the film, not Angela."

"Unfortunately, if you have a vision, if you're doing something you believe in, somebody may get hurt along the way."

It was gratifying to talk with him, and yet, she had not been looking forward to seeing Joe. She had decided the affair would lead nowhere, and had manufactured faults and shortcomings to support her belief. She had written him off, and in the process, he had ceased to be attractive.

In her memory, he had actually shrunk—to five feet ten. In reality, he was six feet two. His hair was blonder than she remembered, and he possessed an air of physical strength, of muscle and sinew, which, against her intentions, she had always found erotic.

They put on bathing suits and walked down the boardwalk, an asphalt path that ran along the oceanfront. They passed people riding skateboards, playing volleyball, lifting weights, flying kites, eating frozen yogurt, rolling on skates.

"When I was growing up, the beach meant one thing—surfing," Joe said.

Lucy felt a sparkling in herself like the sparkling of sunlight on the water. She encouraged Joe to talk, laughing with such genuine pleasure that he felt brilliant and appreciated, she could tell.

Joe said he was one of a breed he called West Los Angeles princes. "Their noses bleed if they have to go east of Doheny." At Beverly High, Joe had been president of the senior class and his brother, Dennis, had been captain of the football team. The Sachs brothers: Dennis the adventurer, always going for the edge, and Joe the charmer, trailing after Dennis, smoothing things out.

Every weekend, Mrs. Sachs would drive the brothers to the beach with their surfboards strapped on top of her Lincoln Continental. "Surfing was the most exciting thing in my life. I *had* to go surfing every weekend."

There was a code among surfers. "You did not get cold. You did not show affection for girls in public—no handholding, you had to walk aloof, like a god. And you did not use a towel or suntan lotion. You didn't need it."

After high school, most of their surfing buddies drifted or went into the Army, but the Sachs brothers went on to UCLA. They joined ZBT, the fraternity of princes: all of them were good-looking, bright and were going to have money. Unlike the jock houses, they found honor in making good grades (they were Jews, after all) but they had to do it not by "booking," like the girls, but winging it on intelligence and character. They liked to quote the don, F. R. Leavis, who, when forced to lecture to a mixed class at Cambridge, had said, "Good morning, gentlemen, do you have that down, ladies?"

Joe earned one of the highest grade averages in the house, but Dennis was not so successful. During his senior year, Dennis married a gentile girl he had knocked up, went into his father's business and moved to the valley. "Within six months he had grown fat and unadventurous. So I became the maverick. I took LSD, mescaline, nitrous oxide. I hitchhiked up to Berkeley to demonstrate against the war, and I

loved going to the Fillmore.'' To his parents' grief, he
dropped his plans to go to medical school. ''I had no passion
for medicine, and I wanted to feel passion for what I did. I
wanted to ride a whirlwind. I just didn't know what it was.''

For a while he drifted, smoking grass and hanging around
the beach, until he fell into a job as an assistant with Hang
Ten Productions, a company making surfing movies. Almost at once, the love he had been waiting for announced itself. He bought a 16-mm. Bolex camera. He went to hear
Stan Brakhage talk about underground film. He built a special rig and took the camera everywhere, until it became an
extension of his body. He shot industrial films, educational
films and documentaries. He lived in a shack in Santa Monica Canyon, which was walking distance from the beach but
he never went surfing anymore. He directed specials for
television, received grants and made a short film, *Rookies*,
about the Los Angeles Rams, that won first prize at the
Cannes Film Festival. Then he was hired by CBS to make
Heroes of the Airwaves.

''You know,'' Lucy said, ''if we had met in high school,
we would not have looked at each other. I definitely would
not have been in your crowd.''

''That stuff was nonsense,'' Joe said. ''Let's go in the
water.''

Lucy looked at the surf.

''What's the matter, don't want to get your hair wet?''

She inclined toward the boardwalk. ''We'll discuss it.''

''We already discussed it.'' He took her by the arm and
walked her in. They stopped where the surf was breaking at
her knees, and as each wave receded, she could feel the
water and sand being sucked out with force.

''Don't worry,'' Joe said, ''you're with an old surfer. After the next one, we'll start swimming. Ten strokes and
we'll be clear. Now . . . swim!'' He counted the strokes
out loud, easy, confident, swimming with his head sideways
so he could watch Lucy. She swam anxiously, faster than he

51

was counting. "Four . . . five . . ." A swell rose up from nowhere and, as she watched, gathered in a wall ahead of them. She was out of breath, helpless, but they were pulled up and through the foaming crest and out the other side. "Seven . . . eight . . ." By the time Joe had counted ten, they were past the swells and had reached the flat sea. "This is wonderful," Lucy said. They floated on their backs and let the deep, subtle rolling of the ocean buffet them.

When they were ready to head in, Joe guided her again, so that she was impelled forward by the waves and never had one break on her. They sat close together on the sand, drying off. Lucy's skin felt clean, tingling.

"It's been so long since I've had a day like this," Joe said, with a sigh of pleasure. "It makes me want to go down to Mexico and find an empty beach."

"Would you go alone?"

He shook his head. "I'd like to go with a woman."

She reached over and touched the small, silver Star of David on his chest. "Where did you get this?"

"My father."

Lucy had never seen one of her friends wearing a Star of David or any jewelry they considered blatantly Jewish.

"Most of my friends felt that way too," Joe said. "Some of the guys at Beverly wore St. Christopher medals. They had their noses straightened, and they all had Christmas trees. We were the only ones who didn't."

"Why?"

Joe said his father had been born in Germany, and had escaped from the Nazis and come to America in 1938. He had taught his sons that they should be proud of being Jews, that they had a special calling to remember the Holocaust—in which the rest of their family had perished. The brothers had been sent to Zionist youth camps, and while Dennis had decided early on he did not want to "throw my lot in with these people," Joe had always found comfort, not in the religion, but in the sense of belonging to an illustrious tribe. In 1967, after the Six Day War, he had sent the first money he had earned for a film—$500—to Israel. He had gone to Israel in 1973, and had always meant to go back but the timing had never been right.

Lucy was puzzled, curious. "I haven't been to a temple since I left home." In the early seventies, she had been drawn to the Eastern religions, with their promised jewel of inner peace, transcendence over the temporal and union with the divine. The Judaism she had known growing up in New Rochelle had been void of soul, a tedious catalog of do's and don'ts that no one seemed to respect. In Jewish theology, as she perceived it, there was always an I—Thou split, an almighty God who sat apart from the world, hurling thunderbolts. The appeal of the Eastern road was the immanence of God: he was everywhere, in everything—a tree, a rock, a killer shark. Every being contained the divine spark, and all one had to do was change the way one was looking and one would *see*. "It's like being in a theater," Lucy said. "If you look at the screen, you see people, animals, scenery, but if you turn around, you see it's only light."

For several years, she had been involved with a Hindu meditation group. "Have you ever heard of Shree Ganesh?"

"Can't say that I have," Joe said. "Did he go to Beverly?"

Lucy laughed, but Joe urged her to continue. "I'm interested in all that."

"There was a time when I felt high, unafraid, certain I was on the right track. I was meditating, and reading almost nothing but spiritual books. I went to Brindaban, India, to study with Ganesh, and I can still remember the feeling of the ashram. Peace was in the air like a fragrance—you could breathe it. There were gardens with exotic flowers. Ganesh would give his talks, and everyone was dressed in orange, meditating, working to develop attitudes of joy.

"I knew my marriage was breaking up, and I had to

change jobs, but underneath everything, I was convinced of the all-rightness of life. Whatever I had was enough. And then I lost it. I came home, to work, to quarrels with my husband, ambition, jealousy, until I was back in the whole roiling soup. I was frightened again, and nothing was enough. And now, the spiritual books sit unopened on my shelf.''

Lucy had been speaking with such absorption that she had forgotten where she was. A wind had come up; she reached for the lavender shirt she had brought and slipped it on.

"Surfing was like that for me," Joe said. "I'm not suggesting surfing was a religious experience, but it was a way of transcendence. When I was out in the water and on my game, nothing existed but the wave. I would feel this rapture all through me. I wasn't doing anything, I was part of something immense and unfathomable. Now, though, if I go out with the board, it never happens. I sit there thinking, this is supposed to be fun." He lit a cigarette. "I don't know if anything can do it for me again. Except the work."

Lucy said, "I can lose myself in work, but when it's over, there's that same hole inside. The problem is, we've seen that you come down from every high—sexual passion, drugs, meditation, political causes, money, work, achievement. Everything. It passes through you so quickly, like Chinese food. And yet, I still have this feeling I need to find my family, my mate, and things will fall in place."

"I think I need to be all right by myself first."

"I've been told that all my life and never been close to it."

"Sure you have."

She shook her head. "I've rarely felt I'm enough. It's largely a waste without someone to share it with."

Joe seemed to wince. "White woman, I know of what you speak."

"What I don't understand," Lucy said, "is why I lost it. I

don't know whether the state I long for, the wholeness I once felt, was a delusion or whether I've blown it."

She looked at him with such openness—everything she was and might be were visible on her face. "What do you think?"

"I think," he said softly, "that your shirt looks comfortable."

She looked down at her shirt, then shook her head and laughed. "Thank you."

"And you look beautiful in lavender."

"For putting things in perspective."

They walked home, and Lucy noticed that they walked with the same gait.

She felt tears forming in her eyes. She was being carried on waves of emotion. She wished she had shaved her legs that morning, she wished she had put fresh sheets on the bed. She was truly surprised about Joe. The night they had met, he had been a stranger, a random sexual partner who flitted through her house. Now, she was seeing him as the embodiment of what she had been longing for: the twin soul.

Here were the things she knew so far: they were in the same field, sharing a passion few people possessed or understood. They were both night creatures. They loved the outdoors, and were interested in development of the spirit. They liked the same books, movies and rock songs. They liked to get stoned. They both drank diet Dr. Pepper. The major difference Lucy could see was that Joe disliked birds and she liked birds all right but hated dogs.

They were lying on her bed, kissing as if they were parked on a darkened bluff, with crickets singing and an occasional headlamp sweeping them with milk-white light. Lucy felt another burst of emotion: happy, grateful. She saw them living together, making films together, having a child.

He entered her and, at the same time, slipped his hands

under the small of her back and began massaging her. He pressed deep, hard with his hands, into the places where the tension coiled, pulling her up to him as he came down.

She was breathless, she could barely open her eyes. "You're going to make me fall in love with you."

"Just have fun with me."

He hoisted her on top and they mirrored each other, so that every sensation was doubled. Something buzzed in the back of her mind but she swished it aside.

"What's the most you've ever come in one night?" he said.

"I don't know."

"Give me something to shoot for."

"I can't think."

"Come on."

"Five times."

"Piece of cake." He had her now. "I love the way this feels. I can feel you getting hotter and hotter."

Yes, she thought. . . . He started to shift his legs and she whispered, "Please don't move, I'm going to come."

"Then I will too."

6

Lucy zipped up the black corset Pam had bought at Frederick's of Hollywood. She looked at herself, breasts pushed up, waist squeezed in, and laughed.

Pam held up a green bra with tassels. "If you wear this, he can pretend you're a circus dancer. Does he like fantasies?"

"He likes games."

"Then try this."

Lucy slipped on a pink satin bra and matching pants with flaps and bows. She glanced at the clock. Three more hours.

Like a Scandinavian woman whose man was coming home from months at sea, she prepared herself: washed her hair, tweezed her eyebrows, shaved her legs and underarms, rubbed lotion on her limbs, filed her nails and tried on several sets of clothes before settling on a white cotton dress . . . one more hour . . . it would look as if she had nonchalantly thrown it on.

She was so excited as she drove to Joe's house, she was afraid she would sweat through the dress. She parked her car, walked through a gate and down a gravel path. Insects were buzzing in the shrubs. Hand trembling, she rang the bell. She noticed, only now, the house was dark. She looked at her watch, he had said eight and it was 8:20. She rang again.

She heard a car, then felt headlamps behind her. A door slammed. "Sorry I'm late." Joe hurried past her, fumbled with his keys and opened the door. "I'll be right there." He motioned her toward the living room while he disappeared upstairs.

Smoothing her dress, Lucy walked into the room. She liked it immediately, which was a relief. There were polished, blond wood floors, a brick fireplace, comfortable sofas, plants, two enormous multidirectional stereo speakers and, on the walls, contemporary lithographs and a photograph of the Sierra by Ansel Adams. The record collection looked similar to Lucy's, heavily weighted toward rock albums from the sixties. On the coffee table was an old electric train set whose pieces had the well-worn feel of toys preserved from childhood. She played with the cars a bit, then wandered off to find Joe.

He was in the study, taking his messages off the phone machine. "I'll be with you in a minute." Something in his posture—the hunch of his back—sent her from the room. She sat on the edge of a couch, feeling an awkwardness that was all the more crushing because it was unexpected.

He walked in and stopped in front of her. "Were you thinking of leaving?"

"I was considering it."

"Don't do that." He hesitated, then reached out to hug her. "Hungry?"

"Not right now."

"You will be."

He opened a bottle of wine and poured two glasses.

Perhaps it was nothing, a mood of his. "How long have you had this place?"

"Four years." He seemed to relax a little as he showed her through the house, which was uniformly pleasing, if anything, too perfect: every piece set, every corner occupied. The kitchen was decorated with blue and yellow Mexican tile. The two bathrooms had oversized tubs, skylights and sinks built higher than customary, so Joe wouldn't have to stoop. There was a sports room with an exercise bicycle, weights, two surfboards, cross-country skis and fishing equipment: feathers, hooks, chenille ribbon and books on creative fly tying. On the second floor was an office with his film awards on the wall and an editing room equipped with a flatbed and library of movies.

"You don't ever have to leave,"Lucy said.

"Except for food. Speaking of which, let's get dinner started."

He settled Lucy in the kitchen with a refill of wine while he prepared the meal, with confidence and seemingly little effort. Two whole trout were pan-fried with butter, lemon and dill, potatoes were rubbed with oil and baked until their skins were crisp, asparagus was steamed, fresh raspberries chilled. They ate in the dining room, making small talk, then sat down by the fire.

Joe got up to put on a record. Coming back, he stretched out with his feet toward Lucy. "Tired," he said.

"That's too bad." James Taylor was singing "Handy Man." Lucy took off Joe's sneakers and began to stroke his feet.

He reached over to touch her but she withdrew, tucking her legs beneath her so her skirt was subtly raised.

Joe caught a glimpse of pink satin. "What's that?"

"Nothing." She pulled the dress down.

"Let me see." He moved toward her.

"There's nothing to see," she laughed, squirming sideways.

James Taylor sang, "I Fix Broken Hearts, Baby."

He grabbed her and slid the white dress up until the panties were visible, with their enticing satin flaps and tiny bows. "Oh, this is great. Where did you get them?"

"Wouldn't you like to know?"

He bent over and kissed her through the satin. "Take off the dress, I want to see the whole effect." She raised herself up on her knees and was about to slip the dress over her head when the phone rang. Joe cocked his head, then hurried to pick up the extension.

"Hello"—his voice sailed out hopefully. Lucy sank to the floor. Joe kept his back to her, but before long, she heard the wind leak out of his voice. When he returned, he seemed to have forgotten the satin underwear. "I should get a new number."

"What's the matter?"

"A couple months ago, I was driving up Sunset and this exotic-looking blonde was driving a jeep in the next lane. She'd pull ahead a little, then I would, and when we stopped at a light, we kind of stared at each other. She had a great smile, which always turns me on, so I made a note of her license plate and found her number through the D.M.V."

"I didn't know they gave out that information."

"For three bucks, anyone can have it."

"That's distressing."

"I called her up and said, 'I'm the guy in the green Porsche and I'm asking you out to lunch.'" He rolled his eyes. "She had the intellect of your average stalk of broccoli. I was ready to leave in five minutes, but ever since then she's been calling all the time."

"Why don't you tell her you've gotten involved with someone and you're not seeing other people?"

He stared into the fire.

"She'll respect you for your integrity."

He shrugged.

"She won't have to take it as a personal rejection."

He looked at his watch. "There's a Fred Wiseman special on channel twenty-eight, let's catch it."

"I don't feel like moving."

He took her hand, led her upstairs to the bedroom and

pulled her onto the bed. He flicked on the show, a documentary about high school, but Lucy's attention wandered. She studied the linens on the bed—beige and brown, discreetly masculine—the stereo table, Tiffany lamp, the books and magazines on the nightstand, his horn-rimmed reading glasses. The bedroom was clearly the center of the house.

Joe fidgeted with the remote control, turning up the volume. Lucy watched him in the mirror. His arm was around her but the rest of him seemed to list away. When the program was over, he dimmed the lights and began taking off his clothes.

Lucy no longer felt like putting on a show with the satin underwear. She removed everything quickly, lifted the sheet and slid under just as Joe was climbing in the other side.

She went rigid. Her foot ran into something that was not sheet, it was slippery fabric, rolled up in a ball at the bottom of the bed. She reached down and pulled it out: a pair of yellow lace panties.

"For God's sake, Joe."

He flipped his head to look, then covered his eyes. "How embarrassing." His shoulders began to shake. "What can I say?"

"This is tacky." She threw it to the floor, as if it were a dead rat.

He was laughing.

"The least you can do is change the sheets between women. You think this is funny?"

He wiped his eyes. "I'm really sorry."

"Women in jeeps, underwear in the bed. You think this impresses me? You're wrong, it's pathetic." She started to put on her clothes. He grabbed her arm.

"Look, I never meant to rub this in your face. I apologize." She twisted free. "Lucy, I think you're a remarkable woman. Bright, successful—in something I respect. You're charming, fun. I love the time we spend together. I'm sorry this happened, but what do you expect?"

"I don't want to be part of a lineup."

"We've been together three times. I haven't asked you who you see or told you what you could do. I see other people."

"Anyone you're seriously involved with?"

He shrugged. "There's a woman in San Francisco, but it's long-distance." She sat down. "The other women don't mean anything. But I have to be honest with you. Whenever I've been in a relationship that puts limitations on me, I've ended up resenting the person."

She drew lines on the sheet with her fingernail.

"I don't want to disappoint you."

"Why don't you let me worry about that."

"I've disappointed people in the past. I'm not proud of my behavior." He hit the headboard with his fist. "Now you've really got me on the defensive."

"I didn't mean to."

"You're making me sound like a complete turd!"

"I'm not making you sound like a turd."

"It's just natural, huh."

"Joe, my life is full and busy, but I feel comfortable with you. I don't have any expectations about what form things will take, but I'd like to find out."

"I would too. Could you be happy having something very casual. Nice when it's happening?"

"Is it because you don't find me attractive?"

"No, I do find you attractive."

"I thought you said you wanted to get together with a woman."

"I'd like to get myself in shape to where I could have a relationship, but I won't be able to do that until I figure some things out. I'm not sure what I want, or what I could promise. I don't see a settled-down thing for at least another two years." He reached over and touched the long, shiny dark hair. "I hope this doesn't turn you off completely."

"No," she said, "but I am interested in . . ."

"I know you are."

"Maybe we're at different stages."

"Maybe."

"Well, it's always better to have things clear."

"Lucy."

She looked at him.

"It shouldn't be so complicated."

"No, it shouldn't."

He took her hand. "My feelings haven't changed."

She raised her eyes, quizzically.

"Let's just leave things loose, okay?" He leaned to kiss her but she was the one to list back.

"I think I'd like to go home."

She hurried across the gravel, got in her car and slammed the door. Bastard. He didn't want me there, I could tell the minute I saw him. I'd like to slash the tires of his green Porsche, I'd like to slash something else.

She drove home, raging, imagining how the conversation would go when he called as soon as she walked in the door.

Just have fun with me. How could she have let that slide by?

Pam and Henry were watching *The High and the Mighty* on television.

"Any calls?"

Pam shook her head.

Lucy told them what had happened, and they turned off the movie and walked down the boardwalk to Chez Johnny for a drink.

"I didn't want to say anything before, but the guy's not a good prospect," Henry said.

Pam stuffed her hands in her pockets. She had watched Lucy run through the cycle so many times. She wished she could shake her by the shoulders and say, "Stop doing this," but she couldn't, and even if she could, Lucy

63

wouldn't hear. "Maybe you'll meet someone tomorrow," Pam said.

Lucy twirled a strand of hair around her finger. "I'm sick of meeting people."

Chez Johnny was a beach hangout, with sawdust on the floor, Christmas-tree lights on the walls, graffiti in the bathroom and a menu written in French. The proprietor, Johnny de Lorenzo, who had a large belly that jiggled over his pants, always gave them the back booth, separated by dividers from the rest of the room. He could flick off the light in the booth and take out a joint, which he did this Sunday night. He slipped his arm around Lucy. "Cheer up, kiddo."

She took two drags before passing it to Henry. Johnny always had the strongest dope. "I'm trying."

"You look like I did last week, until I busted off my diet."

"Johnny, you shouldn't give up."

"I couldn't eat sugar, I couldn't eat salt. No potatoes, no booze. I don't want to live like that."

She laughed, surprising herself.

"Let's have some chocolate mousse pie." He asked the waiter to bring pie, on the house, and a bottle of desert wine.

"What are we celebrating?" Lucy said.

"Your beauty, and virtue."

"Hear hear," Pam said.

Lucy was beginning to feel better.

"What are you guys doing tomorrow?" Johnny said.

"We're having a party," Pam said. "Come by."

Johnny gave a low whistle. "Gotta hold down the fort. Every drunken bozo will be out on the beach playing hero with the firecrackers."

"I hear there's gonna be a gang fight in Venice," Pam said.

"The whole beach is gonna explode," Johnny said.

"Where did you hear that?" Lucy said.

Cries broke out at the front of the bar. They poked their heads around the booth and saw a man with long gray hair, a snake coiled around his neck, coming in the door on roller skates. Johnny leaped up.

"No roller skates inside—can't you read the sign? And no snakes neither."

"He's harmless."

"I don't give a shit. It's long and it wiggles, get it outta here!"

In the back booth they laughed so hard they fell against the table. The munchies had come on, and they ate every drop of the overly sweet chocolate mousse pie. Henry poured more wine.

"I'd just like to announce," Henry said, "that I love everyone here."

"Awwww."

"Let's drink to a partnership for Henry," Lucy said. They raised their glasses and brought them together in noisy clinks.

"A great job for Pam," Lucy said. They clinked again.

"A baby for Lucy." Pam thrust her chin forward.

Then they drank to their friendship, the warm little circle they had created in place of a family, that would go on and on no matter what.

7

The first firecrackers went off just as the sun was rising above the aqua sea. It was promising to be another perfect day, the day that summer would burst into fullness, the day one's destiny for the rest of the year might be fixed.

Lucy could feel the expectancy in the air as she walked down Sea Shell to the oceanfront. There were flags waving on porches. There was a volleyball tournament on Yawl Street, with men leaping in the air and diving in the sand. Music was everywhere, live and from stereos: Fleetwood Mac competed with the Eagles and Donna Summer. Beer kegs were being rolled into place, and on the boardwalk, a woman with a large yellow dog was pacing back and forth shouting, "Poisoned! I've been poisoned! Whenever I get laid I get poisoned."

Lucy found Pam and Henry lying in beach chairs. Henry was reading *The Final Days*. Pam, wearing a broad straw hat and dark glasses, was reading Raymond Chandler, *The Little Sister*.

Pam stood up but Henry remained in his chair.

"You're not coming?" Lucy said.

He put the book facedown and shut his eyes.

"It might be fun."

"This is a rare day off, I intend to stay right here."

The women drove away in Lucy's car, a beige B.M.W. Pam's car was too disreputable—an ancient Dodge that always looked as if Pam had just driven it across country. The seats were piled with clothes, a spare shoe, a towel, laundry, boxes of cookies, hot curlers, books and Pam's mail.

"I've started taking spiritual instruction," Pam said. They were heading for Beverly Hills, to a pool party given by Mark Steinberg.

"In what?"

"Don't laugh if I tell you?"

"Okay."

"Bonsai."

"Those tiny trees?"

"Exactly."

Lucy started to laugh. "I'm sorry, they never did anything for me."

"I went into Yamaguchi's Nursery to buy some fish emulsion, and I saw these little trees. They were clinging to rocks, struggling to rise against all odds."

Lucy's laughter spurred Pam on. "It's my only religious experience. You've got a great long Jewish tradition, but all I've got are some pasty-faced Methodists. So here are these little trees. They live for two or three hundred years. You can become immortal through these little trees."

Lucy was laughing so hard she was afraid she would lose her grip on the car.

"Talk about religious persecution."

Lucy wiped her eyes.

Pam said Yamaguchi had the largest collection of bonsai

in the world. "He gives classes, the third Tuesday of every month."

"How long is the course?"

"Lucy, this is not like a sport where you can say, 'How long till I master it?' This is spiritual development."

"Excuse me."

Pam said she had bought two trees, a Monterey pine she had given to Henry and a Hollywood juniper for Luke. They were five dollars each, untrained. "You have to torture them, hack off their tops, break their branches and tie them down with wire. I wanted to buy one already bent but Mr. Yamaguchi said (she imitated his clipped accent), 'Oh no, you buy straight.' "

"Why didn't you buy one for our house? I don't want to be left out of this."

"Okay."

"Do you have the directions?" They had turned up Coldwater Canyon, which was quiet and leafy, with estates hidden behind electric gates.

Lucy digested the information that Pam was installing trees in both men's houses. Pam kept saying she wanted a home, but she was setting up three homes. She had toothbrushes, lettuce spinners and shoe racks at Henry's, Luke's and Lucy's. She spent most nights with Henry but not a day passed that she did not talk with or see Luke.

"Henry and I don't get along that well," Pam said. She listed the things he criticized in her and the things she disliked in him. Lucy saw that both lists were valid. "Most of the time I was with Jerry, I felt the way you do—critical, ambivalent, restless, with interludes of harmony. Maybe that's the way it is."

"I hope not. You've got a divorce under your belt, but I haven't had mine yet. I want to be married on a green lawn, with flower girls. I want a husband who takes care of me and our children. I want closets filled with linens, and a bright yellow kitchen where there's always coffee brewing. I still have those images in my head, but I'll never get them because no one else wants them anymore.''

"You could have it with Mark Steinberg."

She shook her head.

"Sure you could. People never get over their first loves."

They were signaled to stop at the edge of a driveway by a man wearing a Revolutionary War costume. The women stepped out of the car.

Mark Steinberg had just been made vice-president in charge of production at Warner Brothers. He was twenty-seven, and he interested Lucy because he was a new type: the baby mogul. Mark Steinberg and Pam had known each other at Northwestern, where she had been the flower of Delta Delta Delta and he had been chairman of S.D.S. Mark had fallen for Pam when he had met her in a history class, but he was short, with troubled skin, and Pam had never been attracted to him. Mark had become her puppy-like suitor, always there when she was sick or breaking up with a boy friend, needed a ride or help with her exams.

In 1970, Mark had organized the moratorium that shut down the school after the shooting of four students at Kent State. He was feared by the administration, cheered by the students; he held up the lamp of right and goodness, but Pam still did not want to sleep with him. When he graduated, and the Vietnam War ended, Mark had gone to Hollywood, telling his friends that movies were the way to influence the masses. If he could penetrate the industry, he could make important, socially relevant films.

The political skills he had learned in S.D.S. served him well. He presented himself as having a pipeline to the fabulously lucrative youth market, and was hired as an in-house producer. Mark's first project was a low-budget film written by three guys who had put out the Northwestern humor magazine. The movie was called *Balls*, about a college tennis team, and was full of raunchy, fraternity-house humor: fag jokes, pimple jokes, food fights. It had no social relevance, but it grossed $60 million on a $3 million investment, and as a result, Mark Steinberg had been promoted to chief of production, at $250,000 a year, plus a Mercedes (with a personalized plate—CINEMA), plus unlimited expenses, plus stock options, plus an interest-free loan to purchase the house at which Pam and Lucy were now arriving.

"You know what he told me on the phone?" Pam said. "When you see this place, you're gonna want to ball me."

They walked in the door, through a marble foyer and out to the pool, where a hundred people were standing around poles with streamers and flags flying. Waiters in Minuteman costumes and powdered wigs brought them drinks, hot dogs, cotton candy. There was a giant balloon sculpture in the pool—colored balloons strung together to form a floating American flag.

Lucy recognized many of the people: the men were young producers, directors and agents and most of the women were actresses. Everything looked loose and gay: people were eating corn on the cob, swimming in the pool, but there were rules. It was not good form to talk to someone until you had been introduced. It was not good form to ask anyone what he did, you were supposed to know. Those with the most power did not circulate; they stayed in place and others came to them.

At the center of one of these circles was Mark Steinberg, his squat form clothed in navy shirt, white pants and white loafers. Pam went up to say hello, but Mark merely kissed the air by her cheek. Pam had borrowed a dress from Lucy, a pale blue silk dress that gave her a lambent sensuality, but at this party, Pam did not stand out. The other women were wearing low-cut halters, tube tops, backless dresses, vests unbuttoned to the navel, skirts slit up to the crotch and gauzy blouses through which nipples and bouncing breasts could be seen.

Lucy felt matronly, wearing pleated pants and a tailored Calvin Klein blouse. She noticed a man with a dark curly beard. "Aren't you Alan Edelman?" He nodded. "I heard you speak at Stop the Draft Week."

He seemed to start.

"I remember you chained yourself to a pillar at the Whitehall Induction Center, and the police had to saw the chain."

"Ten of us did it," Alan said, surprised that anyone remembered. "To take a step like that, to put aside your fear of jail, reaction of parents, was incredibly liberating."

"If you did it consciously," Mark Steinberg said, making a quarter turn to butt in.

"But so many didn't," Lucy said, "they were carried along by emotion . . ."

Alan flinched. "Don't remind me."

His wife came up. "I'll be in the shit house with the baby sitter if we don't get home right away."

"Will you excuse me?" Alan said.

Lucy walked off toward the pool, her eyes circling to see if there were any unattached men. It was a reflex, and when she caught herself she was mildly disgusted. The sheets were not yet cooled from the last fiasco.

She found Pam, and they wandered into the house. They heard music coming from the second floor, a piano and voices singing an old rock song, "You Got What It Takes." Their heels clicked on the marble as they walked upstairs. In a den at the end of the hall they found Tim Nash, a rock singer, sitting at the piano with a group around him. Tim had made a cameo appearance in *Balls*. He was called ''Baby Tim,'' his first hit album had come when he was twenty, but now his hair was streaked with gray. When he reached the last line, everyone in the room sang, ''You got what it takes!''

Mark Steinberg came in, carrying a red balloon, ''something special for Tim.'' Tim emptied the balloon on the coffee table: coarse brown powder. Using a razor blade, he divided it into lines.

Kate McCleary, who had been sitting with Tim, said, ''Enough for all us chickens?'' Kate was the ex-wife of another rock singer, and she and Lucy had met frequently, when Lucy had been with Jerry.

''Who wants?'' Mark said.

No one spoke. ''Just us three,'' Kate said, ''isn't that lucky?''

Kate looked like an exotic bird, with a long pale neck and red curls. She spoke in a nasal, tremulous voice that lent itself to comic delivery. ''Oh, Lucy, you're going to think I'm a pervert now.'' She took her turn after Tim and Mark, inhaling a line of brown powder through a rolled-up bill. ''Do you remember when we first met?''

''Monterey,'' Lucy said.

Kate nodded. ''You were wearing your hair in braids.''

''My Indian period.''

Kate inhaled a second line. ''I've been eating my feminist slogans.''

''You're not the first,'' Lucy said.

''I miss Charlie.'' Kate turned her face to Tim. ''Am I pinned?''

''No.''

''What does that mean?'' Lucy said.

''Your pupils are supposed to get narrow.''

Tim looked at Mark Steinberg's eyes, then at his own in the mirror. None were pinned. "Maybe the pinned thing is shit," he said.

"This is shit," Kate said. "I don't feel anything, except sick. I could have taken ipecac."

"Boy we really flyin' now," Tim said, laughing.

Mark became flustered. "I paid two hundred and fifty, it shouldn't be shit."

"We've all been down that road," Tim said.

Pam, who was sitting next to Mark, said she and Lucy had to go. "Thanks for stopping by," Mark said absently.

"What a nerd," Lucy said as they walked down the stairs. Halfway down, she stopped. In the open door was a tall man in an old blue shirt and jeans. He was coming in alone, late, underdressed, and had the personal power to carry it off. He glanced up and saw her at the moment she saw him. It was Jerry Rosser, president of Camel Records and Camel Films.

They had not seen each other in six months. He called her name. She moved down the stairs somehow and he was hugging her. "I thought you were in New York," she said.

"I'm out here a couple weeks. Who's this?"

Pam had come up, wearing Lucy's dress, and was smiling with her chin thrust out.

"This is Pam."

"Of course," Jerry said.

"It's great to meet you," Pam said.

"I know you've heard a lot about me, only half is true. I'll concede half."

"Lucy has only said nice things."

"I wonder if you'd excuse us. I don't get a chance to see Lucy that often." He put his arm around Lucy and walked her away. "There must be some place quiet . . . what an abysmal house."

"It's the house that *Balls* built."

They went into a spare bedroom, closed the door and sat down. "You look great, darling," Jerry said.

"How's the business?"

"Fine. Just fine. What do you weigh these days?"

"The same."

"You look thinner."

"Must be the pleated pants."

"Let's make love sometime, just for the fun of it."

"You son of a bitch."

"Don't be so hard on me. I love you. My heart thumps every time I see or hear your name."

Lucy shook her head, bemused.

"Saw a piece about you in *Variety*," he said.

"What was it?"

"In Amy Moran's column. Some speech you were giving . . ."

"A conference?"

"That's right."

"On 'Women in Film.' What did she say about me?"

"The only thing I remember is, 'lean-faced and bra-less.' "

Lucy burst out laughing. Jerry laughed with her, delighted.

"I work so hard and all she can say is, 'lean-faced and braless.' " Jerry talked about phasing himself out of the music business. It was taking a direction he did not care for, and he wanted to concentrate on films. He had picked a successor for the record company, but it was difficult, "amputating myself from the business after eleven years. It's like a relationship. You don't just walk away, shut the door and never think about it. Especially when the experience was a happy one." He paused. "And the sex was great!"

They laughed again. They began to gossip about mutual friends, to reminisce and joke, and suddenly Lucy was drifting into dark tributaries.

"I'm with you," Jerry said, gesturing over his shoulder. "I have my canteen."

"How's Lauren?"

"Tumultuous. You would not believe the ambition she has. Not like you, not in the normal range." Lauren was off on a job in Alabama and Jerry was not sure what would happen when she came back.

He asked about Skip.

"That's been over awhile."

"I knew Skip was not the end of the trail."

"I want the trail to stop."

"The trail never stops," Jerry said.

"I don't care . . ."

"Darling, when you have a relationship with someone realistic, it will take the focus off of us. The feelings won't go away, I think they'll be with me until I'm ninety. But Lauren does take the focus off."

Lucy sighed. "I should go, we're having a party at our place later."

"Can I come?"

"I don't think that's a good idea."

"I'd love to come to the beach, watch the fireworks."

"Jerry." She made a childlike noise. "Uh uh."

"I don't want to stay at this zoo."

She stood and kissed him. She wondered what he was thinking. "Count on me," he said.

Lucy was silent on the car ride home. Memories were rising and she was struggling to bat them down. It was useless; she was seized with missing Jerry. She remembered the early days, her senior year at N.Y.U., when they had lived in a two-room apartment on St. Mark's Place. They slept in one room and Jerry founded a record company in the second and named it Camel. Lucy embroidered camels on a blue workshirt for him, a gesture which would be repeated by every singer and group he signed. A train of camels would arrive at their home: wooden camels, stained-glass camels, macramé camels, psychedelic camels. Charlie and Kate McCleary had tried to buy them a live baby camel but Lucy had caught wind of the scheme in time.

She remembered magical nights at the Fillmore East when, stoned on the best marijuana, they sat in the first row and could not feel the seats.

She remembered forging youth-fare cards in '67 so she and Jerry could fly to California for the Monterey Pop Festival. With no credentials, nothing but nerve and personal power, Jerry had signed up three unknown artists and within a year, all had made million-selling albums. Camel Records moved uptown, to a suite on Park Avenue. Jerry developed a taste for English antiques, bought a co-op in the West Village and a Rolls-Royce "Silver Cloud" limousine, all of which clashed with Lucy's counterculture values. When he bought the limousine, she made a point of taking subways. The irony, of course, was that she missed the limousine, now that she was older, times had changed and she could not have it.

She missed Jerry as a mentor. When she had been caught up in the *cinéma vérité* movement, working as an editor, then directing her own films, Jerry would go over the rough cuts with her. She relied on his counsel, his taste, as she had not been able to rely on that of anyone since.

She remembered the final years, too, when Jerry was expanding the business and they developed separate friends.

She stopped going to industry parties with him; he stopped meeting her at the airport when she had been away, he sent the limo. In 1973, Jerry moved his base to California and Lucy, reluctantly, went with him. There followed a year of splitting and reconciling, all the while she was longing for something more, something deeper. She went to India for six weeks, and when she returned, there seemed nothing at home to resume.

She spoke to Pam as they pulled off the freeway. "I didn't know what else was out there. I'd been with Jerry since I was twenty. Eight years."

Pam nodded. "You keep thinking you must be missing something, and then you find out—it's Mark Steinberg with his red balloon."

A burst of shots rang out, followed by puffs of firework smoke.

"We talked about having a child together," Lucy said.

"Do you think he'd go through with it?"

"We discussed some odd-ball arrangements. I mean, we couldn't live under the same roof again. So the child would live with me part of the time, with Jerry part of the time, and sometimes the three of us would be together."

"What about Lauren?"

"She doesn't want kids."

"I bet you could convince him. Tell him, 'If we do this, there'll always be a living bridge between us.'"

They turned onto Sea Shell Avenue, but before they could park, Henry came running up. Pam groaned. "The key."

Henry had been locked out and it was not the first time. The key was symbolic: he wanted his own, and Pam had refused to give him one. He had been sitting in his car in the heat for an hour. Pam opened the gate, Henry followed her in and they started screaming. Lucy went into her bedroom and lay facedown. She could hear their voices, muffled through the floor, then quiet. She closed her eyes.

The phone rang. She waited for Pam to pick up, Pam always answered the phone. It rang four times. "Hello?" Lucy said.

"Hello, darling. I forgot to tell you, our new film is being screened next week, I wonder if you would come see it . . ."

She began to cry.

"Easy," he said. "I'm fighting not to succumb to the dark side of the moon myself."

"You don't love me anymore."

"I *do* love you. Why do you think I'm calling?"

"The screening."

"A pale excuse."

"You're moving on."

"Listen to me," he said in the familiar voice he had always used. "I love you."

8

Between seven and eight, the phone rang intrusively, as it often does in the hour before a party. Every time Lucy set the instrument down, it rang. Peter had the flu and couldn't come. Bob and Sandy wanted to bring another couple. Jacob needed directions. Lucy closed all the windows to muffle the drumming of the band across the lane, but the house grew too warm so she opened them.

Guests began to arrive. Pam and Henry drank a lot of wine quickly. Lucy hurried about, introducing people, checking on the pies, and then there was a point when the house was filled with people, talking to each other, and Lucy took Pam and Henry aside. "It's okay, the party's on automatic pilot."

They were a strange mix: friends of Lucy's from New York; friends of Pam's from Illinois, one of whom was a cosmetologist; Henry's attorney friends; beach people; racquetball players; neighbors. Lucy's attention was pulled and split. Bob and Sandy told her they had just decided to get a divorce. Only three weeks before, they had bought a house. Another couple who had recently been divorced arrived together. "Neither of us can handle dating," Stuart said.

Lucy walked outside. Something was rippling in her mind like muscles under the skin. Jerry. She wanted to call Jerry, ask him to come by. Oh, she knew it would not work, and yet, this time, maybe they could avoid the old problems. She would go to the phone in her bedroom and make the call.

The gate opened suddenly and Luke walked in. He came toward Lucy fast and hugged her so hard her feet left the ground.

"What are you doing here?" she said.

"Raising hell."

He set her down and went in search of Pam. Two minutes later, he was pulling her by the arm out the door, but at the gate, she dug in her heels. "I can't leave."

"Don't give me this 'I can't.' It's not that you can't, you won't. I want you to tell me, right now, why you won't come and live with me." Pam turned and saw others watching.

Lucy wondered where Henry was. She looked in the door of the living room but he was not in sight.

"You're going against your instincts, and you're the one who says, 'Feeling is all.' Why!"

"Luke, when I think of a man of thirty-five, I think of someone who's settled, who's learned to do something well and provide for his future. Not somebody living in a shack as a caretaker."

"I can get a job," Luke said. "I can work as an electrician. I can make $25,000 a year. I'll open a business, Goodfellow Electric. We can have a family and you can go back to school if you want."

"I don't want to be responsible for you becoming an electrician. That's the world I come from. Don't you understand? Sometimes I wonder how I've managed to get this far—to California, to Lucy. I've done it by tap dancing, by being funny and seductive, but I know I'm not that original and my breasts are going to drop. I need a home. I can't survive by myself, I need help, and there you are up in the hills with your dogs, watching clouds. Even if Henry . . ."

"Don't compare me to Henry Wexler. Why should I be compared to some tight-ass lawyer, that's crazy."

"Even if I hadn't been with Henry for three years, I still couldn't go off and live with you."

He pinched his lower lip.

"I'll come out Tuesday, we'll spend the day . . ."

"No." He rammed the gate with his shoulder and walked out.

"He hasn't heard. He doesn't know."

"Where was he when Luke came in?" Lucy said.

"Upstairs. Maybe someone's told him. I hope no one's told him."

"Let's get everyone to go out to the beach," Lucy said. She and Pam began coaxing their guests to walk down the lane to the sand. People left in twos and threes, carrying drinks and blankets. Finally, everyone was gone except Lucy's old friend from N.Y.U., Emma Kline, who had sprained her ankle falling on roller skates.

Emma was a psychologist, a large, earthy woman who talked fast and laughed a lot. She was lying on the couch, her legs propped up. "You don't have to stay," Emma said, "I'll keep an eye on the pies."

"That's what I'm afraid of," Lucy said.

"You don't think I could eat all ten?"

"Eight."

"Well, in that case."

Lucy sank into a chair and leaned her head back. "Actually, it's a relief to be sitting down.'' She looked at her friend and smiled. ''Where's Al?''

''The hospital. He likes working on the holidays, he says it relaxes him.''

''Maybe we should check in.''

Lucy enjoyed being with Emma, she was a link back through the years. Lucy could still see the great, fuzzy red bathrobe Emma had worn around the dorm their freshman year. Emma had been with Lucy at Max's Kansas City the night she had met Jerry. For several years after college, Lucy and Emma had lost touch, then met again in California.

''I've been thinking a lot about breaking up,'' Emma said.

''Why?''

''Our sex life is awful.''

''Can't you work on it?'' Lucy was fond of Al, a pediatrician who played the guitar and, when he went to visit children in the hospital, would put on a toy white helmet with a flashing red light. He would rush in the room calling, ''Here comes the doctor!''

''Al's a terrible lover,'' Emma said. ''He won't go down on me. He starts making love when I'm dry and just when I'm getting aroused, he comes.''

''Listen, I've been getting all the sex I want and I'd trade it in a second . . .''

''Who have you been seeing?''

''It varies. I've had a procession of men through my bed.''

''Don't you have a scheduling problem?''

''No. Richard lives in New York, so he's only here once a month. Jeff is a workaholic attorney, he doesn't have many nights free. And Skip doesn't want to be tied down. All of them are expert lovers. All of them like oral sex. I've had them lapping at me like honey bears and half the time I can't come."

"Why!"

"It's not what I want." She went to the kitchen, opened the oven and shifted the pies so they would bake evenly. "I want to be entwined in someone's life. I want to be called every day."

"I'll call you."

"You know what I'm saying." Lucy leaned against the door. "I want to sit in bed and watch movies on television. I want to do errands together, take plane rides together, be bored, be angry and stewing, have dinner, take out the garbage. I want my nose rubbed in the ordinariness of being a couple."

"I have that, and I'm not happy."

"You're just going through a bad phase. Al loves you."

Emma reached for a Frito chip. "I think you're better off than me."

"I don't."

A glint came to Emma's eyes. "No, you win this, you're definitely better off."

Lucy started to protest, but had to laugh at the Confucius-like look on Emma's face.

"Neither of us is happy," Emma said, "but you're getting eaten."

It was dark, and the beach was crowded with people setting off fireworks. The air was whistling with explosives. Eeeeeeeeeee . . . crack! Sprays of yellow burst in the air, turning into showers of red stars, blue stars.

So much smoke billowed over the boardwalk that it was difficult to see. People would emerge and then recede behind white clouds. The smell of sulphur was everywhere—the smell of a thousand matches being struck. Lucy enjoyed the smell, it was exciting to the senses, faintly illicit. She walked through the smoke to the sand and found her friends sitting in a group. Pam was at the edge, next to Henry, who had his arm around Sue Ellen.

Pam stood up. "Want to go for a walk?"

"Sure."

The two women began walking north, toward the Santa Monica Pier, where a formal show of fireworks was in progress. The boardwalk was covered with paper and burning things. "Watch out!" a woman shouted. Bang! A baby started to cry.

"Henry's been after Sue Ellen," Pam said.

A little boy squealed, he had burned his fingers on a black snake.

"We have each other," Lucy said.

The farther north they walked, the more seedy the boardwalk became until it resembled a war zone, with shots, burned-out bodies slumped in doorways and the pervading smell of gunpowder.

"Let's walk down to the water," Lucy said. The sand grew damp under their feet. They could hear the waves now, and just off shore, people were out in sailboats with lights, shooting fireworks from the decks. The line of lights from the boats was like another coastline, from which this beach was being fired upon. When a large rocket was launched, its reflection streaked across the water.

"Lucy."

She started, squinting to see who was calling. A familiar laugh.

"It's Skip." Pam ran up and kissed him. Lucy could see now: Skip was with a woman, Sherry, who had succeeded Lucy.

"Don't I get one from you?" Skip said.

She kissed his cheek. "We're going to walk on."

He smiled.

Lucy took a few steps and turned her head. Skip was star-ing, defiant. She turned away and after a few paces, let out a scream. The sound was drowned by fireworks. She could scream as loud as she wanted. She screamed again and as she did, Pam shrieked. The two of them threw back their heads and yelled, jumped up and down.

A couple nearby turned to see what the commotion was, then lost interest. Lucy howled, Pam screamed, the two of them ground their teeth and hissed until their throats were raw. Exhausted, they went to each other and hugged. They stroked and patted one another, soothing, begging. It's okay, there. Hold me, please. I understand, I'm here. Lucy was hugging Pam, panting as one does af-ter a cry, when she began to be aware of the way Pam's body felt. The springiness of her chest, the softness of her cheek, the scent of herbal shampoo in her hair. The tide was rising, and a wave suddenly foamed up over their an-kles. Pam moaned.

Lucy kissed Pam's hair and felt Pam's lips graze her neck. Lucy shivered. A rain of colored stars showered on them. A door opened a crack, and Lucy felt an impulse—more like a curiosity. Beyond the door was a soft and pleasant land, where they could rest on grassy slopes. She had only to move her lips a few inches and they would be met. She squeezed Pam; the pressure was returned.

They clung together, but the question hung in air for just a moment. Saying nothing, they turned and started to head back, into the smoke.

"I bought some seeds," Pam said.

"You did?"

"Two kinds of lettuce. Pumpkins."

Lucy slipped her arm through Pam's. She had been want-ing a garden ever since they had moved to the beach, but Pam had resisted.

"You're right," Pam said, "we have each other."

"You think pumpkins will grow here?"

"Of course. We'll make jack-o'-lanterns."

"Pumpkin pie."

None of their friends was on the beach where they had left them. At the house, Henry was standing at the barbecue. His eyes looked frightening, but he had a hamburger in his hand and a bite in his mouth. Later, Lucy would remember thinking that nothing bad could happen because he was chewing his hamburger.

Pam stopped outside the gate. Lucy continued walking and Henry brushed past her. "I want to talk to you," he said to Pam.

Lucy went to the kitchen, which was warm and inviting with the fragrance of hot fruit. Emma was gathering forks and plates. Lucy heard a high-pitched cry—Pam—and assumed she was yelling at Henry. Bob Stevens came over. "Shouldn't we break it up?"

"Let them be, this has been building all week."

She cut the pies and began passing plates around. "Apple or peach?"

"Tell you what, I'd like a sliver of each."

She saw Pam come in, shielding her face with her hand. Lucy finished serving the pie, fixed a plate for Pam and took it to her room but the door was locked. "Pam, it's me." The lock was unfastened.

"My God." Blood was running down Pam's forehead, her eye was beginning to swell and the neck of her blouse was ripped.

Pam wiped the blood with a washcloth. "He thought I'd been with Luke."

"Didn't you explain?"

"I didn't have time."

Henry's face appeared in the door.

"Get out of here!" Pam said.

Lucy was mortified. "I'm so sorry, I never dreamed . . ."

Pam yanked a jacket out of the closet.

"You should lie down."

She was hunting for her keys.

"Please, lie down."

"I'm okay." She found the keys in her old jeans.

"Where are you going?"

"I don't know."

"I'll go with you."

She shook her head. "I want to be by myself."

The party was breaking up. Henry was walking back and forth between Pam's room and his car, moving things out: his bicycle, his clothes, his tennis racket. He seemed to carry only one item on each trip, and he spoke to no one.

Bob and Sandy were continuing their quarrel. Bob stood at the door with both their coats, while Sandy dawdled.

"All night," Bob said to Lucy, "Sandy was quiet. Now she's going to be social."

"You're being patient."

"What else can I do?"

"Throw a tantrum, it seems to be the rage."

"Does it work?"

"Not in the long run."

"Forget the long run. All I want is for things to work for ten minutes, the next ten minutes."

Bob and Sandy went out, leaving only Emma with Lucy. When they turned on the overhead lights, the house looked as if a herd of animals had swept through it. Puddles of wine, soggy rolls and cigarette burns were everywhere. Lucy felt sick. Emma assured her it could be fixed. They took garbage bags and gathered up the paper cups, plates, empty wine bottles and half-eaten food. Then Lucy mopped the floor. She could not go to sleep, knowing she would wake up to this.

Emma said she had to leave.

"Why don't you sleep here?"

"Can't."

"There's plenty of room," she pleaded.

"I have to let the dogs out."

Lucy wondered where Jerry was at this hour. Unlikely he was alone. She fixed herself a cup of peppermint tea, got in bed with the tea and a book of Shirley Ann Grau's, *The Condor Passes*. She stared at the opening page.

Me? What am I? Nothing. The legs on which dinner comes to the table, the arms by which cocktails enter the living room . . .

The phone rang.

"Did I wake you?"

"No, who is this?"

"Joe."

Again, she was disoriented.

"I figured things would still be going on at your place."

"Where are you?"

"Home. I just got back, I was at this terrible party."

"Really? It was pretty terrible here too. It was terrible everywhere I was today."

"I felt like we were children left alone, with no responsible adults."

Lucy was silent.

"Funny me calling you like this."

She agreed.

"I guess I wanted to talk to you. Are you tired? Do you want to go to sleep?"

"Yes. And no, not particularly."

"Feel like taking a drive?"

"Where?"

"I don't know, I want to get out of this place. Maybe go up to the Sierras, do some fishing."

The unexpectedness of the proposal made it appealing. Twenty minutes later, Lucy drove off with Joe, leaving the gate locked and the house empty.

9

They drove through the night on Interstate 5, passing Newhall, Valencia, Bakersfield. As the sun was rising, Joe turned onto 65, a little-used, two-lane highway that carried them up into the rural past. There were gray-gold fields in which sheep grazed, but the sheep, being the color of the landscape, could barely be distinguished. Gothic farmhouses stood among cornfields, tomato fields, orchards of lemon and orange trees so close to the highway that fruit spilled onto the blacktop.

Lucy wondered why Joe was taking her on this flight from the city. Watching him drive, she felt, against her wishes, an attraction. A strand of blond hair was falling in his eyes, and he wore faded jeans and hiking boots.

"There's a place in Porterville I always stop," he said. It was a dilapidated green cafe, but Joe went into the kitchen to speak to the cook, who brought them platters of homemade orange muffins and eggs scrambled with cheese and green chilis. The eggs were creamy and spicy, the muffins like buttery cake, with bits of sweet, fresh orange through them. They ate two muffins each and asked for more, along with coffee.

"I haven't been out of Los Angeles in a year," Lucy said. "You get trapped in this town."

"The whole place was once a tar pit. I feel like a mastodon who wandered in and couldn't get out."

He tapped the table idly. "Got a proposal for you."

She wiped muffin crumbs from her lips.

"Have you thought about what you're going to do next?"

"Not really."

"Maybe we should do something together."

"What do you mean?"

"I've wanted to collaborate for a long time, with a woman, but I haven't run across the right person before. Think about it—you and I have similar styles, but we have very different points of view."

"I'm not sure I understand."

He smiled. "I've never been with a woman before whom I didn't feel intellectually superior to."

"Oh you haven't?"

"We could produce a contemporary equivalent of the Katharine Hepburn-Spencer Tracy movies. They were written and performed by man-woman teams. Both sets were worthy adversaries, and you can feel the electricity."

Lucy was intrigued. Having a partner would take some of the pressure off her, and she might learn things she would not on her own. They began to throw ideas back and forth as they drove north, and before long they had left the flatlands and were in subalpine forests.

It was 7 A.M. when Joe took the Wolverton turnoff and parked by the trail head.

Heather Lake	4 miles
Aster Lake	5 miles
Pear Lake	7 miles

"You can do four miles, can't you?" Joe said.

"Think so."

He opened the trunk and began to pack the gear. Lucy stretched, taking in the sweet scent of pine sap.

"Want to come out in the water? I'll bring an extra pair of waders."

"Sure."

He packed the fishing gear in a backpack, then the food they had picked up at a farm stand. He asked Lucy to carry the smaller fishing bag. The trail led through giant sequoias, so tall and thick that only faint shafts of light filtered through the branches. The ground was covered with ferns, deep green clover and chips of red bark. Joe told her the sequoias were part of the giant redwood family, and the largest were more than two thousand years old.

Lucy was thrilled at the lushness and enormity of the trees. Although she had grown up in the city, she had always found a joy, pure and uncomplicated, in the natural world. At the first sight of mountain, or desert, or river uncultivated and wild, she felt a sense of happiness peal through her like a bell. Worries fell away. Sensory impressions became achingly vivid, and she would return from even a brief trip feeling restored.

They walked for an hour, stopping to listen to birds or watch a bobcat, then came out on a rocky plateau. Joe took Lucy to the edge and she gasped. It was called the Watch Tower, and it fell off without warning—thousands of feet to the river below. It did not drop straight but curved back into itself, creating a sense of tumbling so intense that Lucy felt a surge of dizziness. She had to back away ten feet, and even then, had spasms in her stomach when she looked at the drop.

Starting up the trail again, they soon emerged above the tree line in what John Muir had called "the Range of Light." The mountains were gray, capped with snow, and they reflected the light so that everything appeared gray-white and luminous. The rocks were bleached white and smooth, like dinosaur bones. Joe and Lucy went up a path as slick as a toboggan run, then down through a stand of fir and pine and there was Heather Lake.

Joe whooped. It shone behind the trees, emerald green. He began to walk faster until he was sprinting. "I can't believe it." He dropped his pack beside the shore. "The fifth of July and not a soul here."

Lucy sank to the ground. When she had thought of four miles, she had not considered that it was straight up, beginning at seven thousand feet. Joe brought her a canteen filled with icy spring water. "We should get started before the sun's too bright."

"Give me a breather." Lucy swished around her face. "It's so buggy."

"Good sign." Joe clapped a fly between his hands and examined it. "Caddis." He opened his kit and sorted through the dry flies, comparing them to the specimen in his hands. "The trout is so cunning, he won't bite on anything except a certain insect. You have to use a fly that's an exact replica of what he's feeding on, and then you have to simulate the movement of the insect by the way you cast."

He assembled the cane rod, slipped on rubber waders, a vest and hat and slung the fishing bag over his shoulder.

"You look serious."

"Hey, I can be a very serious guy." He walked with Lucy to the mouth of the lake. Where the Kaweah River was spilling into the lake, a trio of rocks stood like icebergs, cutting the water. Lucy saw a flash of silver through the white water behind the rocks. "There!"

Motioning her to stay on the bank, he waded out, cast in front of the rocks and, after a moment, pulled back his line. He cast again, pulled back, cast again, the line making a crisp, slicing sound, and suddenly the still green surface of the water erupted. A rainbow shot in the air: silver belly and crimson stripes. It seemed to skip on its tail, shaking its mouth to knock out the hook but Joe had set it. The fish dove and the line buzzed out, then went slack. Lucy thought the fish was gone, but Joe stood poised. He began reeling again, and then he was pulling the trout above the water and he had it in his net.

"Sachs, I'm impressed."

He climbed onto the bank, water streaming off him.

"Think you got it now?"

"I don't know, you make it look so easy."

He took her arms in his and showed her the movement. "Most people take the rod back too far. You don't need to go any farther than this." He flicked the rod forward with his hands around hers. She practiced awhile, then stepped into the stream. It was slippery, hard to keep her balance in the current. "Don't worry, I've got you." Joe steadied her from behind. The first cast plopped right in front of her. On the second try, the line tangled like a bird's nest. "Easy, it's a wand you're sending out across the water. You wave it and call up a fish."

It was another six tries before she succeeded in sending out the line in a lovely arc. She was so pleased with her cast that she forgot about the fish, but as she pulled back, the rod bent. "Joe, help!" She slipped on the moss and fell backward, still clutching the rod. Joe boosted her up and held her, told her when to let out the line and when to reel in. She was surprised at the power of the fish, she could feel its spurts and lapses.

"Don't be lulled into a false sense of security, he's still got fight."

Her arms were aching, her fingers burned.

"How you doing?"

"Great."

There was less resistance on the line now but her arms could not stand much more, they were shaking. She was debating whether to give the rod to Joe when he leaned out and scooped the fish in his net.

"Beautiful!" He helped her to shore and, seeing her bright eyes and wet cheeks, pulled her close and kissed her.

He built a fire at a campsite just above the lake. While Lucy was drying off, he slit the trout, gutted them, inserted slices of lemon and set them to grill on wood sticks. Lucy buried ears of corn in their husks among the coals. They could scarcely wait for the food to cook. As soon as the fish was crisp, they ate it with their fingers and drank from a bottle of Chablis, cooled in the lake.

The trout was pink like salmon, not white like trout that was raised in a fishery, fed on pellets. It tasted of the stream, of grass and wild herbs. They began to eat more slowly, to sigh and lick their fingers. Joe took a joint from his vest, they smoked it, then he stripped off his damp pants and shirt and lay down on the grass.

"Rosser, you're a good sport," he said.

Lucy sat with her back against a tree. A few puffs had rocketed her into reaches where every image was sharp, every thought seemed magnified and significant. She watched the lake: the burnished trunks of the trees were reflected in the water. She felt infused with hope: out of the carnage, some beauty might rise.

As she often did when she was stoned, Lucy thought about the people she loved and was overtaken by the desire to tell them. She would pick up the phone and call one after another, pouring out her sentiments to the somewhat baffled recipient. If there had been a pay phone at Heather Lake, she would have gone straight to it.

She would have called her younger sister, Leslie, in New York, and asked to talk to the baby, Max, who was one and had just learned to say "door." She would have talked to Leslie's husband, Ryan, a veterinarian, who always made her laugh.

She would have called Pam, and Emma Kline. Henry, Luke too.

She would have called Jerry. She saw his face and felt an

ache. While they had been together, she had not seen a single positive quality; now no one compared. She had never stopped believing it could still work out, and in some odd way, it could. They might yet have a baby.

Pam would help her, Pam would decorate the nursery and sing lullabies. Lucy felt a surge of love for Pam. She would give more time and thought to Pam's career now; they were family.

She slipped off her shirt and stretched out on a smooth rock. She could feel the sun in the rock beneath her, the sun above, penetrating. Closing her eyes, she fell asleep, then started. Joe was kissing her shoulder. She lay still, of two minds. His lips traced a path up the curve of her neck, and her bare skin, which had been warm and lax, began to tingle. It felt fine, lying there on the polished rocks, with the breeze from the lake and the scent of pine. She put her hand on his.

"Did you mean what you said about working together?"

"Absolutely."

"Then I think we should keep things . . ."

He looked up from her shoulder.

"I mean, I don't think I could sleep with you now and then, and see you every day . . ."

"I'm easy."

She searched his eyes.

He smiled, and dimples came to his cheeks above the beard. "We'll be friends." He paused a moment, as if considering something else. "But if you change your mind, don't be shy."

Lucy slept during most of the ride home. Joe had to wake her when they turned onto Sea Shell Avenue, just after 10 P.M. They found the beach possessed by an eerie quiet, like a western town after a shoot-out. A wind had come up, and charred bits of fireworks were blowing in swirls, scratching against houses. The boardwalk was empty. Few souls were out in the lanes, and those who were had a brittle look.

An old car pulled alongside Joe's. The car had been in an accident and never repaired. The windows were cracked, the pieces of glass held together with black tape. The driver, a woman with frizzed hair, called plaintively, "You know where there's any good discotheques?"

Lucy shuddered.

"Sorry, I'm just visiting, wish I could help you," Joe said.

The woman drove away, her car smoking.

Pam was home. Lucy was relieved to see the Dodge. Bleary-eyed and aching, she said good-bye to Joe and went inside.

"Pam?"

The light was on in her bedroom, the door open.

"Pam? Are you there?" No response. Lucy walked across the living room, the oak boards creaking under her feet. "Are you all right, Pam?" Silence.

Suddenly she slowed. Two more steps and she could see into the room.

Pam was standing by her bed. The bed was made. Sitting on the bed was Jerry Rosser. Lucy saw them as one sees figures in a nightmare. Jerry had his arms around Pam, holding her loosely. They had their heads turned sideways, and four eyes stared at Lucy. Jerry cleared his throat. "I have to tell you. I'm going to marry this woman."

II The Desert

July 1977

1

A clock struck twelve, and in the hushed, summer night, the bongs echoed mutedly along Sea Shell Avenue. All the houses were dark except for the pink house, which glowed through its shades and linen curtains. Every room, upstairs and down, was brightly lit. Outside, the oleander blossoms gleamed and each gardenia seemed to wink. The house possessed an almost lurid radiance, as if to suggest the extraordinary events that had taken place within its walls.

A green car pulled into the lane, drove up to the house and stopped. Joe Sachs stepped out, hurried inside and came out moments later with his arm around Lucy. He looked back from the walkway. "Don't you want to turn off the lights?"

Lucy shrugged.

"Wait here." Joe took the keys dangling from her hand, went back and shut off the lights. He returned and helped her into the car.

"This is the most bizarre thing I've ever heard."

Lucy was still wearing the dusty hiking jeans with stains from the trout. "She's going to live in my old home. Cook on my old stove. Sleep in the bed I bought Jerry for a wedding present."

"How did it happen?"

Lucy shut her eyes, and the scene played itself out again, for the first of endless times. Jerry was on the bed, hugging Pam's legs. *I'm going to marry this woman.* He rose, and the three moved awkwardly to the dining-room table. Lucy sat down on one side, Pam and Jerry on the other, as if there were a line running across the table and the room, dividing it into fields.

Lucy looked at Pam. "How did this happen."

Pam fixed her eyes on the ceiling, and began reciting like a pupil who had memorized a report. "After I left the party, I drove around by myself for about three hours. I started to go to San Francisco but the car was acting funny, so I came back. When I got home, there was a message on the machine from Jerry." She turned to him. He nodded. "I called him back."

"Wait a minute. Was the message for you?"

Pam shook her head. "For you."

"Then why did you call?"

"To tell him you were away."

"At three in the morning?"

Silence.

"Go on," Lucy said.

"He asked me to meet him for a drink. Nothing was open, so we went to his room." Her voice changed; her eyes took on the pleading puppy look. "He understood me, Lucy. I didn't have to explain things. The moment I walked in, I felt 'home.' "

"Well said, Pam."

"Oh for God's sake, Jerry, I've heard her do that 'home' routine a dozen times." She turned to Pam. "What do you think this is, *Picnic?*"

"Lucy, you and I have been separated for two years," Jerry said.

"How can you get married after one night."

"Pam's coming to New York, and we'll live together first."

Lucy felt her chin trembling.

Pam crossed her arms and began to pace. "I will not be guilty. You can't legislate what people feel. If we stayed apart because of you, that would be two people denying themselves happiness for the sake of one."

"That would be crazy," Jerry said.

"You told me dozens of times, do whatever will make you happy. Well, this is what will make me happy. This is my chance."

"And mine," Jerry said.

Lucy wanted to scream, "Get out of here," but she thought, if they leave, who can I call?

"When are you going to stop acting like a fucking victim?" Jerry said. "We've fallen in love, it happens in life."

"I feel so alone."

"That's not our fault! We're not responsible for the fact that you're not involved with anybody."

"Why are you talking to me this way?"

"Defensive," Pam said. "Where's a brush?" She went to the bathroom, came back with a brush and began running it through Lucy's hair, which was still in tangles from the Sierras. "How we handle this is so important," Pam said. "Other people will take their cue from us."

"We want you in our lives," Jerry said. "When you come to New York, we'll throw you a party."

Lucy twisted free and hurried from the room. Pam followed. "Do you want to hit me?" Lucy turned, tears clinging to her lashes, and saw Pam, poised like a kitten who's licked herself smooth and sleek. As if at a signal, Lucy kicked her in the legs and struck out blindly with her fists. *"You took my man."*

Pam shrank back.

Jerry came in. "Don't you touch her!"

"I don't mind," Pam said.

"She's a wonderful girl, she doesn't deserve this."

"Are you insane? You've gained nothing by this stunt."

"We've gained each other," Jerry said and, grabbing Pam's hand, left the house.

Joe gave a low whistle. "I'm glad you called."

Lucy had tried calling her sister, tried Emma, no one was home and, desperate, half frightened to, she had dialed Joe's number.

"Listen," he had said, "I'm going to pick you up and bring you over here. Can you hold on? I'll be there in fifteen minutes. Just stay put, I'm leaving right now."

Joe brought Lucy up to his bedroom, put on soothing music and drew her a bath in the large sunken tub. While she was soaking, he called Jerry at the hotel. "This is Joseph Sachs, I'm representing your ex-wife. I understand Pam White is with you? I want you to advise her to have all of her things out of the house by noon tomorrow. That's right, we're changing the locks."

He wrapped Lucy in his robe and settled her on the bed, then brought in tea. He ruffled her hair. "I had a wonderful time with you today."

"Was it today?"

Joe looked at his watch. "Guess not. Yesterday."

She began to cry. He took the cup from her hand, lifted her in his lap and held her. "I wish I could take some of your pain. You're beautiful, you know?" He kissed her forehead and smoothed back the hair. "I was reading a Hasidic tale the other day. It said hearts that have been shattered make the best vessels."

"What does that mean?" she said, sniffling.

"Every human spirit has been broken hundreds of times, and if you haven't, you can't know what life is. You can't feel compassion."

"I took her in off the street, I trusted her."

"I know, I know. If it were me, I'd be afraid to trust

again, and I'd fight real hard against that. I'd also try to see how disturbed these two people are, to do something so crazy."

"Pam says she has no guilt."

"That's her problem. You don't have to live in her skin, she does. And you know, in a strange way she did you a favor, though that wasn't her intention. You can't have any more fantasies about Jerry."

She shook her head. "Finito."

Joe turned back the linens. "Fresh sheets, in your honor. Want to check?" She smiled weakly. "No." The interminable day—it seemed to stretch back forever: fishing, the fourth of July, the parties, the missed night's sleep—was finally catching up with her, and, holding on to Joe as if to a life raft, she fell asleep.

When she awoke, she felt the pain and dread even before she could remember what had happened. She opened her eyes and started. Joe was not in the bed, but she saw: on the pillow was a pink rose.

She burst into tears. Slipping the rose in the buttonhole of Joe's robe, she went downstairs. Fleetwood Mac was singing about the women who will come and go. "Your clothes are in the dryer," Joe said.

"Thanks," she said in a choked voice.

"Bacon's done. French toast will be up in a second. I hope you like bacon."

She nodded. "Jews love bacon."

He kissed her. "It's a gorgeous day. Come on," he said, "you don't have to carry that old baggage anymore."

"How do I stop the pictures? Every time I see Pam with Jerry . . ."

"The pictures will stop. After breakfast, let's go down to the beach and take a walk."

The beach air was salt-tangy and fresh. The winds had blown away the smog, so it was possible to see the sharp outlines of Catalina and the offshore islands. A brown seal was bobbing in the waves, and children were laughing and pointing at it.

"I can't help feeling I'm being punished," Lucy said.

"Don't think like that."

"I sort of encouraged Pam when she was playing Henry off against Luke. I told her, do whatever will make you happy. I guess I found some pleasure, some sense of getting even vicariously, watching her make the two men suffer and crawl back for more. I never dreamed she would use those tactics against me."

"What did you mean when you told her that?"

"That I was her friend, her happiness came first."

Joe nodded.

"Do you think I brought it on myself?"

"I think you have a lot to be grateful for."

Lucy looked puzzled.

"Beauty, brains, a heart, legs that can walk eight miles up and down the Sierras."

"Was it eight? It felt like twenty."

"I never took a woman in the back country before. I had a feeling about you, though. You're the most together woman I've ever known."

"How can you say that?"

He took her by the shoulders. "Don't you understand, those people are idiots. What they did is all about you. Pam wants to be you, and Jerry wants to have you but in a more manageable form. If you weren't in the equation, there wouldn't be anything. The relationship is doomed."

She shook her head. "I think it will work."

"It doesn't matter, let it go."

She sighed.

He grabbed her arm and began running down the beach until they came to a bluff where, tackling her, he rolled with her over and over until they landed, breathless, in the sand. The sun was strong and they lay on their backs and fell asleep.

When they awoke, warm all through, they went to the Seafood Shoppe, where they ate fried scallops and french fries and cole slaw and mugs of icy beer at an outdoor table.

Joe did not drive her home until evening. He told her to wait in the car while he made sure Pam was gone. "Okay, everything's clear. Will you be all right now?"

She nodded. "You've been great."

"I'll be checking on you."

She opened the door but he reached across her and pulled it shut. "I want you to know something. You have a friend in me, Lucy, a friend who isn't going to let you down. I know I've been a disappointment in other ways, believe it or not I've been a disappointment to myself. But I won't disappoint you as a friend."

She nodded. "There's one thing."

"What?"

"You won't . . ." She bit her lip. "You won't go out and fuck my friends?"

He shook his head. "Believe me."

The house felt strange, there were vacant spaces and balls of dust where Pam's furniture and movie posters and grandfather clock had been. Yet something of Pam lingered, like perfume. Lucy decided she would sell the place and move, no she mustn't let them drive her from her house. She would redecorate, pull up the garden, have a Jacuzzi installed. She began to call plumbers and painters, but she could not bear the whispers of Pam that hustled off into the corners of the house.

In the days that followed, Lucy was at home very little. She did errands, she did nothing. She visited person after person, telling her story as if appealing to a jury: hear my case.

Driving, eating, there was a tirade in her head addressed to Pam. "You think if you 'feel' something, any behavior is justified. 'Feeling is all.' Well you have plenty to be guilty about. You think if you marry my husband, live in my house, wear the clothes I do and trace my steps you can have the success I've had but you can't, because you don't have guts. Craft. Discipline. When I was your age, I had produced six shows. Jerry had built a record company. Henry had worked his way into the best law firm in the city. And what have you done? Piddled away your time 'feeling.' "

She imagined Pam and Jerry being brutally killed. She imagined them at home, watching a movie on television. Pam was curled up next to Jerry on the left side of the bed, the side where Lucy had slept. Lucy wanted to smash her head against the wall to stop the pictures.

She found herself in Beverly Hills one afternoon. She walked into a hair salon she had never seen and asked for the first free operator. Normally, she would not let anyone cut her hair unless she knew him.

"I'm Kenji," said a man with a Japanese accent.

She nodded.

He waited.

"I need a trim."

"You like part your hair in center?"

She shrugged.

"You like curls or you like straight?"

"Yes."

He went to work in silence.

Swatches of hair began falling on her smock. She picked up *Cosmopolitan* to read an interview with Robert Redford but could not concentrate. What was eating at her was this: she believed Pam had done something wrong, something she herself would never do. Try as she might, she was not capable of imagining any circumstances in which she would act as Pam had acted.

Yet the jury did not agree. People wavered in their opinions like the needle of a compass in which there was no true North. Those who believed in the credo of nonpossessiveness told Lucy she had nothing to be upset about. "It's not a terrible thing," Emma said. "It's not surprising that two close friends would be attracted to the same man. You should have compassion. Friendships can survive these things, over time."

Others responded with outrage. Lucy's sister, Leslie, said, "I can't believe Pam . . . what a vicious thing to do. I've always made a pact with my women friends there are millions of men in the world, don't get involved with someone I love."

For every vote there was a countervote or an abstention. One man told Lucy she had created the situation, so there was no one to forgive but herself. "You may have to communicate to Jerry and Pam that you take responsibility for creating everything and have no blame."

"They'll think I'm crazy."

He shrugged. "Do you want your life to work?"

Her eyes glanced at the mirror. Kenji was cutting her hair in layers, jagged layers that started above the ear.

"That's too short."

He stopped.

She waved her hand. It was too late.

Kenji sprayed water on her hair from a plastic misting bottle. "I check now," he said, and began to make crisp cuts.

Lucy watched in a kind of stupefaction. Her nose was growing longer, as if she were looking in a fun-house mirror, and her chin, the whole lower part of her face, the part that usually was softened and camouflaged by smooth waves of hair, was being exposed in all its lumpy weakness.

Kenji began fluffing the hair with his fingers.

She shut her eyes. She wanted to know: was there a right and a wrong way to behave? She felt there was, but she was vulnerable to being confused. Notions of "being in the moment," "doing what feels good," "not judging"—these ideas, banal as they were, so permeated the world in which she moved that anyone who professed to have an absolute standard was looked upon with condescension. By what authority did such a person make judgments?

Yet Lucy had seen the consequences of having one standard for Luke and Henry and another for herself. Wasn't it necessary to have a code? Yes, but then, was it necessary to have the agreement of others for such a code to hold force?

Heat lamps were placed on either side of her, and Kenji held up a hand mirror to show her the back of her hair. I hate it, she thought. When she walked out of the salon, she looked as she felt.

Mercifully, she was meeting Henry for dinner. There was a bond of causality between them. Because of Henry, Lucy had started living with Pam. Because of Lucy, Pam had met the man she would marry instead of Henry.

"I'm glad it's over," Henry said, when they were seated in the back booth at Chez Johnny. "I knew I couldn't handle being married to her. I laid her off on you, to take some of the pressure off me. So I'm to blame, partly. I'm sorry."

Lucy dismissed this with a shake of the head.

"How do you feel about Jerry?"

"It's odd, I don't feel much of anything. I guess I expected no better of him. He has a history of seducing secretaries, wives of friends. But Pam! Pam knew my most private thoughts. Pam helped me plan how to win Jerry back. And this is what I can't forget—Pam made the call. When I was away, she went to his room at 3 A.M. and whispered 'home.' She threw away our friendship, me, without so much as a pang."

Henry clicked his tongue. "Back-stabbing cunt. This was the one thing she could beat you at. This was the one thing she'd mastered—making men love her. Nobody can make you feel as deliriously happy and crazy as Pam can, and nobody can make you feel as devastated. She has no conscience. She's malicious, she enjoys finding the weak spot and plunging in the knife."

As he railed against her, though, Lucy began to remember how endearing she could be. Her gaiety and singing in the house. Her face at the back gate. Her dramatic enthusiasms. Her heartfelt empathy.

"She's wretchedly unfulfilled and jealous of anyone who's not. She's weak, in a way you and I aren't.

"I don't know," Lucy said. "On the surface, she possesses nothing—no connections, money, job. But that's what makes her voice so strong. She does what she wants, regardless of what people say. She thrusts out her chin, casts her fate to the wind again and again with complete faith that she'll come out okay."

She ran a teaspoon over her napkin. "God, I loved her."

2

Two months later, on a hot autumn day when
the winds were up and fire warnings were posted, Lucy met
Joe at his house at noon and they worked until late evening.
They did not stop for meals but munched on cheese and tuna
and pastries and Joe drank coffee. They took the same
places they always took: Lucy on the sofa, Joe in a chair,
scribbling on a clipboard.

Lucy had started to work with Joe shortly after Pam's departure. She had not known or cared, at first, what kind of
film they would make, but as weeks passed, she and Joe began to sense that something was there, shimmering, in the
current that passed between them. Like a photograph in a
developing bath, it would gradually reveal itself.

They established rituals. Every day around five, Lucy
would wrap herself in a rose afghan Joe's grandmother had
made and which, Joe said, had magic powers. The sky beyond the deck would turn pink, then silver, dulling to gray
and finally black. Joe would turn on lamps and build a fire,
and it was then, when the vast window glass was dark, like a
screen calling up pictures, that they did their best thinking.

''We should make a film about being single,'' Joe said on

this night in autumn. "It's the primary experience of the de-
cade. Everyone is, or has been or will be alone. I heard a report on the radio that in the latest census, seventy million
people in America are single. That's almost a third of the
population."

"Isn't this a little close to home?"

"Come on, that's what makes great work. Nobody's
done this in a naturalistic way. They do cute specials about
video dating, but nobody's gone into the grit, the compulsion, the loneliness, the incredible highs and lows and how
it becomes a way of life."

Lucy nodded, twirling her hair. "You're right. When I
first split up with Jerry, I thought being single was a transition. I would pass from one relationship to another until one
'took,' so I didn't want to acquire too much baggage. Now,
when I look back, I think my marriage was a fluke."

"I know mine was."

"It's like being condemned to a desert. You're constantly
searching, but all you get is sand through the fingers. I've
become very good at the search. I meet hundreds of men,
sometimes I think I'm running them through my house by
conveyor belt. We get stoned, we exchange a few personal
stories, go in the Jacuzzi and go to bed and maybe it lasts a
week or two and someone calls in sick."

"I can think of any excuse to bolt. Like, I stopped calling
one woman because I couldn't stand her feet."

"What was wrong?"

"They were white, clammy." He made a face.

"Couldn't you send her to the Beverly Hills Tanning
Salon?"

He laughed sadly.

"It's like a disease," Lucy said. "The problem is, all you
meet in the desert are fellow carriers. The longer you stay,
the harder it is to get out. Anyone who does is a source of
wonder to me. How did he do it?"

"I'm looking for the woman who'll end the search."

"What would that person be like?"

"Someone who's very bright, very creative, good at what she does." He smiled. "And lets me walk all over her."

Lucy laughed. "Any particular physical type?"

"I probably respond better to dark-haired women. Someone who takes pride in her appearance. No obesity or baldness." He chuckled. "Someone who enjoys a good cunt lapping at odd hours of the day."

"Hey, that could be me."

"Sometimes at a party," Joe said, "I'll give myself until midnight to choose a woman, and I'll end up going home alone because I kept thinking the great one was in the next room."

Lucy walked into the kitchen to make more tea. "With any man I'm with, there's always a tape running in my head—he's too short, too tall, not bright enough, not warm enough, doesn't read enough, not Jewish, too Jewish. Is he right, would I be happier with someone else? A man I met in India, a man who's an expert on mythology, told me I shouldn't think of marriage as a love affair because all love affairs end on the rocks. Marriage is something else—a surrender to the duad."

Joe clasped his hands like a boxer. "Give me surrender to the duad!"

"The concept is great, but when it comes to specifics, it's invariably surrender to someone who has white feet."

"We've got to capture this in a film."

"How do we dramatize it?"

Joe began to pace. "Maybe we should look at the industries that have sprung up to serve these people. Singles bars. Singles apartment complexes. Club Med. Sushi bars. Racquetball clubs—they've become a scene. Everyone there has frizzed hair and drinks Perrier and likes Woody Allen movies and wears designer gym clothes. While you work out on the Nautilus, you can watch these women in tight leotards jiggling their tits."

Lucy shook her head. "That's all been done, and it's superficial. The real stuff goes on in private. It's the endless affairs, the dates that are disasters, the nights when you bolt awake at 5 A.M. and realize you're stark raving alone."

Joe walked behind Lucy and began massaging her shoulders. "Juicy Lucy. You're cookin' tonight."

"I think we're onto something, if we can figure out how to film it."

"We will. We can do for single people what that documentary about the Louds did for the American family. It made everyone talk and think. It was riveting."

"If we could show men and women living it, talking about it in real language . . ."

"We could sweep the ratings," Joe said.

"A legend in our time," she said wryly.

He leaned down and hugged her. She could smell traces of the cologne he used, musk. "Are you enjoying this at all?" he said.

"I am." She ran her hands over his arms. "I'm afraid I'm going to get addicted to you."

"You will, that's why I wanted to do this. It's going to be more exhilarating than any drug, and when it's over, we're going to feel there's no one in the world who understands us better than the other."

"Then what?"

"Who knows?" He released his arms. "Listen, can we break a little early tonight?"

"Sure."

While Lucy lingered, making notes on index cards, Joe took a shower and dressed. Instead of the jeans he always wore with her, he put on slacks, a cotton sweater and a Giorgio Armani sport coat.

"When do you want to meet again?" She was standing in the doorway of the bathroom, watching him blow-dry his hair.

"I need a haircut."

"No, I like it long."

"You do? The beard needs trimming though. Monday. No, let's make it Sunday. I'll call you tomorrow." He shut off the hair dryer. "Be careful on the road, people drive crazy on Fridays."

"Right."

She was halfway to the car when he ran up behind her, spun her in the air and kissed her.

As she drove home, Lucy began to feel dread. It was the weekend and she had no plans. She wondered where Joe was going. She wondered, also, why he had been so eager to embark on this collaboration.

The truth was, she wanted to be with him. If she could be patient, but that had never been easy for her. If she could wait, though, until they grew to know each other "better than anyone in the world," she could slip through his defenses. Time would do the rest.

At home, she went to check the phone machine. There were always messages but it was never the message she wanted: a new voice, a call to life. Instead, it was: her insurance agent, a plumber doing work on her Jacuzzi. One more. A tennis teacher, canceling their lesson.

She looked in the paper to see what was on television. Nothing good, there was never anything good on Friday night. She went upstairs, thinking she would read *Daniel Martin*, then fix something to eat and sit in the Jacuzzi and that would take her through the evening.

The phone rang shortly after eight. A man she had met at a party many months before—Barry Tamkin. She remembered the party, she vaguely remembered him but she was not sure. He said he worked in advertising, lived in the hills of Mullholland Drive. She ought to think of some polite excuse to hang up.

"I have no memory of you," she said.

"I remember you perfectly. You have blue eyes and a great smile."

"Is that why you waited all these months to call?"

He laughed. "I've been out of town a lot."

"And you've been very busy, working."

"Are you coming up here?" Barry said.

"Right now?"

"If you don't like what you see, you can turn around. It's a beautiful night."

"It's a long drive."

"The jasmine's blooming. I've got a fire going."

"Sounds like an ad for Black Velvet."

Barry laughed. "Hey, are we in love, or what?"

Lucy knew, driving there, that it was a mistake but she could not help herself. She parked in front of his house and smoked a joint to help her through the awkwardness. She walked to the door and knocked.

"Come on in."

Barry Tamkin was watching a hockey game on television. He was tall and freckled, with reptilian eyes and reddish-brown hair. She did not recognize him but she remembered, now, hearing a friend speak of him.

"Did you go out with Gail?"

He shrugged. "Gail and I are good friends."

With the hockey game and its wacky organ music for background, Barry told her his story. He had come out from Chicago three years before. Divorced. Changed agencies. "Always been successful at whatever I touched. But it's been at a price."

"What's that?"

"You don't see a wife and kids around. Sidney!"

A chocolate-brown Burmese cat came slinking across the carpet. He picked up the cat and kissed its face. "Sidney's my family." The phone rang. There were phones in every room and they rang through the evening.

When the hockey game was over, Barry came and sat beside her. "Will you rub my neck?" he said, sounding boyish.

"Does your neck hurt?"

"No."

"You want to be touched?"

"Yes."

She reached over to rub his neck but he turned abruptly and kissed her, slipping his hand under her blouse, finding her breast and teasing her nipple. She liked the way he was kissing her, she was aroused. ("Are you staying?" he had asked, halfway through the hockey game. It always came to that. She had not answered.) From the way he was touching her, she could tell he would be a skillful lover.

"I don't do this very often," she said.

"Neither do I."

"It's hard."

"All good things are hard, sweetheart."

She ignored the double meaning. "It creates a false sense of intimacy."

"Let's go in the bedroom," Barry said. "The outcome is gonna be the same, only we'll be more comfortable."

She walked after him to the bedroom, they began kissing again, removing their clothes and wham, he went right into her. He felt good but she needed more preparation. He came in a short time, grunting, not seeming to have any interest in whether she had.

Selfish ass. She started to roll over and get up but he grabbed her arm, pulled her around and placed her hand on his cock.

"You want some more?" he said.

He entered her again. This time she did come, but only by concentrating on what it had felt like in the past. You remember what it's like, you can do it, yes, you need it, you'll feel better, yes, it's for you.

"I have to leave," she said. He did not protest or even walk her to the door. "See ya later," he called.

At home, by reflex, she checked the phone machine. She walked to the refrigerator and, standing there, began to eat from containers: cold chili, sour cream, cucumbers, leftover apple pie. She ate without tasting, until she realized she had eaten far too much. She went in the bathroom, stuck her finger down her throat and threw up.

3

Six weeks later, Joe and Lucy stepped out of a cab in lower Manhattan, passed through revolving doors, rode an escalator and three express elevators to the 106th floor of the World Trade Center. Swallowing hard to clear their ears, they came out on a landing with blue carpet that ran from the floor up the walls to the ceiling. "We're like merchants, going to Venice to sell our wares," Joe said.

The buyer they were calling on was Howard Ness, founder of the Ness Company, which had amassed a fortune converting apartment buildings to condominiums. Ness sat behind his desk, with a heart-stopping view of the five boroughs below him: toy bridges, tiny streets, little cars. Ness, who had offices in New York, Los Angeles, Aspen and Maui, wore a green warm-up suit with curly gray chest hair spilling out the front. He was forty-eight.

Howard Ness was a fanatic follower of football, and after seeing *Rookies*, had asked Joe to make a television special the Ness Company would sponsor. Joe had said he was about to collaborate with a woman.

"I love it," Ness said.

Joe told him to watch *Carey's Children*, and the next day,

Ness called at 9 A.M. "That was my story, my goddamned story. I have two daughters, and let me tell you." He paused. "Three years ago, my wife and I separated. It was my decision, she wanted to stay married, but I was torn apart inside anyway. The day I moved out, I got in my car, steady, calm, drove two blocks and puked."

"Mmm," Joe said.

The grunt was sufficient to send Ness on. After his divorce, he had led a fantastic life, flying to Aspen and Mexico and Mykonos. He found that when he asked a lady out to dinner, she appeared with her toothbrush in her purse. "Not just the diaphragm, the toothbrush! Then I got married again. Want to know why?"

"What's that?" Joe said.

Again, the pause. "I didn't want to look at another strange vagina."

Joe laughed. This is an orangutan, he thought. But Ness could produce the five or six hundred thousand Joe and Lucy would need and save them going the long, tedious route of funding through local stations and federal grants.

"We'll have a proposal for you in a few weeks." Joe said.

"I'll be waiting."

Now, sitting on Ness's couch on the 106th floor, Joe began, "The name of the film is *An American Hunger.*"

"It's about the hunger of people who are single, looking for connection," Lucy said.

"This sounds a little"—Ness wrinkled his nose—"existential."

"Existential?" Lucy said.

"I don't know if 'existential' is the right word. What is it—some guy pushing a rock up a hill? What I'm trying to say is, I don't sit around thinking about hunger. I want to break forty-five in the ten-k run." He was flying to California the following week for the Beverly Hills Jogathon. He showed them the leaflet. "Jog with the stars through the streets of Beverly Hills."

"It won't be a theoretical show," Joe said. "We're going to follow a woman who's single and a man who's single through one weekend in Southern California. She's a teacher who works with special children, he's an insurance agent. She's fixing up her house, she goes shopping, she jogs, she gets a facial. She has a terrible blind date. It's her thirty-sixth birthday, and she celebrates it with her two close women friends."

Lucy: "He's living in an apartment complex by the beach that's a haven for people in transit. He plays tennis, hangs out by the pool, watches football with the guys, and he's always juggling women in and out, working the phones, filling up every second so he never has to be alone."

Ness fidgeted in his chair.

"We'll cut back and forth between them, starting Friday afternoon when they leave their jobs and ending Sunday night when they're both watching '60 Minutes.' "

"He goes to pick up Colonel Sanders fried chicken and eats it alone in front of the TV," Lucy said. "She's in bed with her cats."

"Wait a minute, why don't you bring them together in the end?" Ness said. "Let them meet at Colonel Sanders, or the pool or something, and watch the show together!"

Joe and Lucy exchanged glances. "I think that would be too contrived," Joe said.

"The point is that they're trapped," Lucy said. "That's their predicament—they can't find each other."

"Sounds kinda downbeat," Ness said.

"It'll be strong," Lucy said. "Because everyone will be thinking, if only they could meet, they're good people and they have the same hunger."

"I guarantee you, it'll attract a lot of attention," Joe said.

Ness pushed up the sleeves of his warm-up suit. "I don't know if you're right, but my instincts say to let you loose. I love the work you guys have done, I'm banking on that. How soon before I see a rough cut?''

''Nine months,'' Joe said.

Ness stood. ''Just make sure it's got heart. No guys pushing rocks.''

''He has no idea what we're doing,'' Joe said.

They were riding in a limousine Ness had lent them, up the Henry Hudson Parkway, past the docks where tugboats were pulling in a French merchant ship.

''It doesn't matter. We did it, Joe, now the fun part begins. We can make the film we want. You know how tough it is getting through the bureaucracy of American Can Company or NEA. Ness doesn't even want to see a treatment.''

''I'm just nervous.''

''It was too easy.''

Joe stretched out his feet. ''I'm starting to have doubts. I thought this was a good idea, but I'm not sure, maybe it won't work. It seems kind of thin, and not terribly significant.''

''Every project seems thin in the beginning. Once we're shooting, we'll be wondering how we can condense it into an hour.''

''You're probably right.'' Joe leaned back. ''I love this car.'' He played with the buttons in the panel of the limousine, rolling up the glass between the driver and them. He pulled Lucy to him. ''You're my lucky lady, Lucy. Let's celebrate. Let's go to the Russian Tea Room and drink vodka and eat red caviar.''

''Now you're talking.''

He chose a tape from the stereo compartment and started Warren Zevon, ''Excitable Boy.''

''The limo makes me feel so decadent. Like tying women up and drinking out of slippers.''

''Want to do that with me?''

He lit a ciagarette. ''If you really want it.''

"Screw lunch. Let's go to that hotel." She pointed to a brick flop house on the waterfront with a sign, "Honeycutt Hotel."

Joe laughed. "You're crazy." He pressed down the intercom. The Russian Tea Room, please."

Joe was staying with a friend in the Village, and Lucy planned to spend the weekend with her sister and Ryan and the baby on Riverside Drive. Lucy could hardly wait to see Max. The first time she had seen him, he was six months old, and not at all like her previous impression of babies—a cranky blob—but playful, expressive. His face was like a Buddha's, with a widow's peak of gold. He had a habit of holding his arms up, like a cowboy surrendering, and opening his mouth in an O of wonder. He almost never cried, he laughed and babbled and he liked to press his head against Lucy's and stare into her eyes.

Such love Lucy had felt for this child! In the mornings, her sister would walk into the study where Lucy was sleeping and lay Max on her chest. "Want a baby?" It was as if, in loving and cuddling Max, she was renurturing herself.

"Loo-dee," Max said, when Lucy arrived from the Russian Tea Room. She was startled: he was standing up, walking—with that endearing baby gait—but he still had the Buddha's face.

Lucy offered to stay with him the following day so Leslie and Ryan could have a break. She fed and changed him, took him to the park, stared into his eyes and sang with him, "Yi yi yi," and gave him a bath. By the time she put him to bed, she was drained. It had been tedious, sitting with him at meals. He had spilled his milk and picked at his lamb chops for an hour, then smeared lamb grease all over the table. Drool ran from his lips, and in his raucous hour before bed, he had dived on top of Lucy, sending baby drool up her nose. It was a relief to hand him back to Leslie and Ryan, and yet, when Lucy went shopping Saturday, she missed him and hurried back to see his Buddha's face.

Saturday night they had a family dinner. Lucy's parents drove down from New Rochelle, her mother carrying a pot of brisket and a Jello mold. Their aunt and uncle drove in from the Island, and their cousins, Barbara and Alvin, came with their mates and children.

Lucy had invited Joe, whom she met in the foyer with Max in her arms.

"What a happy baby," Joe said.

"He's like this all the time."

Joe kissed her, and there was the familiar scent of musk.

"Doe," Max said.

"He's been coached!"

"Come on, wouldn't you like one?"

"There are disadvantages—when he's sixteen and thinks you're shit."

"He'll come around."

"Easy." Joe took her arm as they walked down the hall. "Let's get the work done first."

At dinner, Lucy's mother spooned Jello into Max's mouth as she had once fed her daughters. "Try it, you'll like it, there." Alvin's two children slid off their chairs and ran through the rooms, playing tag. Lucy began to feel shooting pains in her stomach. From the corner of her eye, she saw Leslie huddled with Joe at the end of the table. They were laughing, talking, and suddenly Joe jumped back in his chair. He and Leslie turned and stared at Lucy.

Max said a new word, "Gran-ma," and everyone applauded. Lucy doubled over. The cramps were so intense she could barely walk to Leslie's room. She sank onto the bed, but there was no relief, whether she lay on her stomach or side. Her father came in with a heating pad, followed by her mother with a cup of tea. "A touch of flu?" her father said.

She groaned. "I don't think so."

"Yes," her mother said, "it's the flu that's going around. I had it several weeks ago. I got those griping pains so bad, I threw myself on the floor at Bloomingdale's. I didn't care if I lived or died."

Lucy laughed—which made the pain worse—at the image of her mother facedown in Bloomingdale's. "What department?"

"What does it matter? Third-floor dresses. Drink your tea while it's hot."

Lucy was ashamed, having to be cared for like a baby. "Go and play with Max."

She tried some deep breathing, turned from side to side and somehow, despite the shouting of the children, fell asleep. When she opened her eyes, Leslie was sitting on the bed. "Everyone's gone now."

Lucy yawned.

"Joe said he'll call you tomorrow."

"I'm a wreck," Lucy said.

"No you're not, you look beautiful, you look like an Italian movie star."

"Leslie, what's wrong?"

Leslie was wiping her eyes with a Kleenex. "I feel like the black sheep of the family." Her voice began to squeak. "Joe was telling me about the film you're making. Barbara just got promoted to editor. Alvin's a surgeon. And I have this humdrum life."

"No you don't. You have a fabulous baby and a wonderful husband and a home that's spilling over with warmth."

"Anyone can have that."

"I don't seem to be able to."

Leslie's voice stopped squeaking. "It'll happen, Lucy, I'm positive. You have so much to give."

"What did you think of Joe?"

"He's great, I'd love to have him in the family."

"Don't hold your breath."

"I think there's something there."

"Why?"

"I was telling him about my gestalt group, how I learned these techniques to stop worrying and be less nervous? He seemed interested, so I told him they have a center in California. There's usually ten women to every man, he might meet someone he could get involved with, but I said, you don't want that.

"He said, 'Yes I do, very much.'

"So I said, 'Then why don't you marry my sister?' "

"No!"

"I'm telling you, there's something there."

"Leslie, how could you."

Ryan walked in. "She's right. He looked like he'd been hit with a shovel."

"What did he say?"

"After he stopped choking?" Ryan laughed.

"He said, 'Who knows, stranger things have happened.' "

Lucy covered her eyes.

"It was all in a light spirit," Ryan said. "I don't think he was offended or anything."

"Believe me," Leslie said. "There's something there."

4

Joe was behind one of the cameras, Lucy by the window, making notes. A wordless excitement passed between them: yes, this is great, go on. Lucy thought, we should have a closer angle on Claire, and as she turned to tell Joe, he was already moving in. With the lightweight camera, he could move almost unnoticed by the women being photographed. They were on a beam: Joe, Lucy, the crew and the three women drinking champagne and eating dark chocolate raspberry cake.

At the head of the table was Claire Leigh, wearing a Victorian blouse and skirt of pinkish-buff, which, in the candlelight, seemed one with the color of her skin. Joe and Lucy had been following Claire for weeks. The footage, before tonight, had been disappointing, although she photographed well. While she was growing up, Claire had been told she looked like Brigitte Bardot, not because she was blond, for she wasn't, but because of a kittenish quality to her face, a sensuous pout to her mouth and a pleasing roundness to her carriage. She had always attracted the attention of men, but as most of her friends and younger sisters had married, she had gone on having affairs. She began to lose the kittenish innocence and found herself, by default, building a life of independence: buying a house, writing children's books, living for a time in London and then Idaho.

She had been slow to relax with the cameras, but tonight was her thirty-sixth birthday and the Dom Perignon was working magic. She and her two friends had known each other since high school; their birthdays fell in the same month, and for years they had made a ritual of going out together to celebrate. They took turns picking restaurants, but this year, having agreed to be filmed, they had hired a caterer and were being served in the dining room of Judy's condominium.

Judy sat on Claire's right. She was a medical researcher, a no-nonsense woman with a warm, Semitic face, a head of dark curls and intelligent, merry eyes. Judy was something of a maverick, but she dressed like a suburban matron in polyester pants.

The third friend was Phyllis, a banking executive, who spoke with a husky voice. Phyllis had slightly buck teeth, long fingernails and breasts that pushed out of the V of her silk blouse. She led with her teeth and her breasts.

"To survival," Phyllis said.

"That's not enough," Claire said.

"What should we drink to then?"

"Love, for all of us," Claire said, "and satisfaction in our work."

"Uh oh, that means conquering the biggies—fear of intimacy and fear of success," Phyllis said.

"Without those two, you've got nothing," Judy said.

"To mastery?" Claire said.

"Mastery." They clinked glasses.

"Let's open the presents."

While they began unwrapping boxes, Joe had to change film. Lucy handed him a new magazine, while Tony Burroughs, the second cameraman, covered the women.

Judy had bought her friends gift certificates at Paradise

Now, a new massage parlor for women only. "Clearly an idea whose time has come."

"What on earth do they do?" Claire said.

"The guy on the phone said, 'We give sexual massage, with lotions and rabbit's fur mittens. We also give baths, where the operator goes in the water with you. Vibrators are optional. But by law, we cannot fuck and suck.' "

"I don't believe this," Claire said.

"We'll go togehter," Phyllis said. "I've been celibate so long, a massage parlor sounds good."

Phyllis' present to Claire was a gold bracelet, which she immediately slipped on. "I love gold." Claire leaned over and kissed her.

"Want to hear something funny?" Phyllis said. "When I was buying it, I remembered, that's the same thing I gave you for your Sweet Sixteen party—except it was a charm bracelet."

"You're right. Do you realize, that was twenty years ago?"

"No," Judy said.

"The party was at Scandia," Phyllis said.

"I remember it was raining," Claire said. "I was worried people wouldn't show up, and I wore a blue dress and a white fox sweater and we ate veal birds and I know exactly what was in my mind. I was longing for a boy I could love, hoping one would turn up in the pile of presents."

They laughed. Joe, behind the camera, gave Lucy a thumbs-up sign.

"Who would have dreamed that twenty years later, I'd be longing for the same thing. It's odd, because I always intended to be married."

"Not me," Judy said. "Not since I was twenty-five. I stopped thinking of myself as single, and started thinking I was a family of one."

"I've begun to see how I've sabotaged all my chances to be married," Claire said.

"How?" Phyllis said.

"I have a weakness for artists, crazy men who don't have any desire to be settled. The ones who are ripe for settling down, I don't even see."

"I do," Phyllis said. "Once."

Claire laughed. "Roger was a perfect example."

"The piano player?"

She nodded. "He's not attractive at all, he's short and has a weak chin and a fairly large nose so at first you take pity on him. Then he's so charming, so brilliant, so totally original and witty you're dazzled, you forget the way he looks, he sweeps you off your feet. He makes you totally fall in love with him, and as soon as you do, he withdraws."

"How?" Judy said.

"When he makes love, he's not there. He gets hard but he can't come, while before, he could come all night. He finds fault with you, he knows your insecurities and goes for the jugular. You can't believe it's happening, because at the beginning, he was heaping appreciation on you like you'd never been appreciated."

Phyllis sighed. "It's astonishing what power one lousy man can have. You obsess and cry and people say, 'Over him? He's so . . . nothing.' "

"What Roger does at that point, when you can't let go, is start cheating on you, seeing the next woman he's going to run the cycle with," Claire said.

They fell silent. Joe moved backward, widening the angle, and Lucy signaled Tony to stay on Claire. Lucy felt uneasy; the high spirits had fizzled, and something was bothering Joe.

Judy opened another bottle of champagne. "I think," she said, "there are two kinds of men—those who are able to make a commitment, and those who aren't, and the men who are exciting may not be able."

"I can think of men who are both," Claire said.

"Maybe they're taken. Maybe you won't get one. You should choose one of the other kind."

"I'd be bored," Claire said.

"I used to think Stan was boring," Judy said. "I mean, he runs an auto dealership. I only went out with him because the sex was good. I complained to all my friends about his shortcomings and disgusting habits. Now we're so in love. When I go to his house, he's so happy to see me, and he has dinner ready. I figure, now that I've become like the man I wanted to marry, he's the wife such a man would have."

Laughter.

"Does he have any friends?" Phyllis began applying lipstick.

"They're all married."

"You know any guys I could go out with?" Phyllis asked.

The three searched their minds, threw out names and, for one reason or another, rejected them all. "Somebody called to fix me up with a man whose wife died on the P.S.A. crash," Claire said. "When we hung up, I started thinking it was in poor taste. The crash had only been a month before. But my friend called back and said, forget it, he's already met someone."

Lucy heard Joe mutter. "Jesus."

"You gotta grab 'em," Phyllis said.

The soundman covered his mouth to laugh.

"Well, ladies," Judy stood up, wobbly. "I'm going to make coffee."

Claire and Phyllis had left; Lucy, Joe and the crew were packing the gear.

"Do you think you're going to use all that?" Judy said.

"Hard to say," Joe said, "until we see how everything cuts."

"I'm getting nervous now, that Stan might be offended."

"I don't think he will," Lucy said. "It was all said in a warm spirit."

The doorbell rang. Claire walked in, her cheeks flushed from the wind. "My car won't start. Does anyone have a jumper cable?" The others looked around and shook their heads. "I guess I'll call the A.A.A."

"Why don't you leave it here?" Judy said. "Stan will get it started in the morning."

"Are you sure?"

"Sure," Judy said.

"I can give you a lift home," Joe said.

Lucy watched Joe walk down the outside steps with Claire. When they reached the sidewalk, he placed his hand on the small of her back. They spoke a moment, their heads inclining toward each other. Joe helped her into the car and pulled away.

Lucy took her time driving home. As she walked through the patio, she turned on the Jacuzzi. She opened her mail, straightened the kitchen a little and dialed Joe's number. His machine answered. After the beep, she said, "Hi, it's me, give me a call when you get in."

It took another hour for the Jacuzzi to heat up. Lucy slipped off her clothes and, shivering at the cool air on her skin, stepped in the tub. The water bubbled and she lay on her back, staring at the stars. Dawdling there, she grew weak from the heat. She made her way to the bedroom and tried Joe again. The machine. She hung up before the recording had finished. She read for a while, turned off the light, tossed and switched on the lamp. It was 4 A.M. She dialed again, composing what she would say into the machine.

"Hello?"

She was startled. "Joe?"

"What's going on."

"I was just, uh, wondering, did Claire get home all right?"

"Yes, why?"

"Well."

"Something wrong?"

"I don't think it's a good idea . . . to get involved with subjects."

"What are you talking about?"

"The whole thing changes if the person is involved with the guy behind the camera."

"I still don't know what you're talking about."

"You haven't been home."

"How do you know?"

"I've been calling . . ."

"Maybe I didn't feel like answering the phone. Maybe Claire wanted to talk. What is this, anyway? You're starting to monitor my life? I don't have to answer to you. What I do on my own time is none of your business."

"It is my business when the work is at stake. I know how you can give mixed signals, Joe. If she gets hurt or angry, she might pull out of the project."

"You think I'd wreck a movie for some neurotic cunt?"

"I . . ."

"You what."

"I just couldn't figure out where you could be so long."

"You want to know? I'll tell you. There's a flight attendant who lives near Claire. She's away a lot, but every few weeks I call her or stop by her apartment and if she's there I fuck her. Are you happy?"

Lucy's heart was pounding.

"I think you ought to reexamine what you think of me. We're supposed to be partners, more than that. I gave you my word I wouldn't betray you."

"I'm sorry."

"There's supposed to be a foundation of trust here."

"We never talked about it."

"You should check things out before you leap to conclusions."

"You're right, I'm terribly sorry. I'm still paranoid, I guess. Will you forgive me?"

Joe sighed. "Yeah. We all have our demons."

"The shooting went well, don't you think?"

"I was pretty happy. Let's talk about it in the morning."

"A peace offering," Lucy said, holding out a bunch of poppies and a bag of chocolate croissants.

Joe had no shirt on, and his hair was damp from the shower. He kissed Lucy and put the croissants in the oven. They sat down in the sun on the deck, and after a few minutes, the scent of melting chocolate drifted out from the kitchen.

"I'm excited about the footage," Lucy said. "It could be our centerpiece."

Joe wrinkled his forehead. "Let's see what the rushes look like." He went inside and came back with the croissants, a plate of fruit and cheese.

"When Claire was talking about the guy who seduced her and pulled away, that was strong."

"I'm afraid it's going to sound like a bunch of overprivileged women whining about how men have done them in."

"Claire said she was sabotaging herself."

Joe shrugged. "I don't like whiny girls."

"Every woman will identify with that story. It's the cowboy, blowing into your life with heat and smoke and riding off."

"There's a cowboy in your past?"

"Many." Lucy smiled. "Right back to the first man I loved."

"Who was that?"

"His name was Uzi. Uzi Tamir."

Joe's attention was pricked. "Israeli?"

She nodded.

"How did you meet?"

135

"My freshman year at N.Y.U. He was an exchange student at Columbia, and he came to a party. I couldn't stand him at first, I didn't like his arrogant manner or his name. It sounded like 'ooze,' and it was too Jewish. I pictured Israel as some ethnic backwater, the whole country like Grossinger's. Uzi kept saying it was the most comfortable place for Jews to live, but I thought New York was a comfortable place for Jews to live."

"Was he a Sabra?"

"Born in Austria. His father was killed by the Nazis, and his mother escaped with him and made her way to Tel Aviv. I have to tell you, I had little interest in his story. He wore short shorts when everyone else was wearing bermudas, and he had clunky sandals and a thick accent. But he kept calling every day and dropping by, and when someone is that determined, it's seductive. He knew I liked movies and offered to take me to everything I wanted to see. He made me feel like the most beautiful, desirable creature. We started going out, I persuaded him to stop wearing the sandals, we necked a lot and he was pushing and I thought, well, it might as well be this one."

She broke off a strand of grapes. "Then I fell in love with him."

"What did he look like?" Joe said.

Lucy squinted. She had not thought of Uzi in years, and he was coming to her in fragments: his lean face, his eager smile, his gruff voice, his mispronunciation of English. "He had a wonderful cleft in his chin, and a space between his front teeth, so it looked like there was a rift down the center of his face. It was very sexy. I always wanted to slip my tongue in the niche between his teeth."

"How long were you with him?"

"Eight months." Lucy was feeling the physical memory steal over her. "One night, I called him at twelve and said I was so distracted, thinking about him, I couldn't study. He didn't seem to react. 'Try to work, you need it,' he said. So I opened my books. Uzi was probably tired, I thought. I fell asleep at my desk, woke up and stumbled to the bathroom when I heard the window being forced open. I screamed, but it was Uzi climbing in, looking flushed and happy and gorgeous. He had waited in the snow for an hour, caught the subway downtown and climbed up the fire escape of the dorm.''

Lucy cut a piece of Camembert. "We did crazy things, we hitchhiked to Quebec for Mardi Gras. Then one weekend in the spring, we were going to catch the train for the beach and he didn't show up at the station. I knew right away, that was it. He wasn't at Columbia, he wasn't with friends, but I knew, there had been no accident. I went to the dorm, crawled in bed and shook. The next day he called and said he was with another girl and we were finished."

She cut another piece of cheese. "I wrote him a vicious letter. I had had several dreams about him disappearing like that, and he was always reassuring me he wouldn't. It sent me to the edge, I actually went to a shrink for the first time.

"A few months later, I thought I should talk to him. I'd begun to think I had said or done things that had driven him away, and if I could see him and change those things, I could win him back."

"More tea?"

She held out her cup.

"Go on."

"We met for a drink at the West End, and I sort of apologized for everything I could think of, and he just stared at the floor." Lucy felt tears forming. She wiped them, irritated. "Can you imagine, after all these years? Sometimes I think Uzi was the original blueprint, the one that set the pattern all my subsequent relationships would take. I haven't seen him since . . . 1965. When the Six Day War broke out, I wondered if he was fighting, if he was hurt or possibly dead. He probably doesn't think about me . . ."

"He thinks about you," Joe said, walking to the edge of the deck.

"How do you know?"

"I've been in his shoes. I've left people for no reason I could understand, except maybe it was too good."

Lucy shook her head. "The trouble is, the best, the most thrilling sex I've had has been with men like that."

"Because they can't be domesticated."

She pulled up the midriff of her sweater. "It's getting hot out here."

"Want to borrow something?"

"Sure."

He brought out a tank top. Turning her back, she slipped off her sweater and jeans and, wearing his shirt and her bikini pants, stretched out on a lawn chair.

Joe began to rub oil on his arms. "You're looking awfully good," he said. "Been working out?"

"Tennis." She flexed her legs. "Not as much as I should."

His head came between the sun and her face. He was kissing her, in more than a friendly way.

"What is this?"

"What's the harm? It's Saturday, the sun feels good." He ran his hand up her leg and squeezed her crotch.

She jumped. Lucy had not made love with anyone in four or five weeks.

"What about that flight attendant?" she whispered.

He lifted her hand and kissed the fingers. "The nice thing about them is, they leave."

"I won't, at least for a while."

"Ah, Lucy." He sank back in the chair next to hers. "There you go, poking a hole in the balloon."

"You should talk. You don't care what hole you poke."

Joe laughed. "Like Dr. Johnson said, 'He who makes a beast of himself gets rid of the pain of being a man.' "

A woodpecker was knocking in a fir tree.

Lucy took a breath and exhaled slowly. "Maybe we should go into the station."

Joe smiled. "Or take a cold shower."

5

They drove into Mariners Village just after ten on a Saturday morning. The joggers were already out and the parking lot was filled with the cars of overnight guests. A sign read:

Visitor Parking
Limit—10 Days

"That means you can't have affairs that last longer than ten days," Joe said.

"Ten days is a long time for some people."

"I guess. The world was created in seven."

They drove up North West Passage and onto Captain's Row, passing the hot and cold pools, the gym, the watchtower and the cluster of shops. All the architecture and landscaping were designed to simulate, crudely, the South Seas.

At the clubhouse, they met Tony, the cameraman, Eddie, the soundman and Floyd, the assistant. They walked down paths lined with hurricane lamps, crossed a fake native bridge suspended over a fake green lagoon and entered building 14015.

"Hi, troops." Rich Sampson answered the door of his apartment wearing a sarong Lucy thought she recognized from ads in the back pages of *Playboy*. Rich had a handsome, boyish face and a lank body that gave the impression of always having looked middle-aged: soft and white. At his heels were a Malamute named Fred and a sleepy-eyed young woman, Doreen, who had grabbed a towel to cover herself.

"Just in time for the morning shower," Rich said.

"What's goin' on, what are all those cameras?" Doreen said.

"I told you, they're making a movie, I'm the star."

"I'm not going in the shower with any cameras."

"He's just funning," Joe said. "We'll wait out here."

Joe and Floyd checked the lighting. Next door, someone was playing "The Age of Aquarius" on an organ. Rich's apartment had a nautical motif: grass matting on the walls, an aquarium, captain's chairs and a table made from a ship's hatch cover.

When Rich and Doreen came out of the bathroom, the cameras were rolling. Doreen walked into the kitchen and began squeezing oranges and cracking eggs.

As they were eating, the door opened and one of Rich's neighbors, Ken, walked in.

"Want some grub?" Rich said.

"No, I'll take a beer though." Ken nodded hello to the crew; he had seen them around for a month. Doreen stood up abruptly, gathered her things, kissed Rich and, tossing her head, walked in front of the cameras and out the door.

"Hope I didn't interrupt," Ken said.

"Are you kidding? Doreen's a nice girl, but she's methadone maintenance. She keeps me off the streets."

"I had another blowup with Rita."

"Rita's his main squeeze," Rich said, turning to the camera, like George Burns turning to the audience in the middle of a sketch with Gracie Allen.

"She won't use a diaphragm," Ken said.

"Why not?"

"She's nuts. She can tune up her car, but she can't learn to put in a diaphragm."

"Selective helplessness," Rich said.

"She let me fuck her in the middle of the month with no protection. She said she knows her body. I shouldn't worry. Last night she calls and says she might be pregnant."

"Probably a false alarm."

"She's offered to leave town, but she won't have an abortion."

Rich shook his head, and opened another beer.

"I'm sweating," Ken said. "Because I couldn't walk away from a situation like that, if it happened."

"I told you, buddy, women in their thirties are dangerous. They're so panicked about having a baby, you can't trust 'em."

"I'm not fucking her again until she works something out."

"I wish I could meet a woman who was more . . . appropriate," Rich said. "Self-sufficient, with some brains. I'm tired of methadone, I've suffered enough."

The phone rang. "Bev!" he said. "How ya doin', sweetheart? Yeah. Uh huh." His voice began to sink. "That's too bad . . . Can't you leave him with a sitter? Yeah, I understand." He hung up. "Shit. Her kid's got the flu, that kills tonight." He looked at his watch. "What are you doing?"

"Having dinner with Rita."

Rich walked out on the balcony and stared at the boat basin. Joe moved after him, then retreated as Rich came back and went to the phones. He kept one line open and one to dial. Working through his book, he reached two machines, a service, a woman who said she had a hangover and would call back, another who had company, another who was going out of town.

Ken stood. "Gotta get going."

"Okay, buddy. Try to relax, it's probably nothing." Rich turned to the camera. "I can't sit around this place on Saturday night. I'll feel like a wolf, prowling the frozen wilderness."

Fred lumbered up on the couch beside him. "I got it, Fred. Palm Springs!" He called the Riviera Hotel. "Reservations, please. Guy? This is Rich Sampson, I need a room tonight. Whaddaya mean you don't have any rooms? This is Richie, Guy. Find me a room and it's good for fifty. Hey, any talent around the pool?" Rich laughed. "Call me back."

He tried the Canyon Club, the Gene Autry, same story, no rooms. The phone rang. "Guy! I knew you'd come through. Fred, we're outa here." He started pulling bags out of the closet, throwing in shirts, toiletries, all the while singing an old tune. "What did Delaware, boys, what did Delaware?" He called the Palm Springs Spa to make an appointment for a massage. "She wore a brand New Jersey, she wore a brand New Jersey . . ."

Lucy looked at Joe. "What do we do?"

"We go to Palm Springs."

Lucy rolled up her eyes. "Do we have enough film?"

"We should."

"What about cars?" Tony said.

"We'll take two," Joe said. "Lucy and I'll go in mine, you guys take another, any extras can stay here, they'll be safe."

"I have to call my wife," Tony said. "How long do you think we'll be away?"

Joe shrugged.

"Gonna be a late one," Rich said merrily. "Where has Oregon, boys, where has Oregon . . ."

In a mini-caravan, they drove out of Mariners Village, caught the Santa Monica Freeway straight through downtown and out toward San Bernardino. Industrial suburbs gave way to small towns, then to long stretches of sandy wastes and dunes the color of dog bones. Riverside, Redlands, Beaumont, Banning, Rich doing sixty with Fred in the front seat.

"I'm hungry," Lucy said.

"Have to wait."

"What if I need to pee?"

"Go in a bottle."

"I don't have your equipment."

"That's right, I forgot."

She slapped his shoulder. "How are we going to do this anyway?"

"Shoot first, beg for releases later." He smiled. "That's your job."

"How'd I get so lucky."

"I told you, you're my lucky lady. This trip is a break—we couldn't have scripted it better."

"You like this guy, don't you?"

"He's a lovable putz. And he's right about women in their thirties. I was seeing this lady, Marilyn, a few months ago, and she forgot to use her diaphragm on the exact day she was most fertile."

"What happened?"

"Nothing, luckily. But her period was late, and I had a nerve-racking three weeks. It turned out she wanted to have kids and she wanted to do it *now.*"

He punched on the radio. "Do you mind, I want to hear the scores." The Dodger game was interrupted by a news bulletin: a break in the peace talks at Camp David. "President Carter, holding a press conference with Egyptian President Anwar Sadat and Israeli Prime Minister Menachem Begin, has announced they've reached an agreement for peace in the Middle East." Then came Carter's voice: "This is the first time, ever, that an Arab and an Israeli have signed a framework for a peace agreement. After ratification by their governments, Egypt and Israel will be able to sign a peace treaty, we believe within three months.''

The Dodger game resumed. Joe began switching stations. ''This is incredible. I hope my father knows, I hope some-one called him. Do you realize what this means?''

''I think so.''

Joe could not find any further news reports. ''I can't be-lieve it. Did you know I was in Jerusalem in '73, when the Egyptians attacked on Yom Kippur?''

''No.''

He told her he had been walking through the Old City with an American friend when the sirens went off. Orthodox Jews wearing black suits and tennis sneakers—they would not wear leather on Yom Kippur—had turned and scattered from the Wailing Wall. Soldiers ran through the streets. The state television, which had been shut down for the High Holidays, came back on and the announcer's voice could be heard through every window, droning through the city: ''Unit six, Golani Brigade, report to the Nablus Road, unit five . . .''

Joe and his friend had spent the next three days and nights driving their rented car around the country, picking up sol-diers and taking them to assembly points. Many soldiers had to hitchhike to the front. ''You could see the strain on every-one's face. Every person had a son, a husband, a brother, a best friend who was in combat. I'd go into the Central Post Office, where they have the pay phones, and people would be yelling, 'Mom? Can you hear me? I'm *all right!*' ''

He shook his head. ''Now there's going to be peace.''

At four, they drove around the last finger of the San Jacinto Mountains and saw the desert resort, glittering like Oz. The sidewalks were sparkling white, as they never were in Los Angeles. The grass was greener, the sky bluer, the colors of the flowers a shock to the eye. The air was warm and scented with the sweetness of orange blossoms.

At the Riviera, no pets were allowed so Rich had to sneak Fred to the room, carrying him in a blanket. Rich unpacked, put out the "Do Not Disturb" sign and drove to the Spa for his massage. While Lucy negotiated with the management about releases, the crew followed Rich through the baths: soothing, sand-colored, with elegant mineral pools and eucalyptus inhalation rooms. Then it was back to the hotel for dinner, then to a series of bars and discotheques.

"Hi, I'm Richie, what's your name?"

"Sandra."

"Like some company tonight, Sandra?"

"No."

"Nice meeting you."

Round and round he went. "What's your name, where're you from, what do you do, what's your name?"

"Susan." "Jessica." "Carrie. I work in a dog boutique."

"How interesting. I have a Malamute, I bet we've got a lot in common, Carrie."

"Do you like to party?" Carrie said.

Rich gave her a fixing stare.

"I've got a roommate, see."

"I *love* to party."

Gleefully, Rich escorted Carrie to his car and, trailed by the roommate and the crew, drove back to the Riviera. With a lank arm around each girl, Rich ushered them into his room, then held up his hand to the cameras. "See you Sunday." He closed the door. His face popped out again. "Not tomorrow. The following Sunday. Nighty night." The door slammed.

It was 3 A.M. The crew had started back for Los Angeles but Lucy and Joe wanted to stay over and rest. Along Palm Canyon Drive, all the signs were blinking. "No Vacancy." They passed through town and started back the other way, down Indian Avenue. In the older, less chic part of the resort, there were several places with vacancies. They tried the Sunrise Motel but Lucy thought the rooms were tacky. The Villa Linda had passable rooms but no kitchens. Joe wanted a kitchen. At the Date Palm Manor, everything smelled musty. They stood outside, exhausted, debating whether to take it when Joe stepped out in the street. Down the road was a sprawling old building, recently white-washed. Around it were lawns lit by ghostly yellow lanterns, palm trees, orange trees and hedges of flowers. Above the entrance was a beckoning sign: "The Mexican Inn."

Joe turned. "The Mexican Inn?" It was a name they had not heard, a place they had not seen in many trips to Palm Springs. Cautious, hopeful, they walked into the lobby, which had old Mexican tiles on the floor and, on the walls, faded murals of flamingos. Behind the desk was a white-haired man wearing white bermuda shorts and white suede shoes. A placard said, "Your hosts, Bill and Mary Bingley."

"Do you have a couple rooms, or a suite for a few days?" Joe said.

"Yes, for forty dollars." That was half what they would have paid across town. Was there a pool? Joe asked.

"Oh yes, and a new hot mineral bath." Mr. Bingley said the hotel had formerly been the Palm Springs Ritz. "In its heyday, it was grand. Movie stars used to come here. Jane Russell, Gary Cooper, Betty Grable. There was a nightclub and a cardroom where they played 21. Then it went to seed. My wife and I bought the place last year." Bingley said they had been remodeling it and had completed half the rooms. "Yours is a new one."

He led them out the lobby, under cracked archways and across the pool area. Unlike the newer hotels, which had cement or Astro Turf around the pool, the Mexican Inn had long lush grass. The pool, though, in the ghostly lights, was an overly bright turquoise.

The suite Bingley showed them on the third floor stood

like a turret, with windows looking out on the pool, the town, the mountains. When Bingley opened the door, they had to bite their lips. "Quite a decorating job," Joe said. The carpet was red shag, the furniture green plastic, of a quality found in credit furniture stores in East Los Angeles. Lucy wanted to shade her eyes. On the table was an ancient black phone with a mouthpiece dangling from a hook.

"Does that work?" Lucy said.

"No, that belonged to the Ritz. We have no phone service, but we do have color TV."

Joe smiled. "We'll take it."

The next day, they went to the supermarket, Joe bought the papers to read about Israel and then they went to Savon to buy toothbrushes and a bathing suit for Lucy. Joe had a suit in the gym bag in his trunk. While unpacking it, he found a gift he'd been carrying in a film can—psychedelic mushrooms from Hawaii.

"Let's take 'em," he said when they were back in the turret. "This is the perfect setting."

"I don't know, it's been years."

Joe poured the dried mushrooms onto a plate and divided them into two piles.

"I don't think I'm in shape," she said.

"They're mild, easy on the system."

"Not just physically, emotionally."

"Trust me."

"Maybe I'll take half." Joe put a pinch in her mouth before she could change her mind. "What have I done!" she said.

Joe swallowed his portion.

Lucy sat on the couch, hugging her knees, and soon began to feel a warmth in her stomach that traveled up her torso and down her arms. She went to the table and swallowed the other half. "If you go, I go."

"That's the spirit."

Barefoot, they walked across the grass to the pool and sat in dilapidated lounge chairs. "I feel like I'm on the cover of an Eagles album," Joe said. *"The Hotel California."* Around the pool, they saw no movie stars but an assortment of yahoos: men with tattoos who had driven up on their motorcyles from San Bernardino and drank Ripple in the pool. Women with bleached hair in beehives. One had a bulldog on a leash.

"I think we should go back to the room," Lucy said. The first thing they noticed was the rug. The field of shag had turned to straw, red straw, that rippled in an unseen wind. Lucy went into the bedroom and lay down. She was growing, like Alice, expanding until the turret seemed too small to contain her.

Outside, there was the pool and the desert and the lavender mountains against which the town nestled. The men with tattoos were having a water fight.

"Let's go mingle with the crowd," Joe said.

"Are you crazy? We'll be crushed like bugs."

"Mowed down like grass." Joe laughed. A pair of flies had buzzed into the room and were butting against the window. Lucy swished them. "It's like India here."

Joe laughed again. They laughed at everything the other said, laughed and rolled, holding their sides, until the tears were streaming down their faces.

"Stop, please," Lucy said. They were helpless, but it was healing. The laughter would fall off, burst again and fall until the bursts came less and less frequently, like the diminuendo of a symphony.

It was two in the afternoon; they blinked and it was six. Lucy lay on her back, Joe on his side, their limbs entwined like those of children. To Lucy, Joe looked like a seal.

"A confused seal," he said, "startled to find himself in the center of the ring, with no idea why there's a ball on his nose, or why people are clapping."

Joe said Lucy looked like Pele, the Hawaiian goddess of

mists and fire, who wanders over the crests of volcanoes with her white dog.

Outside, the sun shone, people swam and shook themselves dry and went to the Coke machine and the bull dog barked. The leaves of the palm trees swished like hula skirts.

Later, a powerful wind came up, causing the trees to sway. The bushes leaned, the grass tilted, everything in nature was bending but the people, who remained upright in their chairs. Gradually, the people must have grown cold, for they left one by one until the pool was deserted.

Sand began to swirl across the lawn. A chair flew into the pool. Lanterns swung wildly from their poles, and canvas awnings whipped against the wall. It occurred to Lucy that what she saw out the window were the years ahead of her. She wanted order, rootedness, and could not see it. Only turbulence. Storms. Blowing things. It was like a zone she could not pass through, could not even guess what waited on the other side. She was condemned to stay forever in this realm of howling air.

Tears ran from her eyes. "Take me somewhere, Joe."

"I bet the Jacuzzi would feel good."

"We've got miles to go before we reach it."

"We can make it." He lifted her in his arms, carried her down the steps and across the grass, where he set her down by the pool. Gratefully, she eased herself into the water and closed her eyes.

Joe slid in the opposite end.

Floating on her back, Lucy let her body sink until all but her face was submerged.

"What are you doing?" he said.

"Making a contract with God."

"What's in it?"

"Private."

"Ah."

* * *

150

Darkness came. "You can check out any time you like
. . . but you can never leave." Joe and Lucy were back at
the window; the television was playing in the living room. It
was the sweet finale, when they were sliding back into the
twittering world. They had made tea, and watched the pool
sinking into shadows, lights coming on, Bingley appearing
in his white shoes to pick up trash and fish the chair from the
pool.

Lucy was sitting with her legs hooked over Joe's. She felt
that for ages, she and Joe had merged, come apart, merged,
and now they had hoisted themselves out of the sea to rest on
the rocks.

Joe said he was uplifted by the day. He had looked back
over the years and seen much to be happy about. He thought
he was on the verge of evolving into a new state.

The phone rang, once. Both of them jumped. Joe waded
through the bright red shag and picked up the earpiece of the
old phone. The line was dead. "How the hell did that happen. Oh, God."

"What!" Lucy said.

"Come here."

"I'm afraid."

"No, it's okay, but come quickly. Please."

She hurried into the room and found him staring at the
television.

"Hi, I'm Denny Sachs from Sachs House of Suede. Our
family has been serving you in the same location since
1953."

"That's my brother," Joe said. "My father used to do
those ads when we were growing up. Now my brother's
shilling."

Lucy had to strain to see the resemblance. Denny was
thirty pounds heavier than Joe. His body was stuffed like a
sausage into a pair of orange leather pants and jacket, and
his hair was styled in the manner of Las Vegas entertainers.

In the eyes, though, she saw the identical in-gathering toward the center of the face.

The commercial ended and the station cut back to an old vampire movie. Joe sank into one of the green plastic chairs. "It's humiliating."

"Maybe he enjoys it."

"He does! It makes him a celebrity in the neighborhood. You have no idea how people will worship any moron if they've seen him on TV."

"You're not close with him now?"

Joe shrugged. "He's married to a shiksa. She collects antique dolls."

Lucy looked amused.

"But my brother seems happy, he loves this woman and his dorky kids. He likes to lie around and drink beer and eat frozen enchiladas."

Lucy rubbed his shoulders. "There but for fortune . . ."

"Maybe I should have gone that way. I can't get along, I want too much, or else I'm an asshole. I don't give a flying fuck. I'm no different than that poor putz Richie."

"Joe, you were feeling hopeful."

"False hope. Run in, run out, Richie. At least you've done it once."

"So have you."

"Doesn't count."

"Why?"

"I don't want to talk about it." He cut the air with his hand.

"You've never even told me her name."

"Deborah."

Lucy sat on the red shag, looking at Joe.

"I was twenty-six when we got married. I was desperate to get out of surfing movies and do something serious. I was breaking into television, working eighteen hours a day, and the last thing I wanted after work was more trouble. Debbie was wholesome, she made me comfortable. She was a nurse. I needed a nurse. It actually made me happy to see her get dressed in the morning in her white uniform and white hose. She had blond wavy hair and a madonna-like face, like the nurse Hemingway fell in love with. We'd been going out a year, and she wanted to get married or break up, so I said, I'm sorry but I'm not ready, we'll have to go our separate ways.''

Lucy gave an understanding murmur.

"I went back into the fray, and after a short time I was missing that softness, that comfort. So I took her out to dinner and said, okay, let's do it.''

The wind had come up again, whining through the windows. Joe turned on the old floor heater. "I remember my father's reaction. 'What will you talk to her about in six months?' But everyone else, all my buddies, thought I was lucky. My friend Bernie said, 'She's devoted to you. You can't expect everything in one woman. A, it's impossible, and B, you're insane for wanting it.'

"As the wedding drew closer,'' Joe said, "I grew more scared, but I figured my fears were neurotic and the only way to break through them was to act. When she walked down the aisle, I remember thinking, she looks like an angel. She was wearing a white lace dress and a wreath of baby's breath, and the sunlight behind her was like a halo and I wanted to run out the door, down the street and that way.'' He pointed to the mountains.

"We flew to the Mauna Kea, which has to be the most romantic spot on earth. We had a suite overlooking the ocean, which is the most breathtaking color, nothing like the ocean here. I've never been able to describe it—it's like a Popsicle blue. And the hills are all gold and black where the lava once flowed, and the air is so sweet, it's like breathing the essence of flowers. The night we arrived, after traveling for ten hours, Debbie fell asleep right away. I was lying in this vast mahogany bed, and through the air-conditioning duct, I began to hear the sound, faint at first, of a woman working her way up the orgasmic mountain.'' Smiling, Joe folded his hands behind his head. ''She's down about middle C, rising at a very slow, tantalizing pace. I became riveted to the sound, and I started thinking, how can I meet her, figure out what room she's in? I was imagining what she'd look like when it hit me—Sachs, you're married. It's all over.''

He seemed to blanch under the tan. ''A few months later, Debbie quit her job and started talking about having children, which she'd never mentioned before. I began to have trouble breathing. I had shooting pains in my chest—it was that physical. I went to doctors, thinking I had some lung disease, but I didn't. I'd come home at night and fall asleep in front of the television. We went to dinner parties with other married couples, and all the talk was about kids and schools and I'd be struggling to keep my eyes open.

''Then, this woman came to work with me at CBS, Miranda. She was the opposite of Debbie—crazy, erotic. Home was dull and predictable, but Miranda would tell me how she'd gone to this rock-'n'-roll party and fucked twin brothers in a room lined with mirrors. In no time we were in bed. She was aggressive, tempestuous, where Debbie was passive and ladylike. Miranda had the same hunger I did. She was dangerous, I had to conquer her again and again.

''There was no question of leaving Debbie for Miranda, but it struck me—the fact that I've been married six months and am already having an affair should tell me something. I've made a mistake.''

''Hi again, Denny Sachs from Sachs House of Suede . . .''

Joe swiped at the television, shutting it off.

''Shit.''

Lucy moved to the foot of the chair.

''The sad part is that I didn't meet a woman like that now, when I might be ready for her.''

''You wouldn't find it any less suffocating.''

He sighed. ''My big fear, my nightmare is that I'll find someone I think I love, get into that married state again, and along will come somebody new and exciting and I'll have to have her."

"It doesn't have to be that way, Joe. You were almost ten years younger. That marriage wasn't sound."

"The idea of being a fifty-year-old guy out chasing young women terrifies me, but that's where I'm heading. I'm gonna end up alone in some senior citizens' home."

She climbed onto his lap and put her arms around his neck. "I'll probably be in the home next door. I'll wheel over and visit."

He hugged her tightly. "I feel so close to you."

"I know."

He buried his head in her neck. "Let's be friends always."

"As long as we live."

6

"Hi, Lucy, it's Pam."

It was the first thing Lucy heard on waking. She had the impulse to set the phone back in its cradle but curiosity, or was it perversity—the desire to stick one's tongue in a tooth cavity to feel the pain—made her hold on.

"Did I wake you?" Pam said.

"No." Lucy lifted the phone off the floor and set it beside her in bed.

"I'm just calling to check in."

"Is Jerry there?"

"Jerry's in New York."

Every phrase was followed by silence.

"Where are you?"

"L.A. I'm visiting Luke."

"How long are you staying?"

"I don't know, Lucy. I'm trying to decide whether to move back here, or try Chicago or maybe San Francisco."

"You're not going back to . . ."

"No!"

In the background, Lucy heard water running.

"You're not married?"

156

"No. It's over."

Lucy felt a sudden lifting of a weight. "What happened?"

Pam took a breath. "It was one of the worst periods I've ever been through. I've been living in a furnished room for the last month, trying to figure it out. I wanted to write you a long letter."

She has guts, calling me.

"How's the house?" Pam said.

"Fine. I had the patio remodeled. There's a Jacuzzi now where there used to be piles of dead leaves."

"You never liked those dead leaves."

"I've made a lot of changes."

"Do you have my sheet music, by chance?"

"Uh . . . yes."

"You do!" Pam yelped with excitement.

"The pieces you had framed."

"Oh, no, I meant the black trunk with my collection. Henry doesn't have it, I thought maybe you did."

"I don't. How could you lose your trunk of music?"

"That's the least . . ."

Lucy knew the trunk of antique sheet music, inherited from her grandmother, was Pam's most treasured possession. Lucy thought she herself could not lose a cherished trunk and go on living.

"I suppose we ought to sit down and talk," Lucy said.

"That's why I'm calling. There's so much . . ."

She's left Jerry, Lucy thought. *She must have seen it was a mistake and fled, as she always had. Jerry must be going crazy.*

"Do you want to know about Jerry?"

"Not really."

"He's in New York. Camel Films did great in the last quarter, and he's acquiring a cable network."

A rage came over Lucy. The operator cut in—an emergency interrupt for Luke Goodfellow. "Can we call you back?" Pam said.

Lucy hung up and immediately took the receiver off the hook. She got out of bed, washed her face, brought in the newspaper, all the while digesting: not married. As soon as she set the receiver back, the phone rang.

"Listen," Lucy said, "I have a meeting at ten, but I could see you for lunch."

Howard Ness kept Joe and Lucy waiting half an hour at his headquarters in Century City. His secretary showed them to a conference room. "His awful's being redecorated, oops." She giggled. "I mean his office."

Lucy was thinking, I'm free. She would never have to see the unacceptable sight: Pam and Jerry together. But why had Pam left, why had it shaken out in just a year?

Ness came in wearing a maroon warm-up suit. The curly gray hair stood in puffs on either side of his bald crown. "Okay, let's see what you got."

Joe started the projector. It was ninety minutes of rough footage, but Joe and Lucy were pleased. When the film stopped, Ness screwed up his face.

"I can't put that on the air, it's too downbeat."

"When it's finished, it will move like a rocket," Joe said. "It's too soon to get a sense of the pacing . . ."

"The American people are tired of dreary views. Why can't we give them hope? Those characters are losers. The girl's beautiful, all right, but she's depressed. Who's gonna care?"

"People will care about any human drama, if it's told well," Lucy said.

"Can't you shoot a story about people who are happy and dynamic?"

"The whole tone of this is supposed to be raw, driven, like the world out there," Joe said.

"I don't know what world you're talking about."

"You don't have to look very far. Take the Beverly Hills Jogathon."

"Now that's a great idea. That's upbeat and creative."

Joe and Lucy looked at each other. Perhaps Ness read their condescension, for he lost his temper. "Don't bludgeon me, because I'm a fighter. You push me to the wall and I'll hit back."

"We're not trying to push you. If you don't like what you've seen, we could take the project elsewhere," Joe said.

Ness's voice turned nasty. "Just try that. I do business with all the networks. I'll call Landau. I'll call Fisher. I'll call Albrecht." He ticked off the names on his fingers. "The only one I won't call is Theta Cable. Go ahead, set it up over there. That'll be a perfect audience."

His secretary knocked. "Mr. Amram is waiting."

"Jesus, I gotta move. Bring me the Sunland file." He shot back at Joe and Lucy: "We'll confer tomorrow, I want to look at it again. No, I'm in Phoenix tomorrow. Thursday."

"I can't believe it," Lucy said. "He looked like Bozo the Clown, with those two puffs of hair."

"An angry Bozo. What the hell got into him?"

"He was like a cartoon character—'I'll fix it so you never work again in this town.' Do you think he'll call those people?"

"No, and if he does, he'll sound like a complete asshole."

They had come out of the glass tower and were walking across Century Square. The whipping of wind and gushing of water from fountains drowned out the footsteps of accountants, lawyers, secretaries. A vendor was selling colored balloons, on which were printed sexual advertisements:

> Runners Keep It Up Longer
> Body Builders Pump Harder
> Square Dancers Do It With Eight

People were buying the balloons and carrying them into the towers.

"What should we do?" Lucy said.

"We've got strong footage now, we shouldn't have trouble selling it directly to a network. If we have to, we can raise the money ourselves and syndicate it."

"We can certainly raise enough to finish it. But can Ness block us?"

"I told you we shouldn't have trusted the guy. He has no respect for us, he's treating us like shleppers." Joe suggested they go to his place and call their lawyer. Lucy said she was meeting Pam.

"That's right. Gee, I wish I could be a fly on the wall."

"Don't worry, Joe, we'll get around Ness. I'm more nervous about facing Pam."

"You'll do fine. Going to temple tonight?"

"What?"

"It's Rosh Hashanah."

"I don't keep up with that."

"Maybe you should. Why don't you come with me?"

"Where?"

"Sunset Temple."

Lucy had passed it many times; it was a large, Reform congregation on Sunset Boulevard.

"My folks are in Hawaii and I've got their tickets."

"I don't know." Her hands had begun to tremble. "I'll call you later."

Purposely, she went to Hamburger Hamlet early and sat down on a banquette. It took moments for her eyes to adjust to the darkness. When Pam pushed opened the door, Lucy was able to take a long look at her before she herself was seen.

Pam was wearing a pink leotard stretched taut over her breasts, and a denim skirt with the bottom three buttons undone. She must have had a permanent, for her hair was a mass of frizzed curls, as was the fashion in New York, but it was a style that worked best with an "interesting face," it was not so effective with a face of classic beauty. The curls seemed the wrong frame somehow.

Lucy stood. Pam ran up and hugged her. "I've missed you." She kissed Lucy. Striding out, chin forward, Pam was all confidence as the captain showed them to a table. Men turned.

"I think we both look great," Pam said.

Lucy ordered a bloody mary.

"I'll have the same."

They talked about New York, the record cold wave there, the Scarsdale diet. Pam wanted to hear about Lucy's new film. Their hamburgers arrived, along with zucchini circles and onion rings. They finished eating and Lucy thought, we could be leaving in a few minutes. "Shall we talk about it?"

"I'm . . . not sure."

Lucy lowered her head. "I want you to know that I don't hate you. I think you made a mistake, but people make mistakes." She lifted her face to look at Pam. "I would like very much to be able to see it through your eyes."

Pam was tearing a napkin into small shreds. "This past month, I've been staying in a furnished room in Hollywood. It's tacky. Most of the people are drifters, living on welfare." She was crying now. "But I feel as if I'm waking up from a dream.

"When I was in college, I had boy friends but that wasn't everything, I had my studies, and I always did well. When I came to California, I lost my bearings. I didn't like teaching, and I knew I wasn't good enough to make it as a singer. So what was I to do? How would I live when my unemployment ran out? Even if I found a job, I didn't want to end up like you . . ." She looked embarrassed.

"That's all right, go on."

"I didn't want to be over thirty and alone, longing for a baby. I'd see you out beating the bushes for men, and I couldn't bear the idea of endless years of that.

"I became obsessed—I had to get married. After that, I

could find my career. But which man? Henry? Luke? That was the major decision—the decision I couldn't make—and until I did, I wasn't living, I was in frantic motion.

"When Jerry appeared, he seemed the answer to all my yearnings. He was going to give me a home, security, and at the same time, an exciting life, being the wife of a powerful man in the entertainment business. I made a choice. I was willing to tear up everything. I was willing to lose Henry. Lose you."

"Didn't you think about the consequences?"

She shook her head. "I was willing to gamble. And he did everything to make me feel I was getting a home. He took me to Connecticut and I was welcomed into his family. He called my parents in Lovington and told them he would take care of me. I loved New York. I loved the apartment. I would walk up and down the halls saying, 'This is my home, I can plan the future now,' and he'd say, 'Yes, all that craziness is over.' I spent days sorting through the dishes, cleaning the silver."

"But . . . those were once my dishes, my silver."

"That was just put aside by me."

Lucy shook her head.

"You had some role in this too, Lucy."

She started.

"You talked about Jerry all the time. You made him into a heroic figure, and you painted those years in New York as so romantic and glamorous. You warned me I was going to be attracted to him.

"Jerry says you put the idea in his head too, raving about me. You told him if the two of us had met before, it would have been 'the romance of the century.' "

Lucy vaguely remembered the phrase. "I was joking."

"He never forgot. It stuck in his brain, 'the romance of the century.' How could we resist pressure like that? Don't you know, all you have to do to make people want something more than life itself is to tell them how perfectly wonderful it is and that they can't have it?''

Lucy gave a scornful laugh. ''So that's how you rationalize it.''

Pam shut her eyes. ''It doesn't matter, it wasn't the romance of the century. It was over in six weeks. I didn't move out for a year, but Jerry lost interest after six weeks.''

''Wait,'' Lucy said, ''I assumed that you had left him.''

''No, I wanted to stick it out, go for therapy or something.''

Lucy could not suppress a feeling of victory. Jerry had loved her eight years.

''One thing that helped kill it was that as soon as I arrived, I got herpes. I was in so much pain, and we couldn't have sex. I'd never had herpes, I don't know where it came from and it wouldn't disappear.''

Lucy nodded, feeling surprised and, at the same time, not surprised.

''On the surface, though, things seemed all right. One night we were talking about having three or four children by the Le Boyer method. The next morning, Jerry sat up in bed and told me he wasn't in love with me.''

''What did you say?''

'' 'This comes as a shock.' He said he had thought he loved me, he'd meant it when he told me that, but he'd found out he didn't, and wasn't it lucky we hadn't gotten in too deep. After that, he started calling our relationship an 'emotional adventure.' He started spending more time on the road. Then he asked me to move. He gave me five thousand dollars and a plane ticket to California and said he couldn't be responsible for me in the future.''

Lucy knew the see-saw Pam was describing, knew it better than anyone. She also understood how Pam could have loved him, wanted to hold on, even at the end.

''What I can't understand is why he rejected you,'' Lucy said.

"I can't either." Pam was crying again. "Because I'm a terrific person."

"What did you do after that?"

"I went straight to Henry's doorstep, but he wouldn't have me back. I couldn't stay with Luke, the masks were gone now, so I took a furnished room. And then . . ." Something caught in her throat. "I got stronger. Because what else could happen? If I could live through this, I could live through anything. I felt like God had shaken me by the shoulders. I started going to church. I started thinking, I have talents, I have abilities, I need to use them. I'll never believe in or trust a man again. I'll never be romantic."

Oh come now, Lucy thought. "Why did you want to see me?"

Pam shook her head. "I know things can never be the same."

"No. But I want you to know, even at the worst moment, when I thought you and Jerry were married, I still thought of the year we lived together as one of the happiest I've known. You brought laughter into the house. Your spirit warmed the place. It was as if an angel was with me, and I'll always treasure that time."

Pam's chin was quivering. "That's one of the nicest things anybody's ever said."

"But to the extent I felt an angel had been with me, I felt later . . ."

"I know. Devil."

It occurred to Lucy that Pam indeed might have been a benevolent agent. "I hardly think about Jerry now," Lucy said.

"I hardly do either."

Not the same, Lucy thought. The check came. Lucy debated whether to pay for Pam and decided no. They walked out of the restaurant and across Century Square. Bobbing in the air were the balloons with their sexual messages: "Lady Lawyers Make Better Motions." Pam kept hugging Lucy.

Lucy found herself telling Pam about Joe. "He's the first man I've loved since Jerry, the first man I've ever been with where I've had no doubts."

"How does he feel?"

"I think he wants to be involved, but he's frightened. He's constructed a situation where we could be together all the time, without making a romantic commitment."

Pam looked dubious. "In my experience, once you become friends, it's hard to steal across that boundary."

"This is different. We started as lovers, the attraction is still there."

"The best thing you can do then," Pam said, "is hold back, not seem too needy or available, and that has to seem real."

Lucy was uneasy They had lapsed into their old roles, Pam counseling her as she had once counseled her about Jerry. "I have to go," she said.

Pam's car had finally given out, so Lucy dropped her at the bus stop on Santa Monica. Lucy watched her, waiting by the triangular yellow sign. Standing in her pink leotard and denim skirt, she looked forlorn. In Los Angeles, no one took the bus except children, senior citizens and the poor. Riding the bus was a concrete manifestation that one had fallen.

There was a scent of pine and a crackling of dead leaves as Lucy walked across the parking lot of Sunset Temple. She felt a sadness, thinking how friends could shift and ebb. Joe was waiting by the entrance, looking mature and dignified in a gray, three-piece suit.

He presented their tickets and they walked down the aisle of the sanctuary, which was like a plush civic theater: thick blue carpets, loge seats and a stage covered with flowers. The temple had moved so far from tradition that it did not have a Hebrew name. The men did not wear a yarmulke or tallit when praying, and everything was done to match customs in church.

Behind Lucy, two women were speaking in nasal voices.
"We have a new baby at our house."
"Mazel tov!"
"You heard?"
"What color is it?"
"Blue, with a beige interior."
"A four-fifty?"
"Right, the gorgeous one."

Lucy looked at Joe. This was what she had remembered from Jewish life in New Rochelle. Her parents, like Joe's, had belonged to a Reform temple, which had enabled them to remain in the fold and yet be freed from the ways of the old country. Lucy had been sent to "Sunday school," and before confirmation, her class had gone on a retreat with the rabbi. Seated next to him at dinner, Lucy had asked what he believed God was. "I believe there are alternatives of belief," the rabbi had said. "One belief is that there is a personal God, who's responsive to individuals. Another is that God is an evolutionary force, moving the universe, and another is that God is a moral and ethical ideal."

"But what do you believe?"

The rabbi had tapped his glass to begin the evening's program, and it seemed obvious to Lucy that if there were alternatives, nobody believed any of them.

Her grandparents, who were Orthodox, believed in observing the 613 mitzvot, including the great and puzzling inconvenience of keeping kosher. On occasion, she had been taken to her grandparents' shul, where the air smelled of herring and the services were unintelligible.

The lights dimmed. The choir sang a prayer that sounded like a Christian hymn, and the rabbi, Benjamin Kaplan, came on stage, wearing black robes. It was because of the rabbi, Joe had said, that he continued coming to Sunset Temple.

Rabbi Kaplan was a tall man with sad, sweet eyes. He had been psychoanalyzed, he had had his faith in God shaken and shared his doubt with the congregation. In the sixties, he had spoken so relentlessly about the injustices of American society and the Vietnam War that his congregation had revolted, shouting back from the audience.

If they disagreed with his politics, though, they loved him as their spiritual leader. Kaplan's large, sad eyes expressed gentleness, goodness. He took joy in their marriages and births, grief in their losses. People came away from him feeling consoled and understood.

The candles were lit, and Rabbi Kaplan began the responsive reading. "Once more we meet in the twilight of a vanishing year. Twelve months have disappeared, leaving the dark silence of this night—fresh and clean, new and undiscovered. In these fragile moments of the New Year, when all doors are opened to the beckoning night, everything is possible, and no darkness is too dark for the visions that bring us here."

The service progressed quickly, in English with very little Hebrew, until it was time for Rabbi Kaplan's sermon.

"Friends, I cannot tell you I know how to explain God's work, or how the Torah applies to Jews in twentieth-century America, but I can tell you that I value every one of you."

Lucy winced, yet she felt, as Joe had said, a sweetness that came through.

"This is a special year for us because it's an anniversary. Thirty years ago, this temple was founded. Thirty years ago, in 1948, the state of Israel was founded." He began to evoke a picture of California in 1948, and in the decades that had followed. "The fifties was a time when the sky was always blue. There was a bridle path all the way up Sunset Boulevard. We settled down to have children—our three were born in 1950, '52 and '53. We believed in the importance of early childhood and tried to make it happy and secure. And if we failed, the psychiatrist was always standing by to smooth things out."

Kaplan's voice became strident. "Then came the *dread-*

ful sixties, when everything we believed in and had held without question was overturned. We had to deal with pot, with political protest, demands by oppressed groups for equality, loud music, disdain for the values of family and home, and those confusing living arrangements when our children wanted to *bring people home*. What were we to do? They were agonizing times, but some of us do not regret the decisions and commitments we made.''

Lucy noticed the congregation fidgeting. Back to slap us again? Enough!

''So we moved into the seventies, where we have been left shattered and confused, disappointed with our public life, wanting to retreat into our individual selves.'' As he described the seventies, ''looking out for number one,'' Lucy thought back to her meeting with Pam. She tried to tease apart the contradictory emotions: sympathy, rage, love, closeness, jealousy, desire for vengeance. She did not want to carry anger into the new year, but she had not forgiven Pam. Watching her on the street after lunch, Lucy had been pleased to think the bus was carrying her to a dreary future.

Lucy sighed, turning back to Rabbi Kaplan. ''You've heard me pose the questions before, and again I have no answers. But I believe our coming here tonight, our annual coming together at the High Holidays, is a miracle no less than the burning bush, the parting of the Red Sea or the walking on water. Because it shows that despite affluence and assimilation, there is a greater hand working through us, bringing us together to reaffirm our commitment. We are the children of this fleeting time, and we are the sons and daughters of ancient men and women.''

Everyone rose—parents, grandparents, children—put their arms around each other and began to sing the New Year's song, *''L'shana tova tikatevu.''* Each row swayed back and forth, crisscrossing with the row ahead and behind, until the congregation appeared to be one body with hundreds of rippling bands. Lucy felt an infusion of warmth.

Rabbi Kaplan had been right, there was something awesome about being there, linking herself to this body.

The song ended, people kissed each other and said, "Happy New Year." Joe took hold of Lucy's hand. All doors were open at this fragile moment, and no darkness was too dark.

7

"Did you sleep in your clothes?"

For the third straight day, Lucy was wearing a blue denim jumpsuit. "Why, am I boring you?"

"No, I'm easy. For all I care, you could wear a paper bag."

"How do you manage to look so fresh?"

Joe pointed at her. "Never ask a magician how he does his tricks."

"You know, your friends think of you as the man in the iron mask. Whenever two of them get together, they have different information."

"You're not going to learn anything about me from my friends."

"You've told me more?"

"Definitely."

"And I still love you."

"I can only attribute that to madness."

"You have no respect for me because of it."

He threw back his head and laughed.

"Don't crack up on me, not now," but she broke into semidemented laughter herself.

They were punchy. They had been in the cutting room for four months, having smoothed things out with Ness and received the go-ahead to complete the film. For four months, they had been spending most of their waking hours in a nine-by-nine-foot room with no windows. When they took a day off, they missed each other and would talk on the phone five times. When Joe caught strep throat, Lucy moved in to take care of him. When Lucy was cheated by a contractor, Joe impersonated a lawyer to get her money back. They helped each other pick out clothes. They ate almost all their meals together, went to parties and movies together, and people who did not know them well assumed they were having an affair.

Lucy was utterly and hopelessly in love. Sitting at the flatbed, she would stare at Joe's arms. She studied the definition of muscles, the fine gold hairs that snaked across his tanned skin. She knew the sound of his footsteps, the smell of his shampoo, the way he buttered his toast. She loved everything about him, nothing displeased her, and she thought, if we were together, what would we ever quarrel about?

When Joe's phone rang in the cutting room, Lucy was on edge. She strained to listen, pretending to be absorbed in her work. She measured the enthusiasm with which he said, "Hi." She could tell, and was relieved, when it was business.

"Will you be at the apartment later? I'll call you tonight."

Whose apartment? She would break down, trying to sound idly curious. "Who was that?"

"Oh, this girl I met with Bernie. She's a model for skin magazines." Joe laughed. "Twenty years old and she's out of her mind on coke all the time. I'm too old for this."

Lucy was glad it was not serious, that it would be over soon, which it was. She had been solving her own sexual needs by going out with a stock broker named Gabe

Milander. He was twenty-six, he won tennis tournaments and sailed a catamaran, he had a crush on Lucy and after two dates her skin was crawling. "The more wretched I am to him, the more he hangs on," she told Joe.

"You deserve a spanking."

Lucy had to steel herself when she pulled up to Gabe's house at one in the morning. He did not mind waiting up until she had finished work. I don't want to see him, she thought, why am I forcing myself, he has nothing to say, he's a sponge. Gabe was not unintelligent, but because of Lucy's hard eye, he left sentences unfinished and gave nervous hissing laughs.

Gabe was happy to see her at one in the morning. "Come." He led her into the bedroom, switching off the light so she would not see the piles of dirty clothes, beer cans and orange peels.

He undressed her, holding her with one arm, using the other to caress her. Yes, stroke me, make me moan. She remembered telling Joe how erotic it was to be treated this way, her body the temple and he the acolyte, placing his tongue on her with reverence, raising the current in her softly, easily.

When he entered her, she was swimming with pleasure. "I'd forgotten how good you feel."

"I want you to remember."

"Then you'll have to do this more often."

"Gladly."

Making love, she became giving, appreciative. In the dark, they could reach each other as they could in no other way, although Gabe tried. He bought tickets to *Beatlemania* when Lucy mentioned she might want to see it. The show was silly, four musicians impersonating the Beatles. They sounded close, although not really like the Beatles, but behind them on a screen was a slide show of the sixties: the people in the news flashing by, year after year, to the accompaniment of Beatles songs that had played on the radio.

"Help!" while Martin Luther King was seen after the Watts riots. "Not burn, baby, burn . . ." his voice rang out over the music, "but learn, baby, learn, so you can earn, baby, earn."

The musicians changed from their Liverpool clothes to the costumes from the cover of "Sergeant Pepper." They sang "Lucy in the Sky with Diamonds," while a picture flashed of two young men and a woman, all with shoulder-length hair, lying like puppies on the floor, their eyes glazed with amazement. They looked so innocent, so childlike. Lucy remembered the power of the vision: everyone discovering the secret at once. Today, she thought, those same people would be workaholics, jogging for relief.

"Hey, Jude," they played, while Robert Kennedy was seen in his last campaign. "Some people look at what is, and ask, why? I dream of what could be, and ask, why not?" Lucy's hands flew to her chest. Gabe let out a hissing laugh. She wished Joe was there, he would understand, unlike the hulk beside her.

When the lights came on, she asked Gabe what he thought.

"It was pleasant."

"I loved it."

"You seemed to be having an extreme reaction."

She said nothing the rest of the way home.

In the bedroom, though, the connection was made. The simplest movements felt marvelous with him. "Why do you suppose it's so good?" she said.

Gabe smiled with satisfaction. "Some people fit and some people don't."

At work the next day, she was depressed.

"What do you feel like for lunch?" Joe said.

She shrugged.

"I'll order Chinese."

"No. Oh, go ahead."

"Something bothering you?"

She stared listlessly at the splicer.

"There has to be a pattern to your moods. I just haven't cracked the code yet."

"When you do, let me know."

He put his arms around her. "I can't stand it when you're unhappy. Don't you understand? I can't stand it. If I were an astronaut, I'd cut myself loose, disappear in space."

He looked so distressed, she was touched, and although the source of her unhappiness was unresolved, she felt better.

On Thursday mornings, she took tennis lessons from a black pro named Raymond. She was a strong player, but today she could do nothing right. The balls sailed out of the court. Jeez, Lucy, how could you do that? She hit them long, short, wide. What's the matter, can't you watch the ball? She had not once caught it in the sweet spot. She stood still a moment, trying to compose herself. She swung again and missed completely. Dammit!

Raymond called her to the net. He was wearing Adidas shorts that fit too tightly. "The problem with you, Lucy, is your attitude. You get so down on yourself. So you mis-hit a ball. So you mis-hit two. Slow yourself down, say to yourself, bounce, hit, bounce, hit. Don't think of nothing else. You're your own worst enemy."

"I know, Raymond, but it's so frustrating. All this time and I keep making the same mistakes. I don't know how you put up with me."

"I'll tell you something. I'm in love with you."

She laughed.

"I mean it. The way you crack those balls knocks me out."

She looked away.

"All the work you're doing will pay off. You have to re-lax, it'll come. Listen." She turned. He lowered his voice.

"It's like, if I push too hard in trying to get together with you, I'll blow it. But if I let it be, it might happen. Right?"

She smiled. "Let me try again."

He began hitting her balls from the net. "Take your arm back sooner," he called. "Keep your eye on the ball, you're too late, go to meet it, catch it on the rise, follow through! Don't twist your body, set your feet down square, keep your head down . . ."

She screamed, cracked the racket on the ground and felt a sickening kickback. There was a stab in her lower back. She doubled over.

Thinking it was a temporary spasm, she hobbled home, fending off Raymond's attempts to go with her. She took a shower but the pain was worse, so she called Joe.

"Sounds like a pinched nerve, or else you pulled a muscle."

"I can't stand up straight."

"Call the doctor."

"I did, he's calling back. Could it be a slipped disk?"

"Doesn't sound like it. The best thing is moist heat. Get in your Jacuzzi, then stay in bed. I'll stop by tonight."

When Joe arrived, she was sitting up in bed, wearing a pink flannel gown and drinking amaretto from the bottle. "Amaretto and Valium, a great combo," she said, flourishing the bottle. "The Jacuzzi did wonders too. It was worth all the hassles I went through, having it installed."

"I want to put one in my place."

"I can save you a lot of time. I did extensive research about the benefits of cartridge filters over pumps."

He shook his head, smiling. "I don't know what you're talking about."

"Neither did I, at first." She told him there were Jacuzzi showrooms where it was possible to sit in a full tub and test the system, but the showrooms were scattered around the county. She had driven to the Valley and Long Beach and Anaheim, carrying her bathing suit and towel.

"My worst moment came in Venice. There was a British man there selling redwood tubs at a discount out of his house. It wasn't much of a house, it was a rickety shack on a canal, with chickens walking around. I changed in his bathroom and got in the tub, feeling very exposed. I was sitting there, trying to decide if the tub was comfortable, if the jets were strong enough, if I liked the feel of wet wood, when, plop! He jumped in, wearing nothing but underpants with his big white stomach hanging out."

"Ha!" Joe said.

"I couldn't avoid touching his legs. Then he whispered, 'It's a lovely life, isn't it, ducky?' How do I get in these situations?"

"You have a talent for it."

Lucy laughed, then cried out.

"Easy," Joe said.

She leaned against the pillows and closed her eyes.

Joe went to the kitchen for a beer. "Seen Gabe?"

"I think that's why my back went out," she said. "So I wouldn't have to fuck him."

"That happened to me once."

They looked at each other.

"I should get going," Joe said.

"Where to?"

"Oh, you know."

"Mmm?"

"I told you, I met this woman at the supermarket."

"You didn't tell me."

"I did."

"I don't remember. What does she do?"

He shrugged. "Nothing. She's getting divorced from some manufacturer. Lives in Bel Air. She's forty-three, but she's got style."

"What's her name?"

"Frances."

Silence.

Joe laughed sheepishly. "She's sort of interesting."

"Better not keep her waiting."

Lucy minced back to work the next day, still unable to walk upright. She looked at what Joe had done in her absence and pronounced it awful. Without waiting for his reply, she pulled it apart and redid it. There was an understanding between them that Joe would have authority in the field and she in the cutting room, but they rarely had to exercise it because they were usually in agreement.

Today was an exception. Lucy spoke to Joe coldly. When he made a suggestion, she snapped, "That's ridiculous, this is better." If he tried to protest, she ignored him.

When Joe's phone rang, Lucy listened; she was sure it was Frances. Joe hung up and caught her watching.

"Want to tell me what's going on?"

"What do you mean?"

"Why are you so dogmatic?"

"I don't know what you're talking about."

"You're angry at me."

She kept her eyes on the screen. "Why did you put this scene back in? We agreed it should go."

"I changed my mind."

I'm telling you, buddy, women in their thirties are dangerous.

She ran the film forward. Rich and his friend Ken flickered across the screen at high speed, talking squeaky jibberish.

"It makes a point," Joe said.

"Better made elsewhere."

"No, it's perfect here, it ties in with Claire's next scene."

She stopped the film.

"Leave it!" He tried to push her away from the controls.

"Take your hands off me." She forced her way back and

pulled the splice apart. He grabbed the film but she held tight. They scuffled and tugged at the film, then suddenly she let go and Joe lurched backward. She pulled another reel off the table, took out the center core and hurled it in the air so the film swirled in loops and vines.

"What the hell's gotten into you!" Joe said.

"I can't take it anymore."

"Take what? Don't you give a shit about the work?"

"Don't you give a shit about me?" She grabbed a loop and whipped it across the room.

"Cut that out."

"We're getting everything from each other that you usually get from someone you love, then we go out and screw people we don't care about. It's insane, I can't stand it any longer."

"Jesus! I never know what I'm going to get from you. All I want to do is make a good film."

"We should be walking into the sunset."

"You think I'd be in safe hands with you? You've told me a hundred stories about how you fucked up every relationship you ever had."

"So have you, but you gotta start somewhere."

She hit the switch of the Moviola and Claire was on screen. *He makes you totally fall in love with him, and as soon as you do, he withdraws* . . . Joe lunged for the switch.

"Don't you see?" Lucy said. "We're making this production about people who have a disease, a sickness, and we're the worst of all. We're so sick we're sitting at a banquet table and crying, I'm starving. Food, I want food. And it's there. All the food you could want. And we're not eating."

"Come on." Grabbing her arm, Joe pulled her out of the cutting room, down the hall, out of the building and into his car. He drove fast, running yellow lights, passing in the wrong lane. When he turned onto his street, the car tipped and the tires screeched. Before the motor had stopped knocking, he had her out the door. He was yanking off his belt, pulling at her shirt.

"My back."

"We're gonna cure your back."

He put her over his shoulder and carried her to the bed.

8

Lucy was dizzy, there was a pulse in her throat like a small, shivering animal. The longings of almost two years were about to be realized. Her body shook as Joe lowered himself onto her. Sex, though, can have a mind of its own, and despite her emotions, despite the way they were kissing, she could not let go. She was dry. Like a car that won't turn over, she would strain and strain and the ignition would not catch. She could not believe this was happening. Joe was moving like a jackhammer and she was dead inside, as if she had been shot with Xylocaine.

He slipped out.

"I'm embarrassed."

He put a finger on her lips. "We've been keeping the gates locked for so long, they don't just open. They have to be oiled, softened."

She was relieved he understood. She needed to lie quietly, to feel his skin along the length of hers, to look into his eyes and be assured that this was what he wanted. Joe put on an early Simon and Garfunkel album. The sweet voices, wafting along the cusp of masculine and feminine, filled the room with the mood of another time. Golden children trod the footpath into the greenwood. Triangles rang. Parsley, sage, all was possible, all new.

Joe stroked Lucy's cheek. She traced the soft, ribboned surface of his lips. They touched each other gently, thoughtfully.

Lucy slipped her hands around the back of his neck and began massaging. He murmured with pleasure. She worked down the neck to the shoulders, all the while sitting on her knees facing him.

"I love looking at you," he said. "Your face is always changing. Sometimes it's pretty, sometimes it's funny." He smiled. "Sometimes you look like a little girl."

"I thought I was the only one who'd been looking."

"Why do you think I was picking up women in the supermarket?"

"Your nature?"

"Silly goose." He rested his fingers on her thighs. "Turn over, I'll do your back." She stretched out flat with her arms above her head and lay still, anticipating his touch. He slapped her buttocks.

"Joe!"

He slapped again, harder.

"That stings."

He bent down and kissed the spots where he had slapped. She twisted sideways, kneed him in the ribs and they began to wrestle playfully, sliding over the sheets, until they were locked in a circle, head to groin.

At last, Lucy was beginning to feel her body grow warm. An impulse would run from Joe's fingers into Lucy and through her and out her lips and fingers back to him. It was a kind of exquisite telepathy. Every touch was given and received in the same breath.

Joe disengaged himself and entered her. I love you, she said with her eyes.

He pulled out of her and slid down between her legs. She took hold of his hair. She was rising by notches, moving up, one level, two, like a rocket that had dropped its first stages and was soaring.

His tongue stopped. Her eyes snapped open. It was the subtlest motion, he had merely lifted his tongue but she felt as if ice water had been splashed on her. Joe was smiling mischievously. He started again, and soon she was at the gate, reaching for the latch, when he stopped.

"Joe, please!"

He laughed and resumed. She was writhing, "Please, don't stop," but he did. Each time, she had the sensation of plummeting, but then he would take her higher until she thought she would faint. She shook with what felt like an orgasm but her body was still tight, she was not finished, she would never finish, she would never clear the peak, he was going to keep her at the edge and never let her over.

"I'm going to go insane!"

"Go ahead. Go crazy."

She screamed. He was in her and she was screaming herself hoarse. He was groaning and bucking until at last they lay spent, slumped together like two wet fish in a bucket. He buried his face in her neck. "Finally," she whispered. "Finally."

When she opened her eyes in the morning, a bird was singing near the window. The days had blended together so they had no meaning, but something in the air, a dreamy lassitude, suggested it was Saturday.

Joe kissed her neck.

She jumped.

He laughed softly. "How's your back?"

"Funny, it really does seem better."

"Course it does."

"Dr. Feelgood."

He turned her around in his arms. "I think you should have another injection."

"Mm."

182

They took a shower together and went out to celebrate. They had to pick up Lucy's car, then went to Le Quai, where Joe ordered champagne and lobster and fettucini cooked with basil. They reminisced about the road they had taken to that luncheon. They had gone through the fire together, fought Ness, survived the flood, flown with the gods at the Mexican Inn and worked together to pull something beautiful out of what was formless. "It was ridiculous to think we could go through this and not become involved," Joe said.

"I'm so happy."

He took her hand under the table. "I want you to be happy."

In the afternoon, they drove north along the Coast Highway through Malibu to Ramirez Canyon, where Joe had friends who had a ranch.

The canyon was verdant and lush, with no clue that sandy beaches and surf were so near. Because of the heavy winter rains, fresh water was running and the sound was everywhere: purling over stream beds, tinkling under bridges, squirting and shooting down creeks. It seemed the canyon was as brimful of new life as Lucy. The natural grasses that sprouted on the slopes were not dry and gold as they were most of the year but juicy and green.

At the entrance to the ranch were birds-of-paradise, which stood like laughing woodpeckers with orange plumes and purple beaks. Behind them were fat succulents with names like "hens and chickens." There was the smell of horses and hay, of pollen and sap, and in the first corral, Lucy saw two mares in foal, their stomachs puffed out and pendulous.

Joe's friend, Zack, gave them cans of Coors and their pick of a dozen horses. Joe chose a white Arabian for himself and for Lucy, a gelding named Hawk, who was half quarter horse, half thoroughbred.

"This feels so good," she said as she swung into the saddle.

"Doesn't it," Joe said, tightening the girth. "No matter how often I ride, I always feel that rush of pleasure getting on."

"Is there any sport, any outdoor activity you don't like?"

He adjusted her stirrups. "Downhill skiing. It's too high tech now, people look like they've been dipped in plastic. Give me beaches."

Joe rode ahead of Lucy, taking a trail that led through a grove of poinsettia trees, the branches covered with scarlet flowers. Lucy remembered seeing smaller versions in pots in the snow in New York. The poinsettias were the only reminder in the green and sun-filled canyon that it was December.

"How're you doing?" Joe said.

"Nervous. I've never ridden a horse of this caliber." Lucy had ridden at rental stables, where the horses had been worn down by years of going out on the hour. Hawk, by contrast, felt like an engine that was revved. When they cantered, she was constantly fighting not to lose control, not knowing how fast he could run or if she was capable of bringing him back. "I don't know his limits."

"I'll tell you the best way to find out," Joe said. He turned his horse onto a fire road that ran for miles to the top of a peak. Lucy followed. "Run him uphill—the surface is good, just keep him pointed straight on the road and you won't have problems. That's what you do with a runaway. No matter how fast he goes, he'll get tired before the top."

"Are you sure?"

"Sure."

"Gee-up!" Lucy pressed in with her feet and slackened the reins. With a jolt, Hawk took off. At first she went rigid and clung to the horn. Her hair blew back, the wind stung her cheeks and she could hear Joe's horse thundering behind. Then she began to relax, sinking, pressing the weight down through her legs and into her heels. Hawk's gait was so smooth it was like flying, and she could sit, free of the horn now, flying ahead with him. Halfway up the hill, he began to slow like a motor shifting down. She could see what they were passing: cottonwood trees and live oaks. By the time they reached the summit, he was trotting, wheezing, his flanks wet, and he seemed content to amble downhill from there into the meadow.

It was sunset when they drove back to town. This had been the happiest day, a violet light filled the car like a bubble and she was the happiest woman.

That's my life, she thought, watching Joe at the wheel. "Why don't we stop for dinner?"

He pursed his lips. "Not hungry."

"Drink?"

"Don't think so."

"Music, then."

"Okay."

She put in a cassette of Ry Cooder, leaned back and stared at the sky.

At Joe's house, it was hard to know where to go. Joe collected his mail. Lucy sat down at the dining-room table. He took his messages off the machine. She glanced through *A Rumor of War*, which was lying facedown, its paper spine cracked.

Joe walked in and stood facing her. She smiled. "Listen," he said, "I'm afraid I made some plans for tonight. I'll have to get going pretty soon."

She set the book down. "Couldn't you change them?"

"Not really."

"It's just . . . this is a special day."

"There'll be other days. Plenty of them."

She fingered the edges of the book.

"I'm sorry, I didn't, you know, expect this," he said.

"Well, I could wait here."

He went to the refrigerator and took out a beer. "Want anything?"

"No thanks."

"I think we should call it a day."

She rose and went upstairs to gather her things. She made more noise than was necessary, rattling hangers, shutting drawers. Joe came to the door, which was closed except for a crack, put his face to the opening and peered in.

"I thought we had something more now," she said.

"I'm the same person I was yesterday."

She opened the door and reached for his arm. She felt something unyielding, something that should have told her to back away. Ignoring it, she spoke. "We're so much alike, we get along so well."

"I can't help it, I don't feel ready."

"Have you ever?"

"No, but when I do, I'll know it."

"Joe, you have to learn some time to stop splitting sex and love."

"I can't be your pupil, I'm not going to matriculate. You've fallen in love with a phantom." He walked to the window and pulled the cord, shutting the curtains with a snap. "All you've ever said to me is, love me love me love me, we are the same person. You don't know who I am. You've never seen me. I'm nothing to you but an E-ticket ride at Disneyland."

"In two years, Joe, we've hardly been apart. I think you get to know a person fairly well."

They began moving about the room in an unconscious duet.

"Why do you think I've never left California? Why am I still fucking around with documentaries? Why haven't I made a feature? Because I'm scared. Chicken shit. You have a capacity to jump into unknown waters that amazes me and terrifies me. You court disaster."

"I know you have fears, I do too . . ."

186

"I don't want to merge with someone who's the same as me. I don't want to marry my sister."

"For God's sake, we're not talking about marriage."

"Come on, I know you, once we start on that road that's where it goes. We'll end up fighting over hairs in the sink and who takes out the garbage."

"What are you saving yourself for, the old-age home?"

He cut the air. "We never should have done this, I don't know what was in my head."

"What *was* in your head, what was all that tenderness?"

"You know the pressure, it was intolerable. I thought we could take it all the way and still be friends."

"Look, we're tired, we've been working hard . . ."

"I've never felt more clear-headed. I wish we could wipe out the last twenty-four hours."

"Please don't talk like that. I'm not asking for a life commitment. All I'm asking . . ."

"It's no good, Lucy."

". . . could you try."

"I don't feel it. I never have and I'm not going to change."

Numb, she sat in her car. She could not go home, she wanted to disappear among people. Without planning, she drove to the Women's Garden, a gym she belonged to and rarely used but where there would be people, even on Saturday night. She walked down the corridor, which was like walking into a powder-pink vagina: pink walls, pink lockers, steam rising, Jacuzzis bubbling, water rushing into swimming pools and out of fountains.

She pushed through the door of the dressing room. In the fluorescent light, she saw a Bosch-like vision: a hell of sweat and hair, crinkled skin and sad eyes, rats' eyes. Straps were being closed over veiny flesh, towels were being flapped over saggy bottoms.

In the exercise room, women were lining up to do "the

circuit," in which they passed, as if by conveyor belt, from machine to machine. They raised their legs, pumped their arms, bicycled and chinned to "Yankee Doodle." Lucy stared in horror. The women were strapped in their machines, legs spread, crotches offered. Do they have souls? What are they living for, preserving their bodies for? Do they have children, people they sleep with, sexual problems, money problems, fears and lonely nights?

She went back into the dressing room, put on her street clothes and fled. Then she was in her car again. As if clearing from a trance, she remembered that Emma and Al were having people over for dinner. She went to the gym to use the phone. Was it too late?

"No, come on by," Emma shouted.

Maybe there would be someone there, a doctor, some friend of Al's. When she rang the bell, a couple, Norm and Carole, walked out with their six-month-old daughter.

"Hello, aren't you a lovely creature."

The baby stared into Lucy's eyes. Lucy wondered if her own face as a baby had looked like this: hopeful, trusting, sleepy, feminine, bright. "We love her," Norm said, and kissed the infant.

In the living room, four couples were nestled in each other's arms. Al was playing the guitar. It was the aftermath of an evening in which there had been good food, warm talk, laughter, wine and grass.

"Hey, look who's crawled out of the cutting room."

"Are you hungry?" Emma called. "There's heaps of food."

Lucy waved and went into the kitchen. On the sideboard she found lasagna, spinach salad, chocolate cake. She took a fork and began to pick. Al came in.

"How the hell are you?"

"Not so good."

Al put his bearlike arms around her. "Now you get to find

188

out that being successful and winning awards and producing classy films doesn't make you happy."

"There's one more thing I need."

"Um hmm," he said skeptically. "One more thing."

"Look at everyone here," Lucy said. "Carole and Norm. Robin and Steve. Jane and Bob. You and Emma. How come all of you can do it and I can't!"

"My God, what's wrong?" Emma was in the doorway.

Lucy started. "Nothing." She dabbed at her eyes.

"You've been crying."

"No, I mean, I just got stoned and started to cry. Didn't that ever happen to you?"

Emma nodded. "I get scared when it does, if I don't know where it's coming from."

"Not me," Al said. "I figure there's always more tears in me than I let out."

Lucy gave him a grateful look. "I should go, I'll call you tomorrow." She left by the kitchen door, so she would not have to pass the couples in the living room. She could hear them singing, "Mamas, don't let your babies grow up to be cowboys."

She was going to burst. She began to talk to herself as if to a baby. Hold on, we'll be home soon, then you can cry. She was going to cry until she cried her insides out. She had never let herself cry without holding back, she did not know her limits, as with the horse, Hawk.

She pulled into Sea Shell Lane. Hold on. . . . She walked inside, locked the door, got a towel from the bath room. Almost, hold on. . . . She took off her clothes, curled up under the quilt and, clutching the towel to her face, let go.

Out came pathetic, squalling sounds she would not have let herself make if people were around. Nothing stopped her from howling as loudly as she could. She grabbed the pillow and bit it. The pillow ripped. Joe was not to be her life. All these months of waiting, interpreting small gestures as positive signs, believing things must change yet sensing a reluctance, being afraid to ask. She had blown it all right, blown it royally. Loneliness—she was going to die of it.

The sound of her weeping carried down the lane. Next door, Gino sat up and looked out the window. He wondered if Lucy needed help, if he should go knock on the door, but Edna thought no. The crying sounded like what it was: self-pity. It fell off, started again, made several bursts and faded until there was nothing audible but a ratchety gasping for breath.

In her bed, Lucy, out of curiosity, checked the clock. She had cried for twenty minutes. A mere twenty minutes. She had thought she would cry for days, but she had drained herself of tears in what amounted to no more than a cosmic blip. Exhausted, she sank into sleep.

9

It was the coldest January on record in New York since 1921. A Siberian cold wave had blown down from the Arctic, covering the city with snow and causing temperatures of 30 below with the wind chill. Subway cars broke down and shivering crowds milled in the underground stations. Buses stalled and were abandoned on Fifth Avenue. People improvised outfits for navigating the streets: ski masks and battery-operated electric gloves. It was impossible to find a taxi. On every corner, bundled figures waved twenty-dollar bills to bribe cabs with off-duty lights to pick them up.

Lucy was forced to walk the twenty blocks from her sister's apartment to Columbus Circle, wearing four layers of clothes and two scarves. She entered the lobby of the Henry Hudson Hotel, where National Educational Television had its offices, and, peeling off her outer garments, climbed the stairs to the second floor.

She had shown *An American Hunger* to a dozen staff members, who had raved about it to colleagues and friends. Word went out: Rosser and Sachs had a hot program. It was scheduled to air on a Sunday in mid-February, right after

"60 Minutes." The television writer for the New York *Times* was running a prebroadcast interview with Lucy, as were reporters for the Associated Press and feature syndicates. Meanwhile, Joe was working the Coast. He arranged for advance coverage in the Los Angeles papers, and *New West* ran an item with their picture and the caption "Rosser and Sachs, new team to watch."

Lucy was on her way to meet Norman Silver, the program director, whom she found wearing his customary suspenders and bow tie. In the eight years since she had first walked, green and ambitious, into Silver's office, nothing had changed. The books were stacked several feet high on his desk, only the titles were different. There were piles of magazines, letters, video tapes and, in a cleared island, photos of his wife and two daughters in silver frames. A stereo was tuned to WQXR, the classical music station.

"There she is," Norman said, a cheerful reprove in his voice. She was forty minutes late.

"Oh, Norman, forgive me? I've been misjudging how long it takes to get places, particularly with the transportation out."

"You're surviving the chill?"

"Here to tell the tale."

He motioned her to a chair. She hung her wet scarves and coat on the door hook. "I ran *American Hunger* for Ron Small this morning and he's behind it. Thinks it's controversial."

"Good."

"We're going to start promoting it daily, build a climate of expectancy. Can you give Margaret more background on Joe Sachs? You know, how you two got together, how you found your subjects."

Lucy nodded.

"What's the matter?"

She was hugging herself. "When I left California, it was eighty."

"You may be in for an even greater climatic shock. I have a new project for you."

"Good."

"It's a big project."

"I told you I wanted something I could lose myself in."

"A documentary on the coming of peace to the Middle East."

She made a circle with her lips. "That is a large order. Are there funds?"

"I wouldn't suggest it otherwise. We have a special grant from the Jaglom Foundation. The director knows your work, he says you can approach it any way you want, so long as you find an angle to tell the story in human terms."

"Which means . . . ?"

Norman pressed the tips of his fingers together. "The Egyptians and the Israelis have been bitter enemies for thirty years. Many of them have had relatives killed by the other side. How will they adjust to suddenly becoming peaceful neighbors? You can do two one-hour shows, or one ninety-minute program. You can shoot part in Cairo, part in Jerusalem, whatever you and Joe find . . ."

"I'm not working with Joe."

Norman lowered his reading glasses. "I thought this was the great new partnership."

"Only for this film. Joe wants to develop a feature, and I have other things I want to do in television."

"Make it on your own."

She hesitated. "Joe has the passion for Israel. Are you sure you don't want to offer it to him?"

"You said he's working on a feature. Besides, I know this is a natural for you."

"I'll have to do tons of research."

Norman smiled. It was a good sign if Lucy was resisting. He flipped the sheets of his calendar. "When can you leave?"

The cutting room in California was as Lucy had last seen it, except for this: Joe was standing by the flatbed, rubbing his chin.

"Why did you do it?" she said.

"I wanted to see what was under there."

"How long has it been?"

"Six years."

Lucy took a step closer. She had become so accustomed to seeing him with a beard that without it, his face seemed unnaturally foreshortened. He looked exposed, the newly shaved skin pale and mealy.

He smiled, and his lips pulled to one side. "I didn't know I had such a mean mouth. What do you think?"

"You look a little younger. More . . . straight."

"I'll take that."

"Did you see the A.P. story?"

He nodded, and threw a cigarette pack in the wastebasket. "I'm also quitting smoking. Today is numero uno."

"Good luck. Let's look at the answer print." She took off her jacket, went to the projector and found a box from Paris Pastry with two chocolate eclairs. "Thanks," she said. Joe was trying.

After that day in Ramirez Canyon, she had wanted to be impersonal and had resisted Joe's attempts to lapse back to comradely joking. Fortunately, the only editing that had remained was fine tuning. The professional parts of them, the parts that worked so well together, had taken over.

They decided to watch the broadcast of *An American Hunger* at Joe's house. It was a private moment they did not want to share with others. It was always different to see a film coming out of the set in your home than it was to watch it in a screening room. It played different, sounded different, and the experience was different, knowing that at that moment, ten million people were watching it in their homes. For Lucy, it was like cracking a ball into the culture and having it drive deep into the bleachers, with people scuffling to catch it.

Joe had tears in his eyes. They sat on opposite corners of

the couch in the living room. Discreetly, Joe had moved the set out of the bedroom.

"You were right about Claire, the birthday dinner," he said.

"The color is wonderful, you caught that dusky rose feeling."

When Joe saw their names crawl by at the end, "Produced by Joseph Sachs and Lucy Rosser . . . A Rosser-Sachs Film," he slid across the couch. "We did it," he said. He pressed his cheek to her face and hugged her tightly. "A healthy baby."

She stiffened.

He released his arms.

"Joe, how do you feel about my going to Jerusalem?"

"I don't know. You haven't gone yet."

She edged away. "I wonder if we'll show up in the ratings."

"We can get the overnights at six in the morning, if we call New York. Want to set the alarm?"

She nodded. "I'll call Norman, then I'll call you."

"It seems like it might be a good transition," he said.

"To what?"

"I don't know."

"I'm not sure I should go anymore."

"What are you talking about?"

"I'm thinking of canceling. I have so many things to do and so little time."

"Look, if there's anything you can't get done, I'll take care of it. I'll water your plants."

"It's such an ambitious project, and I'm starting from zero. I don't know anything about the politics, the history. I'm going to have to cram and take language courses."

"It'll probably be the most exciting thing you've done. I wish I were going."

"You could visit," she said, knowing he would not.

* * *

The week before she was to leave, Lucy observed something that had happened whenever she was about to leave a place: life there became perfect. Friendships seemed more dear, new interests appeared and she asked herself why she had to go. In Los Angeles, in the weeks before her departure, she received several job offers, became more friendly with her neighbors, played exceptionally well at tennis and began seeing two new men.

The weather was as beautiful as it must have been in the early days of California. The rains had passed, and it was possible to see the snowy peaks of the San Gabriel Mountains, which, for most of the year, were hidden by haze. The sunsets were dramatic, with sweeps of navy blue, rose and silver. There were Iceland poppies on the lawns, and the lavender petals of jacaranda trees floated down and covered the pavement like carpet.

Everywhere she went, Lucy heard people talking about *An American Hunger*. The show had drawn a larger audience than any program on NET in the previous year. Newspapers ran articles about it; radio and television talk shows devoted programs to it. Ness was ecstatic—his company had been deluged with business and he wanted to sign Joe and Lucy to do another film.

Lucy felt blessed, grateful for the friends she loved, the house she lived in, the opportunities she possessed. Maybe, she thought, living on her own was the way. She had been fighting it for so long, but she did not feel the old desperation.

Her last night, while she was packing, the phone rang at midnight.

"Did I wake you?"

"Obviously not."

"I'm feeling strange, now that you're leaving."

"Only for eight months, Joe."

"It seems like such a distance."

"I know, as long as I'm here, you may not see me but you know where I am."

"You're crazy."

"You're going to miss me."

"I've been thinking about your film. You shouldn't be afraid, trust your instincts. Don't be in a hurry either, try to have some fun with it. I have a feeling there's a surprise waiting for you over there."

"I don't know a soul, I'll be lonely."

"You're like a junkie, anxious before the fix."

"I can't remember why I agreed to do this."

"Look, for nineteen hundred years we've been saying, 'Next Year in Jerusalem.' Understandably, you're a little nervous."

She laughed.

"It's a good move," he said.

In the morning, he drove her to the airport and, after she had checked her bags, gave her a folded slip of paper to place between the stones of the Wailing Wall.

"What's this?"

"If you write a prayer and slip it in the Wall, God receives it."

She looked dubious, then feigned opening the note.

"Go ahead. It's in code."

She unfolded it and read:

SRCR TLV
KOOB

—HLT
RIYKN

"I'll bet I can crack it."

He laughed, then leaned forward and kissed her. "It's all over for me anyhow." He slapped her arm. "Fly."

As she was walking to the gate, a song ran through her mind. "Take a Good Look at My Face."

It was a song by Smokey Robinson, but the version she was hearing was Linda Ronstadt's.

"So take a good look at my face . . ." and Lucy thought, because you're never going to see it again. She felt prickles on her neck. She slowed down and dropped her canvas bag. She hitched it up again and continued walking. It was just a song.

III   The High Mountains

March 1979

1

The American Colony Hotel was a great old stone building, with arches, domes and hand-painted tiles, in the Arab sector of East Jerusalem. The hotel was favored by journalists and tour groups because of its closeness to the Old City—the small, walled enclave in which the West's three great religions had their origins and their most holy shrines.

At night, the outside walls of the Old City were illuminated by yellow floodlamps, which gave the towers and parapets a kind of Disneyland glow. Inside, though, the Old City was a ghostly labyrinth: a maze of walls within walls, shops and places of worship built on top of each other, and narrow, curving alleys down which no one could pass except by foot or donkey.

On a night in late March, a darkness extended from the Damascus Gate of the Old City to the American Colony Hotel. The front doors were locked, and a clerk was dozing on the sofa by the desk.

In a room on the third floor, an American woman was sleeping in a narrow bed. It appeared that she had recently arrived, for her bags were on the floor, half unpacked, and the dresser was covered with maps of Israel, copies of the Jerusalem *Post* and a Hebrew-English dictionary.

The woman lay on her back, under a thin blanket. She had a slender face, with long dark lashes. Her forehead was damp, and her heart-shaped lips were parted slightly.

"Al-lah!"

A man's voice chanting Arabic roared through the windows.

"Al-lahu akbar, Al-lahu akbar, ashhadu anna la ilaha ila-llah . . ."

The woman began to toss, and after a minute she was awake. The chanting was shrill, an assault on the nerves. She fumbled with the light by the bed and looked at her watch—4 A.M.

"What the hell . . . ?"

After five minutes, the chanting stopped. She heard the scratching of a needle. Then it started again, faster. *"Hayyu Ala-s-salat, Hayyu Ala-s-salat . . ."*

She went to the window. The sound was being broadcast, but she could not tell from where. The street was deserted, possessed of that darkness she had noted on the night she arrived. She remembered the taxi driver, who had found the hotel with difficulty, telling her, "Only the dead know Jerusalem."

She went back to bed, put the pillow over her head, but it was impossible to muffle the torturing singsong. Every few minutes it would change pitch, assaulting in another key.

She reached for the phone to call the desk. No answer. She put on a raincoat over her nightgown, slipped on her sandals and walked down the tile steps to the lobby.

Mussa, the desk clerk, was sleeping through the noise. "Excuse me." She touched his shoulder. He opened his eyes halfway.

"Ah, how do you do, Mrs. Rosser."

"What's that loud singing outside?"

"It is the minaret. He is calling the faithful to prayer."

"At four in the morning?"

Mussa shrugged. "They must pray five times a day."
Footsteps sounded in the hall and a tall German, his face
working, hurried into the lobby. "Someone is crying so
loud outside our room. We cannot sleep!"

"I know, sir," Mussa said, still reclining. "All the
guests are complaining. One man, he get so angry, he try to
choke me." Mussa laughed, his shoulders shaking.

"Does this go on every night?" Lucy said.

Mussa nodded. "We have asked them not to put it on
loudspeaker, but . . ." He waved an arm. "What can we
do? It is the religion."

Lucy could not go back to sleep, even when the muezzin
ended at 4:30 A.M. Lying in her room, she wondered how
she had managed to sleep through it on previous nights. Jet
lag, perhaps, but now she was acclimated. The following
day would be the signing of the peace treaty, and she tossed,
worrying about whether to go to Tel Aviv or stay in Jerusalem, or should she go to Cairo with a special plane for journalists?

At six, she dressed and went down to the dining room.
The sun was rising, and pink light filtered through the windows of the great domed ceiling. The room was peaceful,
with fresh flowers on the tables, but the service was mad-
dening. When Lucy ordered an omelet, the waiter brought
it, an hour later, without a fork. "Sorry, we're out of
forks," he said. She made do with tea and pita bread. When
she walked back through the lobby, Mussa flagged her.
"Did you get your message?"

"When?"

"Just now."

"No. What was it?"

"He called."

"Who?"

"That man."

"What man?"

"He said you knew him."

"Did you get his name?"

Mussa hit his head with his palm in an "Oh, I forgot" gesture.

"What did he say?"

"He said, 'Tell her I called.' "

Lucy bit her lip. "Was it local or overseas?"

Mussa waved his arm. "He will call again."

In a corner of the lobby, a corpulent priest in a brown Friar Tuck robe was showing crucifixes to four ladies. "This one's made of Jerusalem stone, and it's two dollars."

"Lovely."

"I'm checking out the day after tomorrow," Lucy said to Mussa. "Can you have my bill ready?"

"That will be difficult for me."

"I know, but it has to be done, unless you want me to leave without paying."

Mussa and the two other clerks began to laugh. Lucy laughed also. If taking a message was hard, what would preparing a bill be? Calculus.

Yael Doron, the young Israeli woman Lucy had hired as an assistant and translator, came to the hotel at nine, with two cameramen and two soundmen. They sat in Lucy's room, working out plans. One crew would go to Maccabee Square in Tel Aviv, the other to the Wailing Wall in Jerusalem.

Danny Modai, the first cameraman, did not want to go to Tel Aviv. "It will be young kids singing and dancing, but it won't be a true reflection of people's sentiments. It's contrived by the government."

"That may be," Lucy said, "but let's shoot it to cover ourselves."

"I think it's a waste."

The phone rang. "The ceremony happens only once,

Danny, we can go after sentiment anytime." She picked up the phone. "Hello?"

"Lucy?" A male voice with an Israeli accent.

"Yes."

"Uzi Tamir speaking."

"Oh my God."

Yael and Danny began yelling at each other in Hebrew.

"Do you think he will hear you?" Uzi said.

"Uzi Tamir." She turned her back and walked as close as she could to the window.

"Welcome to the Holy Land."

"It's been . . ."

"Fifteen years. I've been making calculations."

Her cheeks grew hot.

Danny was shouting in English now. "Go to the occupied territories, go to see the war wounded . . ."

"How did you know I was here?" Lucy said.

"It's a small country."

There was silence.

"Why are you calling . . ."

"No special reason," he said. She heard the door slam. "I tried to contact you a few times before. I've been in the States twice. I saw one of your programs and called the television, but they wouldn't give your number."

She traced with her finger the zigzag pattern in the glass. "I wondered what happened to you, especially when the war broke out."

"I survived," Uzi said.

"And David?"

"He was killed."

The door opened; a burst of Hebrew.

"I'm sorry."

"It was a long time ago."

"What are you doing now?"

"I am professor of Bedouin anthropology at the Hebrew University."

"Sounds impressive."

"I spend as much time as I can in Sinai." (He pronounced it See-nai.)

"I've heard it's beautiful there."

"I have place—rough place, but I love it—at Santa Katarina, where Mount Sinai is."

"I've wanted to see it."

"You will be welcome."

Silence.

"I think we should meet," Uzi said.

"I'm kind of pressed."

"You are working all day and night?"

"Just about."

Yael tapped her shoulder. "Danny's going."

"Wait, I'll be off in a minute." She returned to Uzi. "We're shooting a film about the coming of peace, and tomorrow is the signing . . ."

"But it's in Washington."

"I want to get the reaction here."

"I don't think you will see much. Nobody feels like celebrating."

"I've noticed. Why do you think this is?"

"Personally, I think it's a great step. But most people are complaining, the terms are too harsh, they don't believe the peace will last, so we're giving up Sinai for nothing."

A knock at the door—Mussa with a telegram.

"Can I call you later?" Lucy said.

"Let's meet fifteen minutes for a coffee."

"Miss Lucy, please."

She took the envelope from Mussa. "All right, come by the hotel at five," she said, and they hung up.

At noon, she took a cab to the Jaffa Gate, the major entrance to the Old City. After hours of wrangling with the bureaucrats at Israeli Television, she wanted to check out logistics at the Wailing Wall. Curiously, she had put off going there every day since her arrival. She had been casting a wide net, meeting politicians, writers, army officers, archaeologists, but she had avoided the religious community.

She sat down in a cafe inside the Jaffa Gate and ordered falafel and orange juice. A boy of nine was standing at the juice machine, placing orange halves on a cylinder. There was a bored rhythm to his juice-making: set up, press, lift, throw out, set up. . . . Juice squirted into a glass pitcher, about which flies buzzed.

What am I doing here? Lucy thought. In the spring of her thirty-third year, she had disrupted her life, pulled herself loose from familiar soil and made herself homeless, solitary, unconnected. The film was the most complex job she had ever undertaken. She was running in a dozen directions, arriving nowhere. So many great minds had traveled over this ground ahead of her, what could she contribute?

From her window seat, she watched the people passing into the Old City. There were Israeli soldiers in torn uniforms, carrying clumsy-looking guns. There were Hasidim with curly beards and sidelocks; nuns in gray habits; an old Arab with a cane, dragging a primitive cage of peeping chicks; black women from the Caribbean with rush fans; American teen-agers with backpacks, Italians carrying incense. Arab boys were selling drums and flutes, so there was a constant whistling and beating of drums.

Welcome to the Holy Land. Uzi Tamir. What would he look like now, at thirty-eight? That year in New York they had been students, eating in cafeterias and delis and cheap Chinese, taking subways and sneaking into the Thalia to see movies. She remembered the night they had decided they were in love, sitting in the West End bar, drinking wine while the first snow fell. She could feel the steam heat, see the flush on their young faces.

She paid her bill and walked out to David Street. Every time she entered the Old City, she felt a swell of fear and excitement. There were ancient stones underfoot, and on each side, Arab shops with hanging robes, carpets, beads, copper trays, wooden camels. People swarmed in all directions, while the Arab boys beat their drums and blew their flutes. Down and down she went until there was no sunlight. Two sheep stood in a doorway. The shops changed: tourist goods gave way to lamb heads, whole fish, jellied candies, grape leaves. The street smelled of cumin, rancid meat and urine.

She had never gone down this far before. All the signs were in Arabic, she thought she must be lost, but suddenly she climbed a flight of steps and came out on a large, open plaza. There was the Wall. Its yellow-brown stones reached into the sky and stopped. Caper bushes sprouted from between its stones, and birds whirled and swooped.

Lucy approached, timidly. A metal divider separated the men's area on the left from the smaller women's area on the right. It was 2 P.M., 100 degrees, and only a few people were praying.

"Excuse me, are you Jewish?"

"Yes."

A man in a black wool coat and hat, with a long white beard and glasses, peered at her. "Would you like to spend Shabbat in a Jewish home?"

"Thank you, no." She turned away, but he followed. "How much would it be worth to you to find truth?" She walked faster. "How much would it be worth to learn to live a happy life?" He called louder. "You're American. You've taken est, right? You've been to a psychiatrist? Why not learn the wisdom of your own people—the holy Torah."

She went into the women's section, knowing he could not follow. When she stood before the Wall, sweating, breathless, she saw that there were thousands of pieces of paper wedged between the stones. On the ground was a rain of scraps that had become dislodged. She took from her wallet the note Joe had given her and slipped it into a crevice.

She sat down on a metal folding chair, closed her eyes and pressed her forehead to the Wall. She felt nothing. The stone smelled dank, like a musty floor. She heard a woman beside her, whispering urgently, and from the men's side, prayers being sung in a familiar minor key. She fell asleep.

She awoke with a start, and began to take deep breaths. Lord make me whole, she said silently. She placed her palms on the Wall. She wanted to feel something, but she had lost the thread for so long. She continued breathing deeply, and began to sense a pulsing in the heel of her right hand. As she went on, the pulsing grew stronger, until it seemed there was a current passing between her hand and the stone and she did not care if it was real or imagined.

She opened her eyes and looked up, following the Wall toward the sky. "Do you want me to observe Shabbat and keep kosher?" she asked silently.

"Yes."

"Do I have to?"

"No."

"What will happen if I don't?"

"You'll keep suffering."

"Why do it?"

"To remind yourself always of the eternal."

"I don't believe it will pay off. It's too much trouble. And how do I know the voice answering is you and not my own subconscious?"

A pause.

"You don't."

Smiling, Lucy walked away from the Wall to the edge of the plaza. It was 3:30, she wanted to return to the hotel and change before Uzi arrived. She took out her map, thinking if she could find her way to the Damascus Gate, she would come out a block from the American Colony.

She descended into the shadows, took a right turn, then a left. A man tapped her shoulder and when she looked, blew a lecherous kiss. She hurried ahead, seeing fewer and fewer tourists until she was lost in a soup of Arabic. The crowds had swelled, and there were goats, donkeys, roosters caught in the jam. Two boys were wheeling a barrow cart, the wheels rolling over people's feet.

Beggars stretched out their arms and shouted, *"Baksheesh!"* Heat, darkness. She wedged herself in a doorway and looked at her map. It seemed the street should widen before long, turn and meet the Damascus Gate.

"No, miss, you no go there!" someone cried but she walked on. A shiver passed through her.

"Where you want to go?" a boy said, appearing by her side. He was thin, small, perhaps twelve. He had large eyes with hollow sockets and teeth rotted to stumps.

She shook her head and made a clicking sound.

"I no want money. I just want be your friend."

"Please, go away."

She stopped in an archway leading to a tea shop. "The Damascus Gate?" The waiter pointed.

The little boy took off ahead like a lead dog.

"I don't want a guide."

"I know, I know."

"I'm not going to pay you."

"I just want speak English. Be your friend. Please."

Worn down, she let the boy fall in step with her. They began to chat, where did he live, how was he learning English, and he seemed sweet, she was beginning to feel pleased at overcoming her suspicions. When they reached a crossing, the boy pointed left.

"Are you sure this is the way? I want the Damascus Gate."

"I know. This is shortcut. Much better."

They walked in silence. The boy made another turn and she hesitated.

"You come. Damascus Gate very close." But after another five minutes, they were deep in a sooty alley, so narrow they could barely walk abreast. Lucy stopped. "I don't want to go this way."

"This way good. Why you no believe me? Because I Arab?"

She sighed and walked on, yet with every minute she grew more nervous. The alley was completely deserted and their footsteps echoed. A cat skulked by, flattening itself against the wall like a criminal. They turned a corner and a man on a donkey came clopping toward them. They stood aside. The boy shouted in Arabic to the donkey driver, who grabbed at Lucy's breast.

She looked around. No lights, no shops, only locked doorways. "No scare, I am little boy." He pulled her arm. "Come here, I want talk to you."

"Don't touch me." She yanked her arm from him. "I'm going back." She heard her skirt rip. She looked around and saw the boy's face, black with hate. He was holding her dress with one hand and the other was forming a fist. "Why are you doing this!" She wrenched away and began running up the alley, but there was the man on the donkey. She heard the boy crowing with laughter. "I going to catch you. I going to fuck you!"

The donkey driver turned the animal so it blocked the passage. She slowed; the boy was gaining. All powers of reason flew from her. She started to scream. Both the man and boy were laughing, making bloodcurdling sounds. She backed up against a door and pounded. "Help!" The boy lunged for her, she kicked at him, he screamed in pain but grabbed onto her with grimy little hands when the door gave way.

A fat woman all in black with a black veil caught her, then stepped into the alley. She pushed the boy against the wall. The man was still laughing. The woman approached the donkey and shouted at the driver, who shouted back. The woman shoved the animal's rump, then motioned for Lucy to pass.

"Damascus Gate, can you take me?" she pleaded. The woman gestured, indicating that the way was straight ahead, then right. Her eyes suggested Lucy would be safe, she would watch. "Good-bye!" the boy shouted, still laughing.

She arrived at the hotel with her dress torn and her face streaked with dirt. An Israeli man stood up from the sofa and came toward her. He was wearing jeans and a black military shirt with epaulets. She forgot the Arab boy in her amazement. The young man she had known in New York had been lean and gaunt. This man had a paunch. He was nearly bald. His face was round and lined where it had been narrow and smooth, but in it, she recognized the rift—the cleft chin and the slight gap between the teeth.

He was grinning with a child's uncomplicated joy. He grabbed her shoulder and shook it triumphantly.

"Lucy Landis!"

She looked at her dress, then at him. "Hello, Uzi."

2

"I don't remember your eyes being blue."

"How could you not remember that? It's what people notice first."

"It was not of importance to me, apparently."

"More wine?"

Uzi nodded. "Weren't you plumper?"

"About the same. But you've gained . . ."

"Oh yes."

He kept staring at her, grinning. They were sitting in chairs across from one another in Lucy's room. He had waited downstairs while she had showered and changed into jeans and a light blue shirt. She remembered she had been wearing blue, his favorite color, the last time she had seen Uzi. The blue had been in vain that night, for he had stared at the floor. "Why?" she had asked. He had shaken his head miserably. "You just turned off?" He had looked up and nodded.

At the American Colony Hotel, Uzi consoled her about the mishap with the Arab boy. "You shouldn't be staying in East Jerusalem, you should be in our city."

"I'm moving."

"I am curious about you," he said, patting her arm. "You are married?"

"Divorced. I was married . . . seven years. And you?"

"Married. I have two kids ["keeds," he pronounced it], boy and girl."

She had a sinking feeling. "That's wonderful."

He poured another glass of wine, then grabbed Lucy's hair and yanked it playfully. "In See-nai, I spend a lot of time with Bedouin. We don't talk much, but we have a word, *ahalan*. It means 'Welcome.' "

Lucy laughed softly.

"I don't remember you giggling so much."

"What do you remember?"

"I remember after the first night we made love, you woke up and you were angry. I thought, uh oh, she's sorry she did it."

What was he talking about?

They spoke about their marriages, and their work, and the places they had lived, and where they had traveled and what had become of mutual friends, and Lucy thought, I used to love this man. What was it?

"Do you feel like you know me?" she said.

"Yes. Apparently my memory of you is more complicated than yours of me."

Tears came to her eyes. He took her by the arms and pulled her to her feet. He began hugging her, kissing her damp cheeks. When he kissed her lips, it was completely unfamiliar, she could not recall the feel of them. Tears kept running down her face, and she buried her head against his chest.

"I remember your face from this angle," he said.

"I have to blow my nose."

"No, don't go."

He was running his hand under her blouse. She moved it away and went into the bathroom. When she blew her nose, blood gushed into the tissue. She stared in shock at the bright red liquid.

"Why is your nose bleeding?" Uzi said.

She lay down on the bed, holding a towel to her face. "I don't think you want to know."

He looked concerned.

"It's nothing, really. Just the dryness. It will stop."

"It usually does."

She moved to sit up.

"No, keep down." He made a "down" gesture, as to a dog.

She laughed. When it seemed the flow had stopped, she sat up.

"Why did your nose bleed?"

"I suppose I should tell you, but I don't want you to feel you have to defend yourself."

He watched her intently.

She was crying again. "In my life, there have been, I could count on one hand, the number of men who've meant anything. And you were one."

He nodded.

"I loved you, and I thought you loved me. And then suddenly you didn't love me anymore. It was just cut off. It hurt . . ." Her voice caught. "It was a long time ago, but it's still there, walled up."

"I feel I want to answer somehow."

She wiped her eyes.

"I didn't think it mattered that much to you. I knew it was done with cruelty, but you were this somber person who barely tolerated my existence. You didn't like my accent, my clothes, the stories I told. You didn't think I was smart enough. We were fighting all the time. You were more interested in my friends. You were always about to catch the next bus, and I simply caught one first."

"The other girl . . ."

"She was completely unimportant."

"But you said . . ."

"She was my ticket out."

"This amazes me, that our memories could be so different," Lucy said, and yet she realized, as she listened, that he could have seen things that way. "I thought you didn't love me as much as I loved you. I thought you were incapable of fidelity."

"That may be true." Uzi raised his eyebrows. "But I don't remember fucking around while I was with you."

The irony, Lucy thought, was that he had been married ten years and had two kids and she was divorced.

"You never told me you felt unloved."

"We didn't talk much. I mean, we talked about all kinds of things, but not that."

Lucy said, "I couldn't understand why you were looking me up now. Apparently I meant a lot . . ."

"What a dumb-ass thing to say." He yanked her hair. "Of course."

"I didn't know."

He took her in his arms again and as they kissed, he began to breathe hoarsely.

"I can't make love with you."

He was maneuvering his way on top of her. "Why?"

"I don't want to be your mistress."

"That's a big word."

She pulled her face from his and nestled it in the crook of his neck. They continued to stroke each other and kiss, but the spirit had altered subtly.

"I have a long day tomorrow," Lucy said.

"You want help? Seriously, I am free, and I have car. I can drive you where you need."

"That would be wonderful. If you're sure . . ."

"Of course I'm sure."

She ran her hand under his shirt, feeling his dark, curly

pelt. "I remember the first time we took off our clothes, you asked me, 'Do you like my fur?' "

"What did you say?"

"I didn't know if I liked it or not."

"What did you answer?"

She thought a moment. "Yes."

Uzi laughed. "I probably didn't believe you."

They got to their feet and walked to the door. They hugged again. "I love your fur," she said.

He grinned. "I see you tomorrow."

During the night the weather turned: the 100-degree heat was swept away by winds and icy rain. Lucy awoke to the crack of thunder, which, in her first thoughts, she took for gunfire. White pellets of hail flew in her window and strafed the floor. She shut the window and stared at the storm-darkened street. It was weather for the climax of a drama.

She dug out boots, a sweater and jacket she had brought, having been warned that Jerusalem could be cold. Downstairs, she found Uzi talking to the cameraman, Danny Modai. "He was my platoon leader in Sce nai," Uzi said. "He is tough fellow." He punched his shoulder. Danny, unshaven, was wearing a khaki *dubon*, the hooded army jacket Israeli men seemed to live in.

"So you're old friends," Danny said.

"She was my introduction to American culture," Uzi said.

Uzi's unabashed smile, the wonderful cleft chin, made Lucy feel happy. They drove in Uzi's car to the National Military Cemetery, high in the Judean hills, where teams of high school students were placing pink carnations on the graves. The cemetery was vast, terraced with pines and cypresses. The rain had stopped, and shafts of sunlight were cutting through the clouds, so that patches of the landscape were luminous white while the surrounding earth was dark.

The cemetery was divided into sections for different branches of the service and for national heroes. There was a reflecting pool, under which were the tombs of men who had fallen in the navy. Israelis never died in battle, Lucy had noticed, they "fell."

It was strangely peaceful, walking among the graves, many of which had yellow *Yizkor* candles and flowering plants and little stones set on them to show there had been visitors. Except for the students with pink carnations, the cemetery was empty.

After an hour, Lucy told Danny he could go on to Tel Aviv. She and Uzi continued walking, passing the graves of Theodore Herzl and Golda Meir. It began to drizzle. They came to a clearing in which were seven graves in the shape of a V, with a parachute on each headstone. "Here is Hannah Senesh," Uzi said. "You know who she is?"

Lucy shook her head no.

"She's the national heroine of Israel, like Joan of Arc. Every eight-year-old kid can recite her poems." There was a sudden spray of sunlight in the midst of the drizzle. Everything in the circle turned gold. They sat on a bench under a eucalyptus tree, its leaves sparkling with raindrops, and Uzi told Lucy about Hannah Senesh.

Hannah Senesh had been born in Hungary in 1921, to a wealthy family. Her father was a playwright. In her teens, she had caught the Zionist fervor and left her home to be a pioneer in *Eretz Yisrael,* the Land of Israel. She wrote in her diary, "One needs to feel that one's life has meaning, that one is needed in this world."

Uzi said, "When you study about 'pioneers' in school, you think of them as grown-ups, brave, mature. But when you look at the photographs of them in fields, wearing baggy shorts and funny straw hats, you see they were kids, seventeen, eighteen. They came from bourgeois homes. Their parents wanted them to be doctors and lawyers, and were unhappy that they went so far away. These kids wanted to build a utopia, a safe place for Jews. They wanted to lead a healthy, new kind of Jewish life, not sitting in rooms reading books but being reborn by working with the soil.''

''It reminds me of young people in America who went to live on the land in communes,'' Lucy said. ''Except, the Israeli pioneers built something lasting.'' She remembered how she had felt humbled, her first days in Israel, by the concrete evidence of one generation's work.

''You should read the letters these kids wrote home, to Russia, Hungary, Poland, begging their families to come to Palestine,'' Uzi said. ''But the parents would write back, 'We wouldn't be comfortable. We're too old to start from scratch.' And most of them perished in the Holocaust.''

Hannah Senesh was a sunny, headstrong, exceptionally talented young woman, Uzi said. She worked with the chickens on a kibbutz instead of going to the university, because, she said, ''There are already far too many intellectuals in Palestine. The only thing I'm committed to is building our country.'' She yearned to found schools throughout the land, to become a writer, to go into government, yet she loved to sing and dance and dreamed of finding ''the one.'' In 1943, although she and her brother were safe in Palestine, she volunteered to parachute behind Nazi lines to warn the Hungarian Jews of their fate and organize rescue attempts.

''With the world on fire, it's difficult to believe that personal problems are of any importance,'' she wrote. According to legend, she was fearless, always the first to jump, to lift morale by writing poems and songs, and constructing elaborate paper dolls. She refused to abort her mission when told it was too risky. She was captured and tortured by the Nazis soon after she landed, her teeth were knocked out and she was excuted, refusing a blindfold, at the age of twenty-two. Even the Nazi captain who condemned her to death had conceded, ''She was an extraordinary human being.'' The last thing she did in her cell was write a poem, which was smuggled out by another prisoner. Uzi recited it.

One—Two—Three

One—two—three . . .
    eight feet long,
Two strides across, the rest is dark . . .
Life hangs over me like a question mark.

One—two—three . . .
    maybe another week,
Or next month may still find me here,
But death, I feel, is very near.

I could have been
    twenty-three next July;
I gambled on what mattered most,
The dice were cast. I lost.

Rain began to fall in sheets. The students in the cemetery dropped their pink carnations and scattered. Lucy thought, for a second, they looked like skeletons, with death's heads.

I gambled on what mattered most.

A giant television screen was to be set up on the plaza by the Wall, so the signing in Washington could be broadcast by satellite to Jerusalem. When Uzi and Lucy arrived at eight, though, there was no screen, no explanation. In the freezing rain, the only souls who had come out were tourists. A crude stage had been erected, and on it, Yehudi Menuhin was playing a Bach prelude *a cappella*, but the music was drowned out by soldiers gunning their jeeps.

"It's the Middle East," Uzi said. "Everything that can will get fucked up." He laughed, which made Lucy drop her worried look. He told her the joke about the scorpion and the tortoise ("tor-twaze," he called it). "The scorpion wants to cross the Jordan, so he asks the tor-twaze, 'Give me a ride.' The tor-twaze says, 'No, you will sting me,' and the scorpion says, 'I couldn't do that, because if you drowned, so would I.' So the tor-twaze carries the scorpion on his back and halfway across the river, the scorpion stings him. 'You did it!' the tor-twaze says as he starts to sink. 'Why?' The scorpion says, 'It's the Middle East.' "

"I'm cold," Lucy said. "Where can we go to watch the ceremony?"

They returned to Uzi's car but he could not think of a place. "We can't go to my house, my wife's mother is staying there, and if I take you to friends, it would cause problems." They drove around Mount Zion.

"What about the King David Hotel? They have a TV in the lobby."

"Okay, it's not ideal, but we're running out of time."

They walked in the lobby just at nine, and sat on a couch at the back of the room. Tourists—almost all American Jews—were lined up in chairs, as at a performance, before a single black and white television. The men were smoking cigars, the women wearing bouffant hairstyles twenty years out of date.

On the television, an Israeli woman was singing a peace song, set to a disco beat.

"Shhhhh!"

The scene shifted to the White House. Sadat, Carter and Begin were standing on the lawn, while a band played the anthems of the three nations. No one at the King David, except

Uzi, who chose not to, could sing the Israeli anthem, but they all sang "The Star-Spangled Banner." With each verse, they sang more heartily, and at the end, they broke into applause.

Tears came, involuntarily, to Lucy's eyes. It was bizarre: watching history being made, the fate of the Middle East being sealed in Washington, through the eyes of American Jews in the Holy Land.

Carter began to speak and the picture went dead. Lucy turned. "It's the Middle East?"

Uzi squeezed her shoulders. How could I not have been happy with this person, she thought, and yet she remembered, she had not been.

The picture came back as Sadat was speaking. He was elegant, dignified. "This is certainly one of the happiest moments of my life. A new dawn is emerging out of the darkness of the past. A new chapter in the history of coexistence among nations. Let there be *no more war, no more bloodshed, between Arabs and Israelis . . .*"

Applause burst from the group at the King David, including the two on the couch. Then Begin started his remarks. "I come before you as one of the members of the tribe of Israel, as one of the generation of the Holocaust, as one of the ancient Jewish people who, after 1,878 years of dispersion, persecution, humiliation and ultimately physical destruction, fought for our liberty alone and founded our state."

Uzi made a sour face. "I can't stand him, always beating his breast."

"He has a certain integrity."

"He embarrasses me."

While the documents were being signed, a waiter entered with champagne; people fought for the glasses. Uzi secured two and handed one to Lucy. "So." He clinked her glass. "Happy peace."

* * *

"The Bedouin have a proverb," Uzi said.

" 'The good doesn't last forever;
The bad also doesn't last forever.' "

An Arab waiter brought ten small plates and arranged
them between Uzi and Lucy: humus, tchina, Turkish salad,
eggplant salad, garbanzo beans, bulgur wheat, yogurt and
cucumber salad, pink pickled vegetables, falafel and pita.
These were the first course, brought automatically when
they sat down. Lucy thought it was enough for a meal, but
Uzi cleaned the plates and ordered lamb, rice and a pitcher
of fresh orange juice.

"You eat quickly," she said.

"It's a starving child syndrome. My stomach is afraid it
won't eat again."

The food was one of the first things that had surprised
Lucy about Israel. She had expected pastrami, chopped
liver, lox and bagels, but there was not a deli to be found.
The food in restaurants was Middle Eastern, "Oriental,"
they called it, and at home, Israelis ate simple meals based
around eggs, cheese, tomatoes and cucumbers, olives, fresh
fruit and yogurt.

Uzi spoke to the waiter in Arabic and another plate of
falafel appeared. The door to the restaurant opened. A couple Uzi knew walked in and stopped at the table. He introduced Lucy as "a colleague from America."

"So, what do you think of our treaty?" the man asked.

"Like everyone, I'm a little sad."

"Poor Uzi," the woman said, "he's losing all his Bedouin."

"I had twelve good years." He scooped up humus.

The couple sat down across the room. Uzi told Lucy,
"When you come to Sinai, you will understand. I first traveled through the region with my army platoon, right after the

Six Day War. It was love at first sight. It's a dramatic, wild country, and it was completely unspoiled. I met Bedouin who had been isolated from civilization and were living as they had two thousand years before. They were like our ancestors, when they wandered in the desert, with camels and tents. At first, when you meet them, they seem completely primitive, but they have a highly developed sense of morals. They have beautiful philosophy, and poetry, and a code of hospitality."

Uzi said that if a Bedouin is starving and has one piece of meat, and just as he's about to eat, a stranger appears, "he must offer it to the stranger, and not let the stranger know it's his only piece of meat and he's starving."

"No wonder they haven't progressed very far."

"You're right. They're easily taken advantage of. But they are morally superior to us, I'll tell you."

"Each one? No liars, no thieves in the tribe?"

"I'm idealizing a bit. But you will see."

The remains of the lamb were cleared, and the waiter brought cups of Turkish coffee.

"I came back and read everything published on the Sinai Bedouin and it was terrible. Worthless. Contradicted by what little I had seen in the field. So I set up a project, and for twelve years I've had the most marvelous time. I managed to interview every Bedouin I wanted, and I have enough data to keep me writing for years."

"Funny," Lucy said, "I never saw this side of you."

He paid the bill. "You saw me as a lazy bum?"

"Um hmm." They left the restaurant and walked toward the car. "You were always lying around reading magazines. You were still an undergraduate at twenty-three. I didn't understand the situation you came from—compulsory army service. I thought you'd been wasting time."

"This I remember." He put his arm around her neck and

yanked her close. "Now we are talking, this feeling I remember."

Lucy laughed. The rain had stopped, and the sky was a brilliant dome over the city. Lucy turned her face to his. "I think you're terrific."

Before they could take off their coats he was kissing her. She slid her tongue in the gap between his front teeth. "I've been wanting to do that all night."

"I've been wanting you to do it."

"Haven't others?"

He shook his head.

They stood inside the door, and she thought, this is someone who loved me, loves me.

"Will you be nice to me?" she said.

"How do you mean?"

"Honest."

"How honest?"

"If I ask you questions, tell me the truth. If I don't . . ."

"I can keep quiet. All right, I promise."

"Okay then."

"Great!" He punched his fist in the air.

"What about the light?" Lucy said.

"Turn it off. I'm not that courageous."

She walked into the bathroom, undressed, and when she came out, Uzi was lying in the darkness. She loved the feel of him, massive, warm. He was strange and familiar at the same time. She was still not used to him weighing more, and as they began making love, she was so busy observing and remembering, trying to connect this man to the lover she had had at eighteen, her first lover, that she never came close to letting go.

Uzi laughed gruffly. "Fifteen years later. Same fun."

He began kissing her again, and to her surprise, he was hard. This time, she was concentrating so intently, straining to come, she was scarcely conscious of him and when it was over, she had missed him.

"Let's have a cold drink," Uzi said. She poured club soda into glasses. They sat talking softly, and then they were making love again. "I don't believe this," she said. "How do you do it?"

"It's the inspiration."

The third time was like dancing. He held her tightly around the waist and got to his feet, still inside her. Lucy clasped her legs around him. He spun her in a circle, then dove with her onto the bed. They fell through the air and he fell into her and as they landed, her breath seemed to shoot out the top of her head.

"*Al-lah!*"

Their sighs and moans turned to laughter.

"*Al-lahu akbar . . .*"

They burrowed under the sheets while the muezzin shook the windowpanes. Kissing her cheeks, Uzi said, "I'm glad we did this. It was beautiful."

When the chanting had stopped, he drifted off to sleep, holding her, and Lucy felt blissfully released from an ancient misunderstanding. Lying in his arms, she felt moored, at rest. Hadn't her happiest moments been in a man's embrace, even if temporary? This must be the station, she thought, where masses desert the train, believing they've reached the final stop. When the train pulls out of here, only a few souls are left on board.

Sometime after five, she became aware that Uzi was moving about the room. He had to leave, he said, or his mother-in-law would miss him in the morning. He kissed her tenderly. "I see you tomorrow." He had just walked out and Lucy had curled up, feeling enveloped in softness, when the phone rang. Damn, if it was Mussa . . .

"Lucy?"

"Yes."

"It's me."

"Who?"

"You've forgotten already!"

"Joe."

"What time is it over there?"

"Five in the morning."

"Oh, shit, I'm sorry. My calculations were off."

"Is anything wrong?"

"No, I just had a strong desire to talk to you. How's the film coming?"

Lucy groaned. "Don't ask. I actually managed to put it out of my head the last few hours."

"I talked to Norman Silver, there's tremendous interest in your project. They're expecting it to be the highlight of next season."

Lucy switched on the lamp. "Joe, I'm lost. I don't have a clue where to go, or how to organize this."

"Be patient, you haven't been there that long."

"I may give up."

"Don't do anything rash. I'm thinking of coming over there. Maybe I can help."

She was silent. "This is a surprise."

"That's the idea."

"Why?"

"Lots of reasons. I'm thinking of going to Israel and Greece."

Lucy hesitated; her impulse was to discourage him, but in fact, he was the one person who might be able to help her. "When would you come?"

"About ten days."

"I'm going to Sinai, could you make it after the twenty-fourth?"

"I think so. God, it's great to hear your voice. I've missed you."

"I told you."

He laughed. "Go ahead, rub it in."

She yawned.

"Better get some sleep," he said. "Stay with it, and take care of yourself."

"Okay, Joe. *Shalom.*"

"*Shalom.*"

3

With a suitcase and sleeping bag at her feet, Lucy stood on the corner of King David and Jabotinsky streets. It was 5 A.M., the sky was peppered with stars and the air was intoxicatingly sweet with the scent of orange blossoms. Jerusalem in the spring was bursting with blossoms, most of them purple and gold. On every street there were Judas trees, with weeping magenta flowers, and acacia trees sending out shoots of powdery yellow. Was this why purple and gold had become the colors of the Resurrection?

Where was Uzi? An hour passed, Lucy walked back and forth and the sky was turning pink when he drove up in his jeep. Before Lucy could scold him, he jumped from the car and cried, "Where have you been? Let's go!"

He packed her gear in the trunk and made room for her on the front seat. In back were Danny Modai, Yoram Neged, the soundman, and a military escort who introduced himself: "Shlomo Goldmann." Shlomo had a bushy brown beard, a belly that hung out over his uniform and a gun that looked comically ancient. "I don't know if it works, but if I'm killed, at least I won't be demoted posthumously for being inadequately armed." The other men laughed.

Lucy's instincts had told her she was going to find something important on this trip, and she was in a state of high anticipation. They would be making a tour of the Sinai Peninsula, of all the land due to be returned to Egypt. She had arranged for Danny and Yoram to come along, so certain was she that somewhere in the Sinai, she would find the focus of her film.

"So, how are you?" Uzi said, yanking her hair.

"Great. I feel in the prime of my life."

"You look it too." He patted her bare leg and left his hand there.

The reunion with Uzi had been the turning point in Lucy's stay in Jerusalem. Before he had called, she had been nervous and lonely. Her hotel room with its heavy stone walls had felt like a mausoleum. Bells rang every fifteen minutes from the Church of the Ascension, the Tower of David and other holy places, measuring out her life in quarter hours. Another precious fragment gone forever.

After the meeting with Uzi, her spirits had lifted. She had moved to the Israeli sector of Jerusalem, to Yemin Moshe, a newly built community with cobblestone streets and many artists' studios. The apartment was sparkling white and clean, with a view of the Old City which, from a distance, looked like a fairy-tale kingdom with moats and spires. Children played in the courtyards of Yemin Moshe, and on Shabbat, Lucy could hear joyous singing from synagogues.

She began to feel she was in bloom. Her skin acquired a luster, and her hair, because of the dry heat, hung perfectly straight. Her body grew tight and firm from not having a car but walking everywhere, and from the Israeli diet, in which every meal included local tomatoes and cucumbers, which had a luscious, nutlike flavor that could never be found in American store produce; olives; extra-fresh cheese and ripe fruit. She looked more beautiful than she remembered looking since she had been twenty.

To her surprise, she found pleasure at living, for the first time, in a Jewish society. It was not embarrassing in Israel to have a name like Fishman. It was not unusual in Israel for the most elegant restaurant to be kosher, and for half the men dining to wear yarmulkes. There was a mezuzah on every doorpost, a single rhythm to the week. The Jewish holidays were national holidays, and the entire country shut down.

Lucy felt she was breathing new air. She wanted to learn as much as she could. In the cafes, she studied the dark, expressive faces: people eating sweets, smoking and talking—everyone talking passionately—and cracking sunflower seeds. She spent hours in her white room, reading *The Legends of the Jews*. Louis Ginzberg, in his seven volumes of *Legends*, had gathered all the oral legends and commentaries of the Torah and arranged them into a single narrative. Lucy was enthralled. She read the volume on Genesis, tracing the action on a map of Israel. Then she read Exodus: the slaves fleeing Egypt and wandering in the Sinai Desert, where God performed miracle after miracle to sustain them and still the people kept doubting God's existence.

Lucy's mind filled with fabulous images: the Revelation, when 600,000 runaway slaves, the ragged underclass of Egypt, the Children of Israel, were assembled on the plain at the foot of Mount Sinai. Angels appeared, giving each person a crown of gold and a purple robe. The people trembled when God spoke—from everywhere and nowhere. God lifted the mountain and held it over their heads, threatening to crush them if they did not obey his laws.

The significance of the Ten Commandments, Lucy read, was that it had introduced the notion of one moral standard, emanating from God. The Mosaic code did not charge people to do what they felt, to do what was legal, to follow their hearts and consider circumstances, but to do what was right by decree of God.

According to tradition, the soul of every Jew who has lived or is yet to be born was present at the Revelation on

Sinai. Before God would issue the commandments, he asked for bondsmen to make sure the people would keep their vows. They offered their fathers, but God said no. They offered their prophets, but God said no. They offered their children not yet born, and God accepted. So all the pregnant women were gathered on a hillside, and God made their stomachs transparent like glass. He spoke to the fetuses, asking if they would accept the laws. The tiny, curled fetuses answered from their glass wombs: yea, they said, and nay, to each commandment as required.

A small dark object whizzed in the window of Uzi's jeep, fluttering between Lucy's legs. She cried out. The three men in back jolted forward, and Shlomo's hands went for his gun.

"A bug," Lucy said sheepishly. There was an outburst of derision. Uzi reached over and batted the bug out the window. Danny, cracking sunflower seeds with his teeth, said, "You seem hysterical. What is there to cry about? Maximum could happen is, somebody dies. But a bug."

"She's hysterical because she's not married," Shlomo said. "Loo-zee, find a guy."

She turned in her seat. "We have a word for you. Pig."

He grinned and belched.

Driving east along the Mediterranean, they passed through El Arish, a noisy Arab town where there were camels in the road, veiled women balancing jugs on their heads and donkeys galloping with carts. Then they turned south, plunging into the interior of the desert. Now, Lucy thought, we'll see something. But a *hamsin* had come up, a hot, poisonous wind that drives the temperature up to over 100 and turns the air brown and viscous.

It was 9 A.M., and so hot in the car that Lucy's blouse and shorts were soaked. She was aware, to her dismay, that she was giving off the Israeli smell. She had noticed it among certain people on buses and in the streets, a peculiar body

232

smell against which deodorant was useless. Was it caused by something in the diet, the atmosphere?

They had to stop and wipe the brown film off the windshield. The road was half buried under sand. The sky was beige and the sun looked pale silver, more like the moon.

"How hot do you think it is?" She had to shout to Uzi above the wind.

"About 114. I want you to drink." He thrust a picnic jug encased in Styrofoam at her. "Make sure you drink a cup of water every hour." She raised the jug to her mouth, tasted sand, then passed it back. Uzi started the jeep.

"Can you imagine fighting in these conditions?" he said. "People don't realize when they read about it in the papers. You go into battle and it can be 114, but inside the tank it can be 140."

Danny said, "And a *hamsin* is blowing, and everything is on fire, sand is burning, flesh is burning, and you're deaf from the shooting and you're so fucking scared you're running on adrenaline."

Lucy had an image of her summers in New Rochelle, of Joe and his friends in California growing up on the beach, in peace, perfect peace.

"I tell you, I was in Europe in '73 when the war started and I rushed home," Uzi said. "I don't think I would do that again."

"Look!" Lucy saw the rusty carcass of a tank lying beached on its side in the sand.

"That's nothing, wait." Uzi told her this part of Sinai had been the site of more wars than any other piece of land on earth. It was ideal for battle and nothing else: a sandy waste, with a few mountain passes to make things slightly complicated, no towns or villages, no native population to disturb, except a few Bedouin. Yet this sandy waste was a strategic link between Africa, Asia and Europe. The farther they drove, the more littered the sand was with the detritus of war: bombs, guns, shoes and bits of clothing, broken trucks, grenades, helicopters and planes.

How could she use this? She slumped forward, suddenly nauseous. Uzi and Shlomo were studying the map, and after a few minutes, turned onto a small set of tire tracks. Lucy let herself bump along, indifferent. Her skin and teeth were covered with grit, and her hair felt like sandpaper. She had a headache. "Drink," Uzi said.

"I have."

"Not enough."

They drove around a sandstone cliff and suddenly there appeared a black tent, three men in long cotton gowns— *gelabya*—and women dressed in black and dirty children wearing rags and running barefoot.

"Dok-tor!" the children cried when Uzi pulled up. "Dok-tor Tamir!" Uzi patted them and shook hands with the men. Shlomo came to life, strutting into the fray like a potentate.

Lucy stayed back. Through a feverish haze, she saw, by the tent, filthy creatures with matted hair. The children did not swat away flies, so the insects clustered in the corners of their eyes. The Bedouin chattered in a shrill singsong, like irksome birds. The women seemed haunted, with only their eyes showing and their hair braided into a horn that stood up over the forehead.

"Loo-zee!" Shlomo yelled. Why were they building a fire in this heat? The three Israelis and three Bedouin men sat around it on carpets on the sand. The women retired to the tent. A boy of ten began to mix flour and water in a pot, then rolled the dough on a rock, using an old dirty bottle for a rolling pin.

"Loo-zee." She felt uneasy with her bare arms and legs. Uzi patted the carpet beside him. She went over and sat. "The sheik apologizes. If he had known we were coming, he would have slaughtered a sheep."

The sheik filled little glasses with sugar, then poured tea

with mint over the sugar and handed them around. Lucy placed hers on the carpet. The smoke from the fire was burning her eyes, the heat was awful. The ten-year-old boy brought a sheet of scrap metal to the fire and used it as a griddle on which to cook pita—round, thin circles of flat dough. "This was the original matzo," Shlomo said.

Uzi urged Lucy to drink the tea. She sipped it and, mysteriously, it revived her. Uzi handed her pita, which was light and chewy, with the appetizing aroma of fresh-baked bread. In a moment she was herself again, surprised that hot food would have this effect.

The sheik opened a tin of processed meat, and the men scooped up chunks with the pita. Everyone sat, tearing pita, scooping meat, drinking tea, staring at the fire and the desert and the occluded brown air.

"You look happy," Lucy said to Shlomo.

"I very happy. I like Bedouin, men of the desert."

"Why?"

He pursed his lips. "They are going slow. They are not worrying. They are experts at sitting without compulsion."

Uzi had to forcibly propel Shlomo into the jeep when he wanted to leave.

"*Inshaalu,*" Shlomo said, meaning, what will be, will be.

"I want to reach Refidim by night," Uzi said.

Refidim appeared in the sand like a mirage: a great, pulsating, gray-green city, in which machines were always humming, lights were always burning, people were working twenty-four hours a day. Refidim was the largest army base in Sinai, with three airfields, two movie theaters, a laundry plant, a sports stadium, miles and miles of corrugated metal buildings and radar towers and holding pens for tanks, which were kept in air-conditioned zippered bags, so they would not rust but stay in perfect running order for immediate use. "Just as much, if not more, is built under ground,"

Uzi said. Lucy felt safe in the middle of the camp, though she knew this was illusory—she was in a live target.

At the entrance to Refidim was a menorah made of steel tubes planted in the sand, and above it, the Israeli flag. The six-pointed Star of David was a symbol Lucy had always associated with shame, armbands, defilement, but etched in crisp blue and white, whipping in the air above this outpost, it seemed a symbol of victory, the miraculous.

While Uzi talked with officers, making plans for turning over Santa Katarina to Egypt, Lucy and the crew wandered about. All of Refidim was to be dismantled and moved to a site in the Negev, and crews were starting to pull down buildings. It was interesting but not dramatic. Lucy was disappointed, she still did not know what her story was or what she should be filming. She was beginning to think nothing would come of this trip after all.

They had dinner in one of the mess halls, and were assigned two air-conditioned trailers in the officers' quarters. Uzi claimed one for Lucy and himself.

"I don't think we should sleep together anymore," Lucy said when they had shut the door.

He smiled. "What is this, joke?"

"I'm going to be meeting your family, it's too awkward."

He reached for her hand and shook it. "Okay."

She was directed to the women officers' bathroom, a wooden shack with one shower head. There was a sink and pegs on which uniforms were hanging. She took off her clothes, stood under the shower head, turned the spigot but only a trickle came out. She turned the spigot as far as it would go, but no more water came. She tried to rub off the pungent brown layers with the corner of a towel. When she was clean, more or less, she had an impulse to try on a uniform. She slipped on someone's khaki blouse with epaulets, a skirt, an olive web belt, a cap. She did this quickly, straining to see in the mirror balanced on the sink. The mirror fell to the floor. She froze. She opened the door a crack—no one around—and made a dash for the trailer. Uzi, lying on a cot reading the newspaper, burst out laughing.

"Come here."

She walked to the bed and sat down. "I don't know what it is that attracts me to the army."

"The men."

Lucy laughed. "I was going to give you this elaborate theory about having a purpose in history, being tested . . ."

He started unbuttoning the blouse.

"Uzi."

His hand was inside.

"I don't want to deal with the consequences."

"Don't talk nonsense."

"Can't we just be friends?"

"You think such a thing is possible?"

"Why not?"

"Maybe after the sex has run its course."

She refastened the buttons.

"I think affairs are good for a marriage," Uzi said.

"Suppose you fall in love?"

"You just wait."

"Ah."

"You don't flaunt it. You don't do anything, that's for sure. Unless you're simpleminded, you have to realize, marriage is marriage. It's not going to be that different from one person to another. It's a very efficient system for raising children, that's the main point."

Lucy shivered. The room was icy from the air conditioner. "Can we turn this thing down?"

"There's no control, unfortunately. But we have plenty of blankets."

She left to return the uniform, and when she came back, started to get into her cot. "Don't sleep there," Uzi said.

She pulled the blanket up and turned her back.

"Lucy. Don't make me say it again."

He waited a minute, then went to her cot and pulled off the blanket. Before she could protest, he caught her arms and pinned them together with one hand while the other began to tickle her. She squirmed and kicked but he was too strong, she was helpless. When she had lost her breath from laughing, he began to stroke her, teasing her, still holding her pinned and helpless and she was so aroused she was yelping.

"You want to sleep?" Uzi said, fingering her with tantalizing slowness. "I let you."

"Prick."

A rap at the door. *"Hamesh baboker."* Five in the morning.

Uzi groaned.

"Let's go back to sleep."

"No, we have to start now to reach the Gulf of Suez by ten. Otherwise we will have problems in the Mitla Pass, and you don't want to be stuck there, even with me."

Lucy poked him but he ducked. They dressed quickly, shivering from the air conditioning. Outside, it was already 90, but the *hamsin* had ended. Lucy felt more alert, hopeful. Today, surely, as they pressed farther south, things would begin to fall in place.

As they drove, they listened to Radio Shalom, which played the mishmash peculiar to Israeli radio: Bing Crosby singing "White Christmas," then the Mexican hat dance, then Frankie Lymon's hit from the fifties, "Why Do Fools Fall in Love?" At every break, a tape of Sadat's voice was played: *No more war, no more bloodshed, between Arabs and Israelis.* The jeep rolled past fragmentation bombs, half-tracks. The next song was "No Business Like Show Business." Then Sadat: *No more war, no more bloodshed . . ."*

Shlomo began to talk about his new baby, Shula. "I keep seeing her chubby face, all the time smiling."

Danny said he missed his kids also. "More than my wife. But that's an old story."

"Are you still seeing Tamar?" Uzi said.

"Yes. She and Leah had a meeting last week."

"Oh boy."

"Leah's your wife?" Lucy said.

"Yes. Leah told Tamar one of them has to make a decision. But Tamar said, what my wife and I decide about our marriage is our business, not hers, and the one who should make a decision is me. So the two of them told me to choose."

Uzi whistled.

No more war, no more bloodshed . . .

"I told them, I don't have to make a decision. I'm happy. If you want a decision, you make it."

The three men laughed. Lucy gave Danny an unfriendly look.

Uzi stopped the car. An ammunition train that had been blown up on its way to Cairo was scattered across a wadi. The men wanted to look at it, but Lucy walked in the opposite direction. She was fascinated by the debris: pieces of metal, an old boot. She walked up a rise and from the top, saw a strange object in a gully. It held her eyes, it was different from anything she'd seen. It was five feet long and round, pitch black, with fins that were menacing in their neatness and precise curve at the tip. What was it? Something rare. She wanted Uzi to see. She reached down to pick it up, thinking to swing it like a bat for a joke, calling, "Uzi, look!" But it was too heavy.

She began to drag it, holding it by the blunt round end, across the sand toward the jeep. It made a ringing sound— the metal grating on sand? It was too heavy to drag all that distance, so she lifted the blunt end and stood it on its pointed nose, then leaned on it as if on a walking stick. It sank a few inches in the sand. "Uzi!"

He was walking around the train. Nobody could hear her,

a wind had come up. She stopped again, propped the cylinder on its nose and at that moment Uzi saw her. She laughed.

He raised his hand in her direction. "Don't touch that."

She laughed again, he was playing.

"Lucy . . . it's dangerous, put it down very carefully." He was speaking as if to a child on a window ledge. "Ve-ry gently, yes, go on, just lay it down and come to the car . . ."

"Don't talk like that, you're scaring me."

"Just set it down quietly . . ."

"I can't." She was stuck to it, as in a nightmare, when someone is stuck to an electrical fence. Uzi ran up, took it from her and set it on the sand. Then he pulled her to the jeep, the others jumped in and he drove away fast, checking the rearview mirror. Lucy looked back; Shlomo, Danny and Yoram were sitting rigidly, silently.

They felt it before they heard it: the car shaking; an avalanche of sand and rocks on the roof; the windshield exploding in patterns like a spider's web. Then she heard the boom.

Uzi stopped the car. "So you want to get us killed?"

"What was it?"

From the back seat, swearing in Hebrew.

"What was it?" Her teeth were knocking.

"Are you crazy?" Danny said. "It was an unexploded mortar shell, a dud, that can go off anytime. It would have killed us instantly."

"Are you Jewish?" Yoram said. "You're going to become more Jewish."

"When the army sees one of those, you know what they do? They surround it with boulders so no one will drive over it by mistake. Then they explode it with TNT."

"You have to pray to Allah," Shlomo said.

"I didn't know." She felt the jeep floor rising up under her.

"Common sense should tell you not to pick up something like that," Danny said.

Uzi put his arm around her. "You won't do it again."

Shlomo began to laugh.

She wheeled around. "How can you, we could all be dead."

"When your time comes, it comes."

Lucy opened the car door, tried to take a step but her knees buckled.

"Lucy, wait."

She hit the sand and retched.

4

What surprised Lucy was how little time it took
before forgetfulness set in. She had felt death's hands, and
half a day later, she was bathing in the Gulf of Suez, singing, "Why Do Fools Fall in Love?"

Once she and Uzi had reached the west coast of Sinai,
they had passed from the graveyard into an earthly paradise.
Brilliant red mountains fell away to golden beaches, date
palms and a turquoise sea so still you could hear the slap of a
large fish as it jumped from the water.

They ate fresh-caught langouste in Sharm el Sheikh, then
spent the night in a motel. In the morning, they drove up the
east coast and turned inland, following a torturous gravel
road that wound through the mountains to the remote heart
of Sinai, Santa Katarina.

Loud engine knocking and a pillar of red dust announced
their arrival. Uzi's children came running out of a stone
building. Lucy tensed. The boy was eight, the girl six, and
both had their father's facial rift—the cleft chin, the space
between the front teeth. He caught one in each arm and spun
them in the air. She tried to run a brush through her hair, but
it was gritty and tangled.

"It's a waste of time, Lucy. Better leave it. We all do."
She turned and saw a slim, doe-eyed Israeli woman wearing
a *gelabya,* her dark hair in braids. "I'm Dahlia." She extended a leather-colored hand.

If Dahlia suspected anything, she gave no indication. She
was gracious, witty, and there was between the women, despite Lucy's hesitation, an immediate rapport. Uzi withdrew
behind a screen of politeness, and it was Dahlia who made
Lucy feel at home.

Within days, Lucy was settled in a simple stone room
with windows looking out on the mountains with their star-
tling, deep red color. Before the Israelis had come, there had
been nothing in the mountains except the monastery of Santa
Katarina, a retreat for Greek Orthodox monks built in the
sixth century. After the Six Day War, the Israelis had built
an airstrip, a small army post and a field study center for re-
searchers and young people who worked as guides.

Lucy felt a strong response to "Santa," as it was called,
from the moment she arrived. The place pulled her, spoke to
her, gave her the sense that she was where she ought to be.
She understood at once Uzi's passion for the land, and knew
she would find her film here.

Santa was beautiful, but she had seen many places of
great natural beauty. The pull had more to do with the legends that infused the landscape. Lucy felt a catch in her
throat when she looked out on the er-Raha Valley, a vast,
shimmering diamond of pink sand. In this valley, the Children of Israel were said to have camped while they waited
for Moses to come down with the tablets. In these mountains, Lucy felt a presence of something powerful, watchful.
She mentioned this to Dahlia, who agreed. "I'm living here
ten years and it's still a mystery. I can't explain what it is,
but it is there."

It was Dahlia who escorted Lucy on the obligatory trip to
the peak of Mount Sinai. "We leave at three in the morning."

"Can't we leave at, say, nine?"

Dahlia smiled. "And be carried by porters?"

"Are they available? Seriously, why go at three?"

"Part of the initiation."

Sure enough, at three, when Lucy and Dahlia were leaving the field school, they saw dozens of tourists waiting in the chilly darkness for guides. The climb was steep, slippery, it was difficult to see and hard to breathe the thin air. People walked single file, panting, talking in low voices. "You're not allowed to sing," Dahlia said.

"Only in Israel would you need such a rule. 'No singing on the trail.' "

The narrow path they were following turned slowly and inexorably from black to gray. In the same gradual, almost imperceptible manner, they ascended the mountain, until, when they reached the summit, the sun rose, as dramatic as the rising of a curtain. Out of the darkness appeared a chain of red and black mountains, glowing with paradisal light. The mountains stretched in three directions to the surrounding seas. All was still, all seemed newly formed, as it might have seemed on the day Moses stood there and heard the voice of God. Some of the tourists wept, others dropped to their knees, hands templed like children at bedtime.

"Come." Dahlia took Lucy around the ridge to the Valley of Elijah, where the guides were gathering for a smoke. "Another batch of souls," one said. "Works every time."

About thirty Israelis were living at Santa when Lucy arrived. Uzi and Dahlia had their own cottage, but the others stayed in a compound, sleeping in small rooms, sharing a common bathroom and eating together in a dining hall. It was in this compound that Lucy and her crew were given rooms. The compound had electricity from a generator and running water from a tank, but no phones, no contact with the outside except the mail once a week. Supplies were brought in by jeep from Eilat, and outdated movies were shown once a month.

Many of the guides had been in Santa for years. They had come when it was virgin wilderness, had helped build the field school, explored and marked trails, drawn maps, conducted digs, learned Arabic and come to know the Bedouin, whom they spoke of as their "close friends."

Lucy still could not understand their reverence for the Bedouin. She thought they were patronizing, like white civil rights workers who had gone to live among poor blacks in the South. The Israelis filled their rooms with Bedouin artifacts: camel bags, iron cooking utensils, baskets and women's black clothing, decorated with bangles. They loved to visit Bedouin in their tents, where they would sit for hours, drinking sugary tea, eating fresh plums and dates. Even Uzi's children spoke Arabic and played with Bedouin children.

This life was to end soon, and a sadness hung over the compound. They were tasting the last drops: the last Passover in Sinai; the last trip to visit the Bedouin storyteller at Wadi Firan; the last Bedouin wedding, a three-day feast with chanting, dancing and camel races. Dahlia said, "I can't believe something so beautiful can just stop. I've always believed Israel should give back the land—Sinai, the West Bank, everything—for a real peace. But it's painful."

Dahlia had built, on her own, a small museum of Bedouin culture next to the field school, and was torn whether to leave it for the Egyptians or transfer the exhibits to Jerusalem.

Lucy saw, at last, that she could use the turnover of Santa Katarina to tell a story about the coming of peace. She would film the final days of the Israelis, the transfer of power, the arrival of the Egyptians and, behind it all, the unchanging mountains with their legends and the Bedouin who had been there thousands of years and recognized no government.

Now that she saw the story, she sent Yoram and Danny back to Jerusalem with plans to return with a larger crew for full-scale shooting. She stayed on, making arrangements, doing research. She felt compelled to see as much as she could of the region, not knowing why, except that something more important than the film might be at stake.

Uzi, who was trying to conclude twelve years of field work, apologized for not spending more time with Lucy. He gave her a map of nearby trails, and urged her to walk by herself or go out on day hikes with groups. One night, Lucy was having coffee with Uzi and Dahlia. She sat closer to Dahlia, and avoided Uzi's eyes.

"There's a place I want you to see before you leave," Uzi said. "Mount Sirbal. It's something special." He said a group from a moshav, a collective farm less structured than a kibbutz, had reserved a Bedouin guide and string of pack donkeys for a three-day hike during Passover. "You can join them. Two friends of ours, Zal and Ruthi, who used to be guides here, are coming from the moshav."

"Will I be the only non-Israeli?"

"Never mind. Moshavniks are the best people in Israel. You'll be welcome."

"But Israelis are in fantastic shape. I've been sitting in an editing room all year, I'll slow the group down."

"No worries," Uzi said. "You just walk at your own pace and join the group at the end of the day."

Lucy looked dubious.

Dahlia said, "Which of our guides is going?"

"Giddi."

"Maybe I'll substitute for him. It could be my last chance to see Sirbal."

Uzi raised his eyebrows. "Giddi will probably agree. He has work to do at Bir Iqna."

"Would you look after the children?"

Uzi nodded.

"Then it's settled."

* * *

Lucy's heart sank when she saw the truck with the moshavniks pull into Santa. Out spilled eight rugged, fit young men and women, wearing shorts and combat boots and khaki flak jackets, the men carrying rifles. They laughed and raced about, while Lucy stood shyly, fitted out in borrowed gear: a belt with two canteens, Israeli desert boots, a Bedouin scarf of thin white gauze wrapped around her hair and Uzi's *dubon*, for the high mountains. She introduced herself, and learned that three of the men had just been released from the army. She thought of dropping out right then, but Dahlia coaxed her into the truck and they drove to the trail head.

They began the hike at six the next morning. The sun had not yet risen, the air was dark blue. All the gear and food were loaded onto donkeys, driven by a tall Bedouin with a saber dangling from his waist. They walked in a straight line on flat ground, and after fifteen minutes, Lucy was winded. How long would they keep this up before a rest? They hadn't even started the ascent.

At the foot of Mount Sirbal, they met another Bedouin, Suleiman, who was to guide them up the mountain, as there were no trails. Dahlia walked after Suleiman, followed by the moshavniks in single file with Lucy near the end. By 8 A.M. the sun was scorching; the men took off their shirts and tied them to their rifles.

"Why guns on a hiking trip?" Lucy asked Zal.

"It's a holdover from the army. You learn to take it whenever you're out in the country and don't know what can happen. You know, five wars, six million killed, et cetera."

Dahlia kept reminding people to drink from their canteens. "You sweat a quart of water an hour and you have to replace it."

They came to a steep set of switchbacks and in minutes, Lucy was red in the face. When they reached a plateau, she stepped out of line. The whole line stopped.

"Go ahead, I'll catch up," she said, wheezing. But the group stood patiently, pretending to admire the yellow and purple wild flowers. Zal motioned her in front of him. "We push you." They started walking and she got a little farther this time before she ran out of breath. She looked at her watch, five more minutes I'll keep on, maybe they'll rest. She stepped aside and doubled over. Again, the whole line stopped. Zal took the day pack from her back. Another man, Avner, slipped the belt with the canteens off her hips, so she was unencumbered. She saw, with a start, that Avner had one arm that did not hang right. He told her, later, his arm had been amputated at the shoulder after a grenade accident.

There was no way out. She would have to transcend the pain, the panic of being winded, or the whole group would not complete the hike. They moved her up to the number three spot behind Dahlia. It was easier psychologically, they said, to walk at the head of the line.

For three hours, they walked straight up, no rests. It was not a hike at all, it was a forced march. Lucy did not see the mountains, the views, she could have been walking through New Jersey. She kept her eyes on Dahlia's feet, concentrating all her powers on stepping in her tracks. When Lucy's nose bled she used the Bedouin scarf to press against it and kept walking. She thought of Hannah Senesh walking across Hungary. The pain in her lungs was a sensation to tolerate, like the heat. She thought only of matching Dahlia's steps, and when she did, all sounds—boots crunching on rocks—disappeared. It was hypnotic, she was being pulled up the mountain in a human train, drawn from ahead, pushed from behind.

A Jimmy Cliff song ran through her head: "I Want to Know." Over and over as she climbed, she sang to herself, "I want to know." She crunched ahead. "I want to know." She inhaled the fragrant herbs that grew wild in Sinai: mint, camomile, oregano. "I want to know."

At noon they stopped by a spring to fill their canteens and

248

have lunch. "Most of the climb is over," Dahlia said. Lucy was astonished. Her throat was burning, her lips were blistered, but she was there. It was 100 degrees and they crouched in the shade of rocks, pouring water down their throats as if down a car radiator.

Lunch was laid out—Israeli trail food. There were loaves of bread and an assortment of cans containing eggplant salad, humus, falafel, stuffed peppers, sardines, olives, stewed pears and peaches and a jar of chocolate the consistency of jam. The Israelis spread the canned food and the chocolate on bread, making a variety of open sandwiches.

When Lucy had hiked with other groups, she had found that once the food was opened, everyone grabbed, and if you didn't hurry and elbow your way toward the choicest cans, you would get only dregs. But this group was different. Each person took a small amount, making sure everyone had an opportunity to taste some of everything. They were always counting and watching. "Is there enough tea for a second cup? Has everyone drunk? Where's Nava, has she eaten fruit yet?"

At first, the group had seemed an undifferentiated mass to Lucy, but in a short time, the faces became distinct. Each person played a strain, as in an orchestra. Lucy was the greenhorn, the soft American, a figure of good-natured fun. Zal was the leader, towering and confident. He and Ruthi planned to marry in a few weeks, and they revolved about each other like twin stars. David was the oldest, a father of five, and his wife, Orit, was the mother hen. Yossl was the inarticulate hunk. Nava was the prettiest, with angelic blue eyes and blond braids. Avner with his missing arm was the martyr, who needed special attention, though he usually refused it.

Lucy, who generally disliked groups, had never experienced such caring and thoughtfulness as with the moshavniks. It must have been the way they had been raised. No one was unfriendly or selfish, no one was outcast or the butt of jokes. They were so helpful it was unnerving. If Lucy tripped on a pebble, three hands would reach for her. If there was a tricky spot to negotiate, each person would turn, after passing, to help the next one across.

In the evening, after supper, when the Israelis had spread their sleeping bags, Dahlia and Lucy walked to a rock where the Bedouin had built a fire. Suleiman poured them glasses of tea, and they sipped it in silence. The Israelis down the valley began to sing.

"How do you find Uzi?" Dahlia said.

"Improved with age."

Dahlia laughed.

"Actually, I was surprised to learn he had stayed married so long. I wouldn't have expected it."

"I didn't expect it either, but then, I didn't really look ahead," Dahlia said. "If Uzi and I had lived in the States, it probably wouldn't have lasted. Here, people are more forgiving. Life is so hard, you need your family."

Lucy was thinking, if she and Uzi had married, this might have been her life.

"Are you alone, Lucy?"

She nodded.

"Why?"

She told Dahlia about her strange history with Joe, and how it had prevented her from becoming attached to someone else. "He's still my closest friend, the person whose company I prefer to almost anyone's."

"Is he a kind man, a giving man? Would he make a patient and understanding father?"

Lucy was reticent. She had not considered such questions about Joe, or, for that matter, any of the men in her life. Why had she not, and why was the answer not a clear yes, if yes at all?

"We can bring our sleeping bags here," Dahlia said, "it will be warmer." Dahlia rose, but Lucy sat hugging her knees. "Come. We have a long day tomorrow."

* * *

The second day in the mountains was the eve of Passover. At dawn, the group set out to climb to the summit of Sirbal. There was a harrowing stretch where they had to scale a sheer rock face, with a drop-off of two thousand feet. Lucy looked down, despite instructions not to, and her legs began to tremble violently. She said she was too frightened, she would wait behind, but the group would not hear of it. Zal, David and Yossi stationed themselves at crevices in the rock, and Lucy was passed up from arm to arm. Smiling, whispering encouragement, the men held her by her hands and feet, and although she knew they were like ants on a wall, she felt secure.

The view from the summit was incomparable. They could see the Sinai Peninsula as a map: a triangle, with Sharm el Sheikh at the bottom, Saudi Arabia to the east, and to the west, Africa. Lucy had driven along both coasts, had looked up at this saw-toothed peak from both sides and now she was on it. Sitting above the clouds, she was grateful that Uzi and Dahlia had pressed her to come and that this caring, loving group had pulled her with them.

As they climbed back down, Dahlia told them to gather dried brush for a fire. Each person collected an armload of wood and used his free arm to maneuver down the steep rocks. Yossi dropped behind to help Avner, who was using his good arm to hold wood. Lucy stayed with Yossi; they supported Avner while he reached with his feet for holds in the sliding rocks. It was cumbersome, they would have been able to move more quickly if Avner had let the others carry wood and used his arm to balance himself, but that was not the point. The point was to carry wood.

When they reached the camp, the men built a fire and the women improvised materials for a seder. Ruthi grated horseradish, Nava cut up apples for *haroset* and Orit sliced cucumbers to be dipped in salt water. Dahlia gave Lucy flour to help Suleiman make pita, for matzo. Lucy sat with him, trying to learn to pat the balls of dough into large, thin round sheets. Suleiman did it with ease, but each time Lucy began patting, the dough would collapse like the work of a beginner on a potter's wheel. She thought of Pam, struggling with the pie crusts on the fourth of July. She felt a pang. Wasn't she now in the very position Pam had taken? There were distinctions, she told herself: she had been Uzi's lover before meeting Dahlia. She was not Dahlia's closest friend.

"Lucy." The group was calling her for the ritual burning of *hametz*. Lucy watched them walk before the fire and, one by one, toss in scraps of bread.

"Why are we doing this?" she asked Dahlia.

"It's a symbolic act. The yeast in the bread is a symbol of man's imperfections. So at Passover, we have a chance to purify ourselves. We break with the past and start fresh. We stop eating bread made with yeast, we eat only matzo, and before the seder, we burn any bread left in our possession." She handed Lucy a crust. Lucy walked to the fire and, pausing a moment, feeling the heat on her face, threw the crumbs in.

The ceremonial foods were laid out on a rock, and as the sun was setting, the group sat down, joined hands and sang the Israeli folk tune *"Hi-ne ma tov u ma nayim . . ."*

How good it is to dwell together as brothers.

Lucy remembered the song from Sunday school. As they swayed, repeating the simple melody, she thought of Passovers in her childhood: people clowning and making wisecracks through the seder, everyone impatient to finish the service and start the gargantuan meal—gefilte fish and hard-boiled eggs and matzo-ball soup and stuffed cabbage and turkey with dressing and giblet gravy and potatoes and spinach and Jello mold and Passover honey cake with fresh strawberries. Then there was the rush for the card tables.

The moshavniks sang another song, and Lucy watched the full moon rise over Mount Horeb, the mountain of God.

Zal, who led the ceremony, said, "This seder tonight is different from all other seders, because on all other Passovers, we didn't have peace with Egypt. Tonight, for the first time in four thousand years, we do."

Yossi, the youngest male, began to chant the four questions. As Lucy listened to the words, foreign and familiar, she was filled with emotion. She was sitting with Israelis in the very mountains where the events being recalled had taken place. This might be the spot where the pregnant women had stood before God, their stomachs like glass, while the fetuses had spoken through the wombs, promising to obey the unbending moral laws.

Zal proceeded through the Haggadah, they sang more folk songs and drank the four ceremonial cups of wine. Then they passed around the stew made from corn, potatoes, onions and mushrooms. When the food was gone, they continued drinking wine. Ruthi and Dahlia led a medley of Passover songs with dozens of verses, but they started tripping over the words. Lucy saw, with bemusement, that the seder was degenerating into pagan rowdiness. There was drunken laughter, roughhousing; Yossi and David pulled down their trousers and peed off rocks.

She took a walk by herself and sat down on a ledge. The sky was the most extraordinary color: royal blue. The symmetry of forms—of mountain and moon, sand and stars—was breathtaking. Her eye was caught by a streak of blue light. A falling star? She felt unbearably happy.

For the first time in her life, Lucy felt she was linked to a people, a group, and this link would not require sleight of hand to maintain. The group was not founded on emotional affinity or passion, which could fade, or on political belief, which could shift with the next wind of public sentiment. It was a group that embraced a wide range of individual belief and levels of practice, including denial and nonpractice. Yet by blood and lineage—parents to children and children to their children—the group was sustained.

Membership would not require of Lucy that she chant Sanskrit or wear a dot of sandalwood paste. No allegiance had to be sworn to any person or leader. If there was allegiance, it was to a set of ethical ideals, a code, that taught respect for life, kindness and social responsibility. The Jews had carried this code on their scrolls through centuries of wandering, with a stubbornness that bordered on the pathological. Each member might not adhere to the precepts, but the code remained unaltered. It was true North.

There were those like Hannah Senesh, who had given her life for the greater good, and those who had cheated on their income tax and left the Holy Land for a bigger house and car in America. There were those who had stood up to torture and those who had converted to escape it. There were parents who had rejected the tradition, only to have children who embraced it. Into this multifarious community, Lucy had been born and, regardless of her ranging and seeking, would remain.

As she stared into the blue-black night, she saw herself part of this living chain that reached all the way back to the nomads who had wandered in this desert. Within this chain was threaded the line of her own life. She saw herself as a girl, a young woman, moving freely over the earth, then a mother, growing old. She imagined the chain continuing ahead through her children and their children, and she thought, Lord, don't let it end in me. Don't let me be one of those dead stumps on a family tree, a line that stops in a dry ball while the others continue to fork and branch. I want to be connected to the river that flows on . . .

She cried out with all her soul, and she heard an answer: You will.

The next day was the descent. The group went straight down a spill of rocks that poured from the top of Sirbal to the valley floor. At first it was exhilarating, springing from rock to rock, but after an hour, Lucy's shins were aching from constantly braking and starting.

She grew faint. She began to see chickens, giant red chickens, where she knew there were only rocks. "I feel like I'm drunk," she said.

"Zal! Lucy feels like drunk."

"I was kidding."

"That little joke will cost you," Zal said.

The group stopped while Lucy was made to drink a full canteen.

She still felt dizzy, but she was not the only one to lag. Avner moved painfully slowly, and Orit had a cramp in her foot. When they reached the valley floor, it was not over. They had to walk another two hours across flinty rocks and scree. Lucy could feel every rock through the soles of her boots, and by the time they reached the field school, she was ready for the stretcher. She said an exhausted good-bye to the moshavniks with feeble promises to stay in touch.

In the bathroom, she was shocked at what she saw in the mirror. Her hair was wild and covered with red dust. Her skin was cracked like the skin of the Bedouin. She stood in the shower for an hour, washed her hair twice, brushed her teeth twice. As she came clean, she began to feel the euphoria that follows physical exertion. She hobbled to the kitchen, where she found Uzi setting out plates of roast chicken, olives, tomatoes.

She fell upon the food. "I hear you had great trip," Uzi said.

"It was fantastic, especially Passover on Sirbal."

Uzi made a face. "I can't stand that holiday."

"Why?"

"It's so stupid. The symbols are so stupid. The bitter herbs, the egg."

Lucy smiled and shook her head.

"You don't look like the girl I picked up in Jerusalem. Nervous, jumping at bugs."

She laughed. "Something happened up there, I feel healed. I'm filled with love, for God, for the Jewish people, for humanity."

"Good on you."

"Good *for* you."

"You still insist on improving me?"

"Sorry, an old habit."

Dahlia walked in, looking scrubbed and rosy, and Lucy felt a sudden loneliness. Where was her group?

"Don't you become attached to the people you take out on trips like this?"

Dahlia cut a piece of cheese and placed it in a pocket of pita bread. "I think you had an advantage over me because you didn't speak Hebrew that well."

"Why?"

She scooped tomatoes into the pita. "It was a terrible group, the worst I've ever hiked with. They were quarreling all the time." Lucy's mouth fell open. "Nava was having an affair with David, so she and Orit were sniping at each other. Orit and David were quarreling too. Avner was sour, complaining all the time, and the others couldn't stand him. Zal and Ruthi are fine, but they were off by themselves at every chance. The only good moments for me were with you and the Bedouin. They know how to sit and be quiet. Israelis have to cry and sing."

"I thought they were the nicest people. I thought I was floating in a soup of love and kindness."

Uzi laughed huskily. "If you could capture this in your film, you would have something."

"It's a pity you have to leave tomorrow," Dahlia said.

"I'll be back."

Lucy ached all over, just getting into bed was an effort. She stretched out, expecting to fall right asleep but she did not. She was tense, sore, overly fatigued. She began to wish for someone's arms to curl up in, that would help, that would be a completion. Unconsciously, her hands slid down between her legs. She could go to the tent where the moshavniks were sleeping, find Yossi. She could go knock on one of the guides' doors. Some of them had been alone in the mountains for months.

Her door opened suddenly and someone stole in. "Hello, love." He was on her cot, kissing her, running his hands under the sheet and she was quivering.

"Uzi, please don't."

"You want to play games every time? Just don't make too much noise."

He kissed her breast.

"Dahlia."

"She's asleep. She won't know."

He was probably right. She felt her body arching up to meet his. She pushed his head away. "I'll know."

He threw his weight onto her. She struggled but that only seemed to excite him.

It was hopeless to fight so she stopped and lay flat, inert. After a moment, Uzi sat up.

"You're married."

He made a clucking sound. "We go deeper than that stuff."

She switched on the bed lamp. "I'm terribly sorry, I shouldn't have started again with you."

"Okay, so life is short. We have to take love however it comes."

She shook her head.

He gave a disapproving smile. "It's a pity."

"It's better."

"That's a difference of opinion."

She lifted his hand and kissed it gently. "Please understand."

He rose, tucking in his shirt. "I'll just wait."

5

Passengers arriving at Ben Gurion Airport are met by soldiers with rifles, escorted into buses and driven to the terminal, where they wait in long lines to pass security clearance. In the warm, languid air, passports are checked against lists of suspected terrorists, photographs and faces are matched, questions are asked. The Israeli agent, who wears tight jeans and sandals, stamps her forms, and the passenger is then free to collect his luggage, pass through customs and out the swinging doors where, behind a metal barrier, throngs of Israelis are waving and shouting, "Welcome home!"

Lucy stood in the crush outside the terminal, watching the doors. Joe's plane had been due at five, but there was no way to tell when he might pass out the doors.

"Are you coming from New York?" she asked a woman in boots and a fur coat.

"No. Paris."

Lucy took a drink from a soda bottle. Every time a new tide of people surged out the door, she felt her stomach tighten. She had flown in from Santa Katarina that morning, and within hours, the calm she had carried from the desert had evaporated. She had gone to the Super Sol to restock her kitchen for Joe's visit. The salesgirl had overcharged her and refused to give her bags.

Lucy went to another store to buy a nylon shopping bag, waited in a long line, went back to Super Sol and found her groceries had been returned to the shelf. She gathered them again, waited in another line, got into a shouting match and was walking home when a boy on a school bus threw a plum at her. The fruit splattered and purple juice ran down her blouse. The children laughed as the bus rumbled off down the Gaza Road.

"Are you coming from New York?"

"London."

She scanned the arrivals: Yemenite Jews in leggings and braided hair; young Swedes volunteering for kibbutz work; American Jews in leisure suits, maybe that was Joe's plane, there! He was unmistakable, with his tan and sun-bleached hair and open-necked shirt and sneakers. He was carrying a leather shoulder bag and walking with his customary springy step.

She called his name.

He spotted her, and instead of proceeding down the ramp, let go of the cart with his luggage and leaped over the barrier. She laughed. He spun her in the air and kissed her. "Great to see you."

"How was the flight?"

"Grueling."

They began walking arm in arm. "Any progress with the film?"

She held up two crossed fingers. "Just beginning to take shape."

"I knew it would." He looked around. "I forgot how hot it gets here." It was 7 P.M. and 95 degrees; most of the Israelis were wearing shorts.

"Better get your bags," Lucy said.

"Holy shit." He jumped back over the barrier, found his

cart and pushed it down the ramp. Lucy went to hire a taxi, and when Joe rejoined her, he was walking with an Israeli in a steward's uniform.

"This is Raffi . . . my friend, Lucy."

Raffi gave a cursory nod, then said to Joe, "You see how beautiful Israeli girls are?" He gestured toward a trio of female soldiers, wearing tight khaki pants. Joe said something under his breath to Raffi, and they laughed. Lucy got in the cab.

"When you want to meet some people, you just call me in Tel Aviv," Raffi said.

"I'll be in touch."

Joe's luggage was tied on top of the cab and they drove off.

He stretched out his legs. Lucy's face was turned to the window. "Hey," he said.

"Are you tired, hungry?"

"Tired." He looked at his watch. "I've been on the road for twenty-six hours, but Raffi let me sit in first class, which made things more pleasant."

"I'm sure."

"I had a rough time with El Al in New York. They interrogated me."

"They do that to everyone."

"No, they took me in an office for special questioning. It was embarrassing. They asked why I was going to Israel. I said to visit a friend. They wanted to know your name, and they said, 'What is your relationship to this woman?' "

"What did you say?"

"Hard to explain. Particularly under duress."

She rolled her eyes. "Did you really come to visit me?"

"What do you think?"

"You wanted to see Israel again."

He ruffled her hair, and she felt a constricting in her chest. "Could you roll down the window?" In came warm air, along with exhaust fumes from military vehicles and wheezing old buses. The taxi driver drove right up to the bumper of the car ahead and banged on his horn. The car ahead pulled over and the taxi sped on, weaving and honking.

"Israelis are the worst drivers."

"I have something for you." He took from his shoulder bag a florist's box. Lucy opened it and found, carefully wrapped in cellophane, a gardenia, still white and firm, exuding a rich jungle scent.

"You brought this all the way from home?"

"Never ask a magician how he does his . . ."

They pitched forward as the taxi stopped abruptly at a roadblock. A soldier put his head in the window and asked to see their bags.

"What's the trouble?" Joe said.

"Terrorist attack in Hebron."

"Anyone hurt?" Lucy said.

"Quite a few. Six dead so far. Did you just arrive to the country?"

"I did. She's been here awhile."

The taxi driver untied the bags and threw them to the ground.

"Did somebody give you a package to deliver to anyone in Israel?" the soldier said.

"No."

"Were the bags out of your sight at any time?"

"No."

"Could somebody have put something in them?"

"No."

The soldier signaled to the driver to tie the bags back on top when Joe turned. "Wait. At the airport, I did leave them alone in the cart a few minutes, but I don't think . . ."

The soldier asked him to open the bags and check. "Anything there you don't recognize?" Joe rummaged through the suitcases and shook his head.

"Okay. Good night, and have a good visit."

"You didn't have anything strange in there, did you?" Lucy said.

"Absolutely."

"Oh, Lord."

He put his arm around her. "You know I missed you."

"That's nice to hear."

They lurched forward again as the driver slammed on the brakes. Holding the horn down so it honked continuously, he made an illegal pass on the right.

"Hey, pal, take it easy," Joe said. "We're in no hurry."

"Excuse me, I have to make two more trips tonight. I need to feed four kids."

"You won't feed anybody if we don't get there in one piece."

The driver muttered in Hebrew. They were climbing up from the coastal plain to the hills of Jerusalem, and the air grew cooler, the trees taller. Before long, they had arrived at Yemin Moshe.

With the excitement of a child moving into a new house, Joe walked through the flat, looked out the windows, tested the chairs, opened the refrigerator.

"Beer!"

Lucy set the gardenia in a bowl of water. She showed him the room where she slept, the alcove where she worked and the guest bedroom. "This is yours."

He caught her arm. "You look wonderful. Beautiful."

She fixed her eyes on the third button of his shirt. "Let's sit in the living room."

While he drank several beers, she told him about her visit to Santa Katarina and her idea for the film. She described her meeting with Uzi and their conflicting memories.

"That's amazing, that you misunderstood each other so completely. What's the story with Uzi now?"

"The story is that he's married, and I like his wife enormously."

Joe pursed his lips, nodding.

"What do you think of the film?"

"Great idea. You should go to Cairo and meet Uzi's counterpart, clear it with the government, so on the day of the changeover, you'll be set."

It felt comfortable, talking with Joe about shooting schedules and story sequences. She was relieved he had offered to help her do some shooting. "The cameramen here are impossible—when I tell them what I want, they argue, then do exactly what they please."

Joe laughed. "It's the national character."

"Can you spend three or four weeks at the field school?"

"Sure. It'll be good to get back to work. I haven't done anything since *American Hunger.*"

"Why?"

"I've been putting together some ideas for a feature, but every time I set up a meeting to pitch one, it doesn't seem that promising." He hit the empty beer bottle with his palm. "I lose my confidence. I don't know if I'm capable of pulling it off."

"You have to act as if you believe you can, push ahead anyway."

"Lucy, have you become involved with someone here?"

"No, why?"

"Something about you, I can't put my finger on it."

"Have you?"

He watched her intently, then smiled and shook his head.

Jet lag caught up with Joe and he slept for fourteen hours. Lucy kept looking in on him, waking him to drink water. In the heat, Joe kicked off the covers and sprawled in his underwear on the sheets.

Watching him sleep, Lucy felt a surge of tenderness. The sands were shifting, she was losing her bearings; she longed for the clarity of the desert.

When Joe woke up, she fixed him an Israeli meal: cucumbers, tomatoes, olives, humus, pita and fruit. Joe took a bag of grass from his suitcase.

"That was risky."

"Calculated risk."

They smoked a joint, and Lucy felt her mood take a dizzying upswing, intensified after so many weeks' abstinence. Joe suggested they go to the King David Hotel and swim. When they opened the door, it was like opening the door to an oven. Hot wind blew in their faces, blew back their clothes, blew the two of them like bits of paper down the baking white street.

At the King David, they sank into deck chairs on the grass. It was incongruous: sitting by a pool with lifeguards and cocktail waitresses while across the valley, they could see the Old City where men in *kefiyas* rode donkeys.

Lucy watched Joe swim laps. *Was he a kind man, a giving man?* At first Joe was swimming in a lane by himself, but the pool began to fill with Israeli families. *Would he make a patient father?* Joe was doing the butterfly, his arms plowing, his back arching up over the water, but at intervals of increasing frequency, a child would crash into him or kick him. He got out of the pool and came, dripping, to sit beside Lucy.

Children were splashing, singing, dribbling ice cream, riding on their fathers' shoulders, and suddenly the atmosphere changed, as if a green lens had been dropped over Lucy's eyes. She saw herself and Joe as two aging, overindulged Americans. Their stylish bikinis seemed absurd. She looked at her body: it was tan and slim, but it felt dry, sapless.

Damn, it was this city, the mood swings. She stared at the hedge across the pool and for a second, thought she saw terrorists crashing through the bushes.

"I think we should stay off the dope," Joe said.

"You think that's it?"

"Being stoned here is different from being stoned in California. Your guard is down, and it shouldn't be."

The hottest hours were coming on, and they walked home to rest. Lucy had adopted a modesty with Joe, which he was respecting; they were careful not to intrude on each other or walk around without clothes, as they had so often in the past. They lay down in their separate rooms to sleep, and when they awoke, Yemin Moshe was in shadows.

Lucy sat on the front stoop, enjoying the special sights and sounds of the city in the afternoon before Shabbat. She saw people rushing on last-minute errands, buying candles, washing their children's hair, picking up loaves of twisted hallah, gathering flowers. The activity would rise until, at a signal, the city went into glide. No buses, trains or planes would run. Nobody—no one at all—would be working. No shops would be open, and a dreamy quiet would descend onto the streets.

She and Joe set off for the Old City, intending to be at the Wall for the coming of Shabbat. They found the narrow alleys crowded, for it was Friday of Passover week and Good Friday for the Greek Orthodox. At the start of the Via Dolorosa, there was a burst of sound: human cries, bird cries, flutes, drums, wagons. Greek women dressed in black were crawling along the dirty stones, carrying wooden crosses on their backs. Choirboys were chanting, swinging urns of smoky incense. The muezzin was blasting, and Arab vendors were selling vials of water from the Sea of Galilee.

The last time Lucy had been in the Old City, it had been menacing, but today with Joe, it seemed a place of wonder. They shared the sense that everything had been placed there for them and they embraced it all: the tawdry, the sacred.

Joe bought them bags of fresh almonds with furry green shells so soft they could peel them with their fingers. The almonds tasted like crunchy, ripe cherries.

They wound their way to the Jewish quarter, where they

saw a wedding couple who had just had their photograph taken by the Wall, as was customary. The groom wore a tight-fitting gray suit, the bride an overly frilly gown. Both appeared to be in their teens.

"Have you noticed how obsessed this country is with marriages, weddings, births, families, bigger families?" Joe said. "It makes me feel like I should get in step."

"Better not stay too long," Lucy said lightly, but she felt a growing uneasiness.

When they came out on the plaza by the Wall, they saw thousands of people milling about, like the audience at a theater on opening night. Tense, expectant, wearing their best, they craned their heads and looked at watches.

"Where are the dancing yeshiva boys, Gladys?" one woman cried.

"They'll be coming down those stairs."

"I've been here three times already and I haven't seen them."

Lucy saw there were two groups: the spectators and the worshipers. The spectators stood on the plaza, while the worshipers descended to the enclosed area before the Wall. On the men's side, there was a swarming like that of bees. On the women's side, there were relatively few people. Some of the women stood on folding chairs to stare over the divider at the revelry on the men's side.

In front of the Wall were the most Orthodox men, wearing black suits, davening, pecking forward at the waist like jerky animals. Behind them, groups from different synagogues and schools prayed in clusters. A hundred melodies clashed in the air. A hundred dancers bumped each other. Men formed lines that snaked and swirled through the crowd.

"I'm going down," Joe said.

From Lucy's viewpoint, Joe looked strange and out of place. He walked among the men in suits and prayer shawls with his sun-bleached hair and a skimpy tank top that left

part of his chest and shoulders bare. In a few minutes, he
was back, repelled by disapproving looks. "What gives
them the right . . ."

Lucy took a white Bedouin scarf from her bag and
wrapped it around him. "There. A prayer shawl."

He returned to the Wall, and Lucy fought to keep her
place. The crowd had swelled, people were pushing and she
had to use her elbows. In an idle moment, turning, she saw
there were two small girls behind her and she was blocking
their view. Chastened, she let them slip in front.

This was something she had noticed in Jerusalem: all her
deeds and thoughts were immediately reflected back at her.
She came to think of it as moral theater. Acts which, in California, she might not have been conscious of now stood out,
inviting judgment. She could not say a cross word to a shop
clerk without feeling the sting. She could not leave water
running longer than was necessary. She could not pass a
beggar on the street without offering a coin.

Joe emerged from the men's side, and told Lucy,
"You've got to go down there."

"Nothing's happening on the women's side."

"Just go and feel the Wall."

He put his hands on her shoulders and sent her off.
Women were standing three deep in front of the Wall, but as
Lucy approached, a wedge opened and she walked straight
up to it. She pressed her hands and face against it and was
shocked: the stones were hot, alive, as if with the force of all
the prayers. She could not think or pray, it was too intense,
she turned her head aside for relief.

Looking up, she said, "Is Joe my mate? If not, who? I
want the question to be settled."

She turned her face back and the Wall had gone cold. Her
eyes blinked open. Her selfish asking had done it. She
closed her eyes and began to rock back and forth. "Work
through me," she said. "Let me learn to be more giving."
She began to see people she loved, and to see a luminous

267

thread binding them to her: her sister Leslie, Ryan, Max, her mother and father, her friend Emma, Joe, Uzi, Dahlia, the people from the moshav. She saw the golden thread linking them in a circle, linking them in a place where completeness could be found, in infinite love, and the Wall was alive again. And she thought, is there anyone I need to bring into this light?

She saw Pam, wearing a low-cut black dress. After a moment, Pam's image dissolved and Lucy stood still. When she turned to leave, she found Joe sitting on the ground.

"I wish you could see yourself," he said. "You're glowing."

Night was approaching, and the singing and dancing before the Wall grew more fervent. Lucy saw that the spectators were rising as well. They had been waiting, watching, and suddenly it was dawning on them that nothing was going to happen. No overture would begin, no players would come on stage. And yet, something was happening, had happened, the night was different. *They* were the show they had been waiting for.

This understanding swept over the faces in the crowd like a shaft of light playing over the Jerusalem hills. The Sabbath queen had descended, touching every soul. People hugged and kissed joyously.

Joe drew Lucy to him and rested his head against hers. "I don't take these things seriously most of the time," he said. "I feel very serious tonight."

Slowly, they walked back through the darkened Old City, out the Jaffa Gate, along King David Street and over to Yemin Moshe.

"I'm tired," Lucy said when they had reached her flat. "I think I'll go to bed."

"Is something wrong?"

"No, why?"

"You don't seem thrilled to have me here."

"That's not true."

"You're a million miles away."

She went to the kitchen, opened the refrigerator and took out a bottle of club soda.

"Would you like me to leave?"

"No, I want you to come with me to Santa." She poured two glasses and handed one to Joe. "My head's wrapped up in the film, that's all."

She got in bed but did not turn off the light. She opened a book, *The Israelis;* through the wall, she could hear Joe moving about the flat. She picked up the phone and asked quietly for long-distance information. "Los Angeles, do you have a listing for Pamela White?"

There was no listing in Los Angeles, or in New York or Lovington. She tried Chicago and decided to give up, then took a last stab—San Francisco. A number was found. Ten minutes later, she heard Pam's voice.

"This is Lucy, I'm in Jerusalem."

"Lucy! I can't believe this, oh, I'm so glad to hear from you."

"I thought of you tonight, and I wanted you to know, I forgive you."

The connection was as clear as if they were on the same street. Lucy heard Pam suck in her breath. "I needed this."

"I couldn't forgive you before, because I thought what you did was directed against me. I couldn't see that it was your own need to find a small resting spot for yourself."

Pam began to cry. "I've felt like an ex-con these past two years. I didn't understand about marriage, Lucy. I suffered losing you."

"I know."

Pam told her she was studying drama for children—which she loved—but was having a hard time financially and was in debt.

"That won't continue long. What's important is that you've found work you enjoy."

"I want to hear about Israel."

"I'll tell you when I see you. I'm going to Sinai to shoot this film, but I should be home in the fall."

"'Do you think . . . we could be friends?"

Lucy answered without hesitating. "Yes."

6

The day after Shabbat, Lucy and Joe flew out of Jerusalem with Uzi in a Cessna 402 he shared with two other scientists. They had to take off by 6 A.M., Uzi said, or they might have problems with the plane in the heat.

Sitting beside Uzi, with the controls and steering yoke in front of her, Lucy felt a surge of excitement. The propellers started. The small plane taxied to the runway and turned into the wind. Lucy held her breath as the plane gained speed and imperceptibly lifted off the ground. Joe sat behind Uzi, and a short time after takeoff, the combination of noise and motion and high air put him to sleep.

"Listen, Lucy," Uzi said, "I don't know what you and Dahlia talk about, but I told her nothing happened between us. Since you've been in Israel."

"Do you think she suspects?"

"She didn't before she met you, but now . . ." He tipped his palm from side to side.

"She has less to worry about now. We've been so virtuous."

"It was a complete waste."

Lucy laughed. "Virtue is its own reward."

"There is no reward in such virtue, believe me."

"I'll have a talk with her."

"Please don't."

They had been flying south along the coast of the Red Sea, but at Dahab, Uzi headed west for the mountains. Joe stirred in the back seat. Lucy turned and waved. Because of the engine noise, they could not hear each other unless Joe leaned up to the front.

"Dahlia's had a difficult year," Uzi said. "Her brother was killed in January. He was in the army, and after a terrorist attack, his unit went into Lebanon in pursuit. He was ambushed. They found him hanged, with his testicles stuffed in his mouth."

"Good God. Dahlia never said anything . . ."

"She wouldn't."

Lucy covered her face. "How ghastly."

"It really brought home to me that there's no pleasant way to get out. Either you're sick, or you're senile, or something violent happens. Nobody ever dies when he's feeling well, he's with people he loves, it's a marvelous day, the sun is shining."

He reached over and yanked her hair. Looking out the window, Lucy saw a day such as Uzi was describing. There were no clouds, the sky in its entirety was a brilliant blue. They could see the black peak of Mount Katarina rising above the chain of red granite mountains.

Uzi turned and cupped his hand around his mouth so the sound would be directed: "Joe!"

Joe leaned forward.

"Want to see the most beautiful spot on the earth?"

"Sure."

Uzi banked the plane and changed course, heading not for Santa but a spot farther south. They were soon flying over mountains the Israelis had not penetrated with roads, army posts or radar stations.

"Look to the left, between those two peaks, you see a

high valley? That's the place—Farsh e-Tuteh. I first came here in 1967, with a girl from my army unit. God, I can't remember her name."

"Shame on you," Lucy said.

"My memory was never that good."

He shouted back to Joe. "You see how beautiful it is?"

He made a low pass over the valley, and Lucy saw pools of water surrounded by floury pink sand. There were date palms, fig trees, grape vines.

"Everything you see was planted hundreds of years ago, by the first Christian pilgrims."

"It does look enchanting," Lucy said.

Uzi took the plane up over the ridge, circled and made another pass.

"You have to fly so low?" Joe said.

"No worries. Look that mulberry tree is four hundred years old."

They were so close that Lucy could see sprays of blackish-purple berries. The rocks below the tree were stained red from falling fruit. They rose up over the ridge once again and flew back down. Joe tapped Lucy's shoulder but she was straining to hear Uzi. "Dahlia and I try to come here once a year. It's five days' walk from Santa, and it's the best trip you can make. It's so remote, you can stay for weeks and not see anyone, not even Bedouin. You just eat the fruit and bathe in the pools and walk in the mountains."

"Uzi!"

He was taking the plane up for the turn but he had not counted on a downdraft, which caught the plane and pushed it down. Lucy's stomach lurched. They cleared the ridge but the plane began to buzz and shake violently.

"What the hell's going on?" Joe said. Every surface was vibrating.

"Propeller strike."

"Where?"

"Not sure." Uzi looked out the window and saw it was

the right propeller. He shut down the right engine and the plane yawed and pitched until he could stabilize it.

Lucy looked from Joe to Uzi to the wing. The sight of the propeller blades, motionless in air, was terrifying.

"Relax, this is standard maneuver in flight training—you fly on one engine," Uzi said.

"Not at eight thousand feet," Joe said.

"We can make it to Santa." Uzi steered the plane over a saddle and began following a wadi to the north. The vibrating had lessened; there were clicking sounds as Uzi worked at the controls.

"How's the oil?" Joe said.

"Leaking. We're losing altitude."

"Shit!"

"Try to be calm. I'm going to take her down in the wadi."

Lucy felt a shock of fear, like adrenaline, rattle through her. We're going to crash, we're going to be hurt badly. No, it can't be!

"Radio our position," Joe said.

"It won't work, because of the mountains."

Lucy watched in stupefaction as the rocks on the ground grew larger. Joe and Uzi were shouting but she did not hear. Joe put his mouth to her ear. "Undo your seat belt, get in back, away from the windshield. Now!" She put her hands to the buckle but her fingers were shaking. Joe stood up, reached over her and undid the belt.

"Stay quiet," Uzi yelled.

Joe was yanking her through the opening in the seats. Her leg was caught in the yoke, she was being twisted and tugged and then she was strapped in the seat beside Joe.

He pushed her head down. She began reciting the *Shema*, and braced. As the plane hit the ground, her jaw was smashed against her knees. The plane rose up, banged again and kept racing. There was a terrible shrieking of engines, glass breaking, metal crunching, swirls of rocks and sand and she blacked out.

For five minutes, no sound or movement came from the plane, which had lodged, nose down, in the wadi. A fire began to sputter in the engine. There was shuffling inside, a faint knocking, and then the left rear door opened with a jerk.

Lucy stepped out. Holding a hand over one eye, she looked in both directions. The flames flickered intermittently, but she could smell gas. She started down the steps, hesitated, and bolted back. She threw out her purse and a canteen. She crawled into the cabin where Joe was lying, groaning. She pulled his arm, took hold of his shoulders and tried to move him. Tears were streaming down her face. In front, Uzi was slumped, dead, his head twisted at a piteous angle. "Joe! We have to get out!" She took a deep breath and tugged as hard as she could. At last, Joe began to move.

From the darkened plane, they emerged into molten sunlight. Weaving, stumbling, they ran toward a cliff and sank down under an overhanging rock.

Lucy looked back at the wreck. The fire was still sputtering, she had time, she got to her feet when, with a whoosh, the plane went up in a hideous ball of orange flame. She reeled backward. "Dahlia, the children! What are we going to do?"

Joe did not answer.

She began to notice things: a warm, salty liquid in her mouth. She spit: blood and fragments of tooth spattered the sand. She was dizzy and her head ached. She felt inside her mouth, and found that all her front teeth were broken. She winced when she touched the sharp ends.

Shading her face, she wanted to test her right eye. Cautiously, she opened it and grew more dizzy. The images waved or appeared double. What did it mean to have blurring in one eye?

She reached for the canteen and found it half full. She took a sip, then handed it to Joe. His eyes were glassy and his face chalk white. "Where are you hurt?"

"Don't know."

She began examining his body. She could find only superficial cuts on his head and chest. His Rolex watch was smashed, and, she saw, his thumb was gashed to the bone. She took the Bedouin scarf from her head and started wrapping it tightly around the thumb.

"Cut that out!"

She tensed. Red seeped into the white scarf, until it was saturated. "I want to stop the bleeding." She tried again and he did not protest.

She asked him to move one arm at a time, then his legs. "Does your head hurt?" Silence. "How many fingers am I holding up? Joe, please, look at me."

"Two."

"What's the date today?"

"Don't know." She was not sure herself.

"What day of the week is it?"

"Monday."

It was Sunday. But in Israel, Sunday felt like Monday, it was the beginning of the week.

She felt the shadow of a large bird pass across them. An Egyptian vulture, she had seen them before at Santa.

"We have to think carefully," she said. She was waiting for Joe to take over, to tell her what they must do.

"Nobody will miss us in Jerusalem," she said. Her pulse was racing, adrenaline was still pumping through her. "We're not expected back for weeks. There's no phone at Santa, and Dahlia won't be concerned when we don't show up. Uzi's notorious for changing plans at the last minute. It might be days, even a week, before we're missed. What do you think?"

He grunted.

"If we follow the wadi, it should wind down from the

mountains to the sea. But which direction?'' The wadi was flat, and the cliffs on either side were a thousand feet straight up. If she could climb to the top of the cliffs, she could tell in which direction the sea was, but that was not possible.

"Dammit, Joe, don't just lie there, I'm hurt too. Tell me which way, I don't want to make the wrong choice."

"Doesn't matter."

"What's wrong with you? You know how to read stars and catch fish and . . ,"

It was occurring to her that Joe might be in shock, or have internal injuries. She broke down. "I'm sorry, if it hadn't been for me, you wouldn't be here, you'd be sitting somewhere with a floor under you."

He waved her to stop; his words came out scrambled: "Strength save you,"

"We're going to get through this, we're going to walk toward the Red Sea and find help." Joe wanted to stretch out in the sand and sleep. She put the canteen to his mouth, then took a sip. "We'll wait until it's cooler. We'll find water, too, I know how, they taught me at Santa."

She pulled her knees up and rocked. *You can stay here for weeks and not see anyone, not even Bedouin.* Sweat was running down her arms and legs; it was 140 degrees. Why hadn't she paid more attention when the guides had talked about finding water? She remembered, vaguely, they said to look for certain plants, but there were no plants here. Unlike Uzi's hidden valley, this wadi was enclosed by black volcanic rock, inhospitable to life. *There's no pleasant way to get out.* She struggled to push Uzi from her mind.

Sunlight ricocheted off the black rock, creating a glare so intense that all color disappeared. She was growing faint. Her head began to peck forward and she fell off.

* * *

When she awoke, the heat seemed to have lessened. It was minutes before she realized—both eyes were open and she could see. Relief washed over her.

Joe was drinking from the canteen.

"Feel better?"

He shook his head no.

She emptied her purse except for a few items: matches ("Hiro Sushi," she read absently), wallet, first-aid kit. She saw a shadow move across them—the vulture again.

She gathered rocks and formed an arrow in the sand, pointing away from the wreck. "We're going to start now," she said, and, supporting Joe under the arms, helped him stand. "Can you walk on your own?" He nodded. Holding the canteen, she went ahead of him, limping, noticing only now that she had injured her knee in the crash. Joe moved mechanically, stopping when she stopped, starting again at her prodding.

From the point of view of the vulture, they were specks moving badly over the sand. The Red Sea was relatively close to their wadi, but they were walking in the wrong direction.

Lucy was weaker than she had realized. She wanted water and it was more than wanting, it was a compulsion, like the compulsion to take a breath under water. The pressure builds until the urge becomes desperate.

Before they had walked very far, it was dark. Twice, Joe sank to the ground. Twice, she coaxed and reassured him and pulled him to his feet. The next time, he would not respond to her pleading. Exasperated, she started to leave, then turned and yelled, "Where's all that macho strength when it counts? Who cares how many girls you can fuck, how many surfboards you can ride? Don't you understand? This is the desert, this is not some goddamned singles bar. You can't get by on your looks and charm and acting *so sincere.* You can't go limp at the first sign of trouble and hope the lady gets the message. Run away and wait for the dust to clear. Because if you go limp here, you'll die." She took him by the shoulders. "This is not a movie, it's winner take all and loser is dead. So get up off your fucking ass!"

With a groan of rage and pain, he rose. They struggled on, and after two hours came to a spot where the wadi seemed to join another and fork. Lucy told Joe to wait, she would test the two courses. She tried the right fork but became aware she was moving uphill. She limped back and tried the left. There was a slight uphill grade to this also, but she thought she could make out the forms of trees. Soaked with perspiration, dragging her leg, she made her way toward the trees, praying this was not an illusion. If there were trees, there had to be water. The black shapes lengthened and shrunk, was her vision blurring? No, they were trees.

She stumbled back to tell Joe and found him crouched on all fours. His body jerked like that of someone retching, but nothing came. She kneeled and took him in her arms. She put her lips to his forehead and became alarmed—his skin was dry and papery, unlike her own, which was wet. She gave him the last water in the canteen. "We're going to take it slow," she whispered. "We're going to make our way back. We will, Joe. I found trees." She was so dizzy and weak herself that it was difficult to sit. "We'll have water . . . when . . . the light comes."

Lucy had no watch, so she was aware only of vague demarcations: periods awake and periods unconscious; periods of light and periods of dark. When next she awoke, it was becoming light and she had a piercing headache. Joe was leaning on a rock, holding his head at a strange angle. He said he had a headache also, and was nauseous, but every time he tried to throw up, he had dry heaves. She remembered, headaches were the first sign of severe dehydration. She urged him to walk—it was more like creeping —until they reached the trees, where he lay down in the shade.

There were four trees, and the ruins of a pink stone wall that once must have enclosed a Bedouin garden. There had to be a well or spring, but how to find it? She searched along the stone wall, in the overgrown plot, around the trees, under rocks, but she could find nothing. She picked the youngest tree and began to dig beside it.

She went rigid; she turned her head, cried out, then clapped a hand over her mouth.

Ten yards away stood a figure, a man. He stared at her without moving. He wore a torn *gelabya,* and around his head was a filthy white *kefiya.*

She stole a look at Joe, who was watching.

"We've been in an accident," she said in English, realizing instantly her foolishness. The figure walked toward them, hardly seeming to touch the ground. Her heart pounded. He stopped, then said what sounded like "Alicka licka licka . . ."

She shook her head.

He repeated, louder, "Alicka licka licka!"

"What's he saying?" Joe whispered.

"I don't know," Lucy said. His eyes were flat and small. She thought of the eyes of the Arab boy in the Old City. Would he hurt them, had he been provoked by the sight of her in a blouse that showed her arms?

"Do you speak Hebrew?" she said.

"Ktzat." A little.

"Water," she said in Hebrew, putting her hands to her throat. "Do you have water?"

He handed her a goatskin bag. She drank, then crawled over to Joe, not taking her eyes off the Bedouin. Joe reached out and gulped greedily, but after four swallows, he threw up. She looked wildly at the Bedouin, who motioned for Joe to take a small amount and stop.

"Try just a sip," Lucy said.

He did. Another. The Bedouin came toward them and Lucy stiffened. He dropped to his haunches, tore a strip from his *gelabya*, soaked it in water and motioned for Lucy to bathe Joe's skin. She had Joe lie down and pressed the cloth to his face. His body was shaking.

Lucy struggled to retrieve the Hebrew she had studied.

"We were in . . . plane . . . broken."

"Plane?"

"Yes."

"Where?"

She pointed in the direction of the wreck. She drank again from the bag, and removed Joe's cloth, which was steaming. She poured water on the cloth and replaced it.

"You have friends?" the Bedouin said.

Was he trying to determine if they were alone?

"Friends . . . in plane?"

She looked in his eyes. "Dead."

7

The Bedouin built a fire, made tea and all day he fed Lucy and Joe from a little shot glass, sips at a time. They were so debilitated that they did not move from the shade of the trees. By late afternoon, Lucy was able to stand, and Joe could drink a glass of weak tea without retching.

The Bedouin told them his name was Achmed. He had learned Hebrew in Eilat, where he had worked a short time as a dishwasher. He was on his way from Gebel Umm Shumar, where his family spent the spring and summer months, to Bir Miar, to visit relatives.

"Where are we now?" Lucy said.

"Ein Hereta."

Why had she asked?

"We want to go to the Israelis. Where is the closest place?"

"Santa Katarina."

"Can you take us? We will pay you."

He seemed shy at the mention of money. She tried to give him what she had in her wallet, $30, but he waved his hand. *"Beseder."* It will be all right.

"How long will it take to reach Santa?"

"Four days. Maybe five, if you can't walk well. Perhaps we will rest here another day, so you're stronger."

"No, let's start tomorrow."

"*Beseder.*"

When night came, he smoothed a bed for them in the sand. He gave them his blanket, which Lucy spread over Joe and herself. Hugging Joe, she whispered, "A few more days and it will be over." She lay down on her side. After what seemed hours, she dozed, but only for an instant. She saw Uzi, grinning. Uzi yanking on her hair. Uzi in the pilot seat and she was awake, whimpering in pain.

She saw Achmed, a creature from the Stone Age, watching her.

"Dream," she said.

He nodded.

Just after dawn, Achmed tapped her. She was glad, she could not bear tossing, thinking, any longer. Joe was not asleep in his place, he must have walked down the wadi. The sky was overcast, but she did not notice, she merely felt something pearly and dreamlike in the air.

"I know this sounds ridiculous, but it looks like it's going to rain."

She started. "You look better, oh, Joe, I'm so relieved."

"I feel like I've been in a coma. How long has it been since . . ."

She considered. "Two days?"

He nodded.

"What happened to you?" she said.

"I got the shit beat out of me when we landed. Then, I don't know. Exposure and dehydration, I guess. When I started to get some liquid in me, I started to come back."

Achmed was building a fire, gathering branches of dried broom plant.

Joe tore a strip from his shirt and asked her to help rebandage his thumb. Achmed brought them glasses of tea laced with sugar, and as soon as they had finished, they set out.

They walked single file, Achmed leading, Lucy in the rear, limping. She noticed the sky was completely gray, and they were retracing the course he and Joe had walked the first night. So she had been wrong.

"It's a good thing Achmed found us."

"I just hope we can trust him."

"It's also good he speaks a little Hebrew, it's our only link, and a thin one."

"How old do you figure he is?"

She shook her head. "He could be twenty-five or forty."

Achmed had lost many teeth, and the few remaining were caked with brown scum. He was thin and his face was covered with sores. He seemed never to have washed his hair or clothes, and he walked through the mountains in flimsy plastic sandals. The gap between them was so great, Lucy thought, that little of substance could pass between them.

After an hour, they came in sight of the wreck—black and charred. Lucy faltered, and said a silent prayer. "Let's move on."

Before another hour had elapsed, they reached a pool of water, surrounded by fruit trees. "This Gassuba," Achmed said. "Oasis." Water had been this close! Lucy sat by the pool, soaking her swollen knee, while Joe tried to clean the gash in his thumb. Although the sky had darkened and a wind was blowing, Lucy felt feverish. Achmed told her to sit under a rock. She propped her leg up while he gathered broom plant to make a fire.

"Are you hungry?"

She had not thought of food in two days. "Yes."

Achmed took flour and salt from his bag and mixed it with water, using the hollow of a rock for a bowl.

"What's he doing?" Joe called.

"Making pita."

This was not the flat, fried pita she had tasted before, the pita made for Passover on Mount Sirbal. This was pita "for the road," Achmed said. He molded the dough into a round loaf, about two inches thick. When the fire had burned down, he dug a hole beside it, buried the dough in the ground, covered it with hot coals and covered them with dirt. His movements were graceful, mesmerizing. Periodically, he floated his palms over the mound, testing the temperature. Joe came and sat nearby. Achmed dug up the mound: the moist white dough had turned to a crusty brown loaf. With a rock, he scraped the cinders and dirt off the loaf, tore chunks and handed them to Joe and Lucy.

The appearance of the hot, fragrant bread from the earth seemed miraculous, Joe said. Lucy nodded, biting with the side of her mouth to avoid the broken teeth. She tried to communicate their pleasure to Achmed but he seemed preoccupied, getting up every few minutes to stare down the wadi or up at the sky. The wind began to whistle in the trees, and soon it was drizzling.

"I thought it doesn't rain in the desert," Lucy said.

"It won't last long." Achmed smiled. "But . . . there is something . . ."

She was translating for Joe.

"There may be *shitafon*," Achmed said.

"What's that?" Joe said.

"I don't know the word."

Achmed tried to explain, using other words. "Much water."

"Rain?"

"No."

"River?"

"No. *Shitafon.*"

It rained harder and wind blew the spray under the rock, stinging their faces. "Ask him what we do if it doesn't stop," Joe said.

"I know a house, good house, where we can wait," Achmed said.

"Nearby?"

Again, Achmed smiled.

"How far?" Lucy said.

"Two hours."

Achmed walked away from the rock and after a moment, came rushing back. "Quick, we must go. *Shitafon!*"

At that moment, Lucy heard a roar. She stepped out and, to the right, saw a spout of water rising up over a ridge and crashing down the face of the rock. It looked as if a giant pitcher of water was being poured from the sky.

"Holy shit," Joe said.

Lucy stood transfixed. Achmed grabbed her arm and began pulling, half dragging her up the side of the wadi toward higher ground. Joe climbed after them. In minutes, the stream of water had struck the wadi floor and was racing in the direction of the wreck. Lucy strained against Achmed's arm, but he held firm. As she watched, the water in the wadi rose to a depth of eight or nine feet. Anyone caught below would have drowned.

She had the impulse to laugh. It was like a monstrous joke. Bam, take this, bam, take that. Like Eliza fleeing over the cracking ice, they scrambled from rock to rock, wading at times through water up to their thighs. It was funny to Lucy that she was not afraid. The rocks were slick, the drop-off was fatal. Was she losing touch, like divers who succumb to rapture of the deep, believing that they see mermaids and no longer need their air? She felt no pain, she felt nothing in her knee. When they reached a high saddle, Achmed released his hold. *"Beseder.* The water won't come this way."

"How does he know?" Joe said.

"I know the mountains," Achmed said. "I know where the water runs, where it's dry, where there are good houses."

Looking down, Lucy saw a scene of supernatural beauty. They were standing on the crest of a ring of mountains whose peaks were enfolded by clouds. Water was tumbling down the ridges forming a dozen waterfalls. The rain and clouds created an optical illusion so that everything appeared double. There was a double ring of mountains, double edges of rock, double trees, double falls of water—and everything was pearlized through gray-green mists. They were treading in the Valley of the Gods.

They did not reach the "house" until late afternoon, and it was not a house at all but a giant red rock. The rock was hollow, like a cave, with a small opening. Bedouin passing that way had made it into a shelter by fashioning a little door out of wood and attaching it to the rock.

Achmed, Joe and Lucy had to crawl, stomachs low to the ground, to get inside. It was still pouring and they were drenched. It had taken five hours, not two, to reach the "house," and the rapture of the deep had worn off. Feeling had returned to Lucy's knee, and it was not good feeling. Every movement brought pain. Her head ached, and judging from the breath coming out her nostrils, she had a fever.

Joe was shivering. They could not make a fire—all the brush was wet—but in a few minutes, the cave grew warm from the heat of their bodies.

Achmed said he was going to find a Bedouin who lived nearby, and left Joe and Lucy the blanket from his bag. Lucy took off her wet clothes and slung them over a pole running down the center of the cave. Wrapping the blanket around her, she urged Joe to do the same.

He began to swear and rage at the flood, the desert, small planes, stupid Israelis, stinking primitives. "I don't know where the hell we are. I can't communicate with Achmed or anyone else in this shithole. What if you and I got separated? Even if I had a map, I couldn't read it. What if this guy doesn't come back?"

"He'll be back."

"What gives you such goddamned blind trust? What if he brings back friends, they could kill us for thirty bucks."

Lucy tried to reason with him. She repeated what the guides at Santa had told her—that Bedouin possessed a highly developed sense of ethics, that in twelve years of Israeli occupation of the Sinai, there had not been one incident of violence involving Bedouin.

"What if he can't find the cave again?"

"You can't be serious, Joe. He grew up in the mountains, he knows it the way you know State Beach."

Joe laughed, grudgingly, and began removing his wet clothes. Lucy spread the blanket over the two of them. "You were right, it does feel better," he said.

"Why don't you lie down." There was just room for the two of them to stretch out on their backs. "You have the window beside you," she said. At Joe's head, there was a cluster of holes punched in the rock, like the holes in the top of a salt shaker.

"You call that a window! You have lost your grip." He laughed darkly. The cave had grown pleasantly cozy, but outside, it was still raining and thundering. "I feel like we're in a space capsule, cut off from the mother ship," Joe said. "This is not how I pictured the end."

The cave, which had been suffused with gray light, was becoming utterly black. Lucy and Joe stared at the granite ceiling. Lucy began to cry quietly. "I don't feel my life has been much of a success."

"What are you talking about?"

"You know."

"Not everyone has the knack," Joe said. "It's like, not everyone can ski."

"Everyone else in my family has it—my parents, my sister. My grandparents were married for sixty-two years. For the last twelve, my grandmother was senile and living in a nursing home. Every day, my grandfather would go there to feed her, brush her hair and take her outside in the wheelchair. For twelve years, he didn't miss a day. He kept saying she was beautiful, and when she died, I'll never forget, he stood by the crypt and called, 'Sleep well, darling.' ''

"It's the same in my family," Joe said. "But when the cards were dealt, it wasn't given to me."

"I don't think it's luck. You can tell right off, when you meet a person, if he wants to become involved or not, if he's interested in a family or not. I've been saying I want one and going for the other, again and again. Every man I've loved has been unavailable in some way. It's doomed, and when it fails, I become more driven to reverse it with the next unsuitable man."

Because of the dimness, she could not see Joe's face.

"Everyone has some pattern," Joe said. "If a woman is too loving, I can't feel anything. And I torment myself, why don't I feel it, I should?" He shifted his weight. "You remember the day we spent at the beach right after we met? It seems a lifetime ago. I taught you to swim through the waves?"

"Yes."

"You said you could fall in love with me. It was only the second time we'd met. You hardly knew me, and you had such intensity. I thought, who is this woman? I went home scared shitless."

"Of what?"

"Being consumed. Too much was being asked, nothing of me would be left. If you really came close, you would see me for the piece of shit I thought I was. I had to back away. But I was attracted to you too, so this strange dance began."

"The crazy thing is," Lucy said, "we're compatible in every way except this."

"And this is the kicker. Without this, the machine won't go."

"It makes a lot of smoke, though." She clicked her tongue. "How could I have believed for so long that we were perfect for each other?"

"In every other way," Joe said, "I guess, we were."

The rain had stopped, but water was still streaming over the ridges. In the darkness of the cave, Lucy and Joe were seeing a truth about themselves they had not known. They said nothing that was notably original, but often, a problem that is easy to observe in a third party is most difficult to see about oneself.

They gave no advice, for what was the point? They might analyze the problem from different angles, but that would not accomplish much. All they could do was listen, and understand, and say good night and hope that someday, there would be better weather.

Lucy sat up suddenly. Rocks were falling outside the cave. "Who's there?" The small door opened.

"Achmed." She squeezed closer to Joe to make room. Achmed had brought back another blanket, pita and water. "You have matches?"

Lucy looked in her purse and found the matchbook, Hiro Sushi.

"Light one." When she did, he began to perform a feat. Among some garbage on the floor of the cave, he found a piece of tin that had been the top of a can. He punched a hole in it, tore a strip off the bottom of his *gelabya* and threaded the cloth through the hole.

Lucy noted that everything Achmed did had a lightness, whether it was making pita, tearing cotton, collecting twigs. He walked with lightness, there seemed no tension in his body. Even in the flood, he had seemed to float up the rocks, and at one point, moving across a sheer, wet cliff, he had given Lucy a hand, not bracing or clutching but with grace, as if escorting a lady down an aisle.

He took from his bag the little shot glass and filled it with cooking oil from a goatskin container. Then he set the flat tin piece on top of the glass, struck a match to the piece of cloth poking out the hole, and he had an oil lamp.

The atmosphere changed: light danced about the walls

and ceiling of the cave. They ate dry pita and sipped water. "In America," Achmed said, "you'll tell your grandchildren about this." Lucy and Joe began to laugh, hearing the familiar concept uttered by a Bedouin in broken Hebrew. Soon they were howling, and Achmed laughed, not knowing quite why.

"Lucy," he said, "I'm going to be married in two months."

She stopped laughing, and wiped her eyes. It was the first time he had offered any personal information.

"How old are you?" she said.

"Twenty."

"And the girl?"

"Fourteen."

Joe said, "That's great, tell him congratulations."

Achmed said the girl's name was Sultana, and he had known her since she was a baby. Their families had planned the marriage.

"Do you love her?"

He smiled. *"Ktzat."* A little.

"Ask him if they can spend time together alone," Joe said.

"Not too much," Achmed said. "We meet sometimes in the mountains, when she's with the goats. I think I will love her more after we are married." He asked Lucy, "Have you been to Amsterdam?"

"No. Why?"

"I hear it's beautiful. Water runs in the streets."

"Yes, canals. *Shitafon.*" They laughed.

"I want to go there," Achmed said.

She asked why, but Achmed would only make shy references to "friends" he had met in Eilat.

"Maybe he's had some relations with a Dutch girl," Lucy said to Joe. "I've heard the Scandinavian women come to Eilat for winter vacations, and sunbathe nude on the beaches. Can you imagine the reaction of Bedouin? Their women cover everything but the eyes.''

Joe gave a surprised laugh. ''They might never recover.''

Now that Achmed had opened the door, Lucy rushed in, eager to learn about his life. She asked question after question, which he answered directly: he had four sisters and two brothers; the family had twenty goats, seven sheep and one camel. The camel was eight years old and would live, *Ham du Leilah*, to be twenty-five.

Joe was falling asleep, soothed by the steady murmuring in Hebrew. Achmed was telling Lucy that his grandfather was a healer who cured people with herbs. His uncle was a *shofet*. Lucy did not know the word. Achmed said, ''If a man steals, they take him to a room.''

''Prison?''

''No, *shofet* is not prison. A room where a man asks, 'Did you do this?' ''

A judge, Lucy thought.

Achmed said his uncle was the most respected *shofet* in the tribe. Bedouin came from all parts of Sinai to have him settle disputes or give them advice. Achmed was his favorite nephew, and he liked Achmed to sit with him while he heard people's cases.

''I have a tape recorder I bought in Eilat,'' he said. ''I'm making tapes of my uncle. I want to make a record of Bedouin life, because it's going to disappear. Another twenty years and''—he made a snuffing gesture—''that's it.''

Five years ago, he said, Bedouin had traveled only by foot or camel. ''Now they have trucks. Radios. Men work in the towns for six months to make money, then go back to the desert.''

It was surprising to Lucy how much they were able to communicate with a limited vocabulary, both of them using the wrong tenses. Had they been more fluent, they would have been aware of how crude their statements sounded, but as it was, they were happy to succeed in passing an idea across.

Achmed's appearance had undergone a transformation. His eyes were no longer flat but warm, kind, teasing. There was a glow about his face, and his smile was all sweetness.

"What are you thinking?" she said.

"I don't think."

"Really?"

He nodded.

"I think all the time."

"Even when you're walking in the mountains?"

"Yes. I have a bad habit; if I'm walking up one mountain that's beautiful, I'll think, maybe it's better over there."

Achmed smiled. "I know what's over there."

"No . . ."

"I know," he said. "I also think like that. Tonight I'm thinking about the wedding. I want to go to Amsterdam. I want to go to London, America. I want to see the whole world, and if I marry, I won't leave Santa Katarina."

I know what's in the rest of the world, Lucy thought.

"Sultana will not travel. We'll have many children, and I won't do other things. I don't want to get married right now, but our families, everyone in the tribe is pushing. Everyone says I'm a good young man, I speak nicely, I behave nicely, they love to have me around."

Lucy wanted to tell him, marry, don't leave, the desert is beautiful, our ways are not necessarily better, and yet, she understood the need for voyage and discovery.

He asked if Lucy was married, if she had children.

"Not yet."

"Why? You have gray hair." He pointed to the strands at her temple.

"You're not supposed to notice that." She laughed, and brushed the hair back. "I wanted to make films, I wanted to have experiences, I wanted many people to see my films and I didn't think I could do that if I had children. I wasn't ready, but I am now. I will have children, if we manage to get out of here.''

He looked at her with complete understanding. ''Then you will have children.''

She had a brief fantasy of bringing him to California, having his teeth fixed, giving him English lessons. He would learn quickly.

She spread the second blanket over the three of them and they lay down, like teen-agers at a slumber party. The improvised oil lamp flickered; rain pattered on the roof of the cave.

''Achmed,'' she said softly, ''are you sleeping?''

''No.''

''You want to sleep?''

''Yes. But I also want to talk.''

''Do you believe in God?''

''Yes.''

''Do you pray five times a day?''

He made a clucking sound. ''I don't have time. But I know there is a God.''

''How do you know?''

''I know.'' He raised a dark hand. ''And he will take me to Amsterdam.''

8

As rain drummed on the cave, Lucy slept peacefully for the first time since the accident. Her last thoughts were of Achmed and his fourteen-year-old bride, setting out on foot for their honeymoon in one of the Sinai wadis.

In the morning, Achmed was lying to her right, breathing rhythmically, but Joe was gone. She took her damp clothes off the pole and slipped them on. Using a piece of tin for a mirror and her fingers for a comb, she tried to untangle her hair. As she was braiding it, Joe crawled through the door.

"As terrible as it was yesterday, that's how beautiful it is today," he said. She followed him out and blinked in disbelief. The sun was shining, there was no hint of cloud or rain, as if the calamities of the day before had been a hallucination. For a moment, she felt a wild hope, but it passed.

They spread their clothes on the rocks and while they were drying, took stock. Joe's thumb was swollen, the nail was black and pus was oozing from the gash. "It doesn't hurt unless I bump it." To prevent this, they tore another strip from his shirt and made a sling. Lucy's knee was still sore, and she had intermittent shooting pains in her head.

"As soon as we get some rest," she said. "I'm sure everything will heal."

Achmed was lying in the sand, twirling a leaf in some rainwater that had collected in the hollow of a rock.

"I think you kept him up too late," Joe said.

She turned to Achmed. "How are you today?"

A smile lit his face. "Good. I'm always good."

"Always?"

"Well. Yesterday was a little . . ." He jiggled his hand.

Lucy smiled. "Thinking about the wedding?"

"I'm thinking about what will happen when Santa Katarina goes back to Egypt. There will be less work for us, less money, because there won't be so many tourists. And if I don't marry, I'll be drafted into the Egyptian Army."

He drew two lines in the sand and pointed to the space between. "I'm here. This is Sultana, the other is the army. I don't know which way to go."

When their gear had dried, they started off down a slope that was covered with black rock. Lucy was moving more slowly than the day before. The heat was rising, she could feel it through her sneakers. The sun beat on her head and from time to time, her left leg went numb. Joe, also, was walking with difficulty. As they neared the wadi floor, the path grew muddy, full of brush uprooted by the flood. The glare on the rocks hurt their eyes and they began to stagger. Achmed decided they should head not for Santa but a Bedouin settlement to the west, where he had relatives who could care for them.

Toward noon, the heat was menacing, the light was shrieking like an air-raid siren. Achmed found shade under an acacia tree, raked a bed in the sand and told Lucy and Joe to rest. They sank into a dull sleep, from which he woke them.

Lucy was irritated, why wouldn't he let them be? She was stiff and sore, and when she tried to stand, her leg gave out. "You two go on."

Achmed shook his head. He lifted Lucy and, with his arm around her, half carried her, while Joe walked behind. She was short of breath, her heart was pounding, and her gums, her ears, her fingers—everything had the rapid hammer beat. "Good," Achmed kept saying, "you're doing good."

Just before sunset, they entered a canyon and Lucy began to acquire a second wind. As they descended, the black rocks underneath gave way to red granite, then to soft pink sand. Plants appeared, and the intoxicating fragrance of mint and sage piqued her senses.

Achmed took a small mirror from his bag and held it so that it reflected the light.

"What's he doing?" Joe said.

"Saying hello," Achmed said.

Lucy looked up toward where Achmed was aiming the light a red peak.

"Listen," he said.

"I don't see . . ."

He put a finger to his lips.

Faint and far away, there was a sweet whistling.

"Look, where the light hits the ridge."

Lucy squinted and saw, beside the diamond point of light, the tiny figure of a girl. Moving to the right, Lucy's eyes began to pick out little black dots—goats. They were rolling down a slope, one at a time, like toys on wheels.

"Do you know who it is?" Lucy said.

"My cousin."

"How can he tell?" Joe said.

"The way she plays her flute."

They walked on, and began to see more signs of human habitation. There were date palms recently harvested, gardens with pink stone walls, irrigation ditches and neat rows of trees—apple, pomegranate, plum. In one garden, Lucy saw a scarecrow dressed as a Bedouin woman, in black robes and face covering. She smiled, she had always thought of scarecrows wearing overalls.

The canyon spilled out onto a wide plateau, and they saw the Bedouin settlement: a dozen pink stone huts, open on one side, covered with roofs of palm. There were camels feeding on acacia trees, donkeys roaming in the upper valley, chickens and roosters pecking about. Bells tinkled. Women tended cooking fires and girls in long black veils were bringing the goats down from the mountains, playing flutes and crying, "Esh! Esh!" to their charges.

"I feel happy," Joe said.

The sun was setting, and as they watched, the colors of the mountains changed. Lucy stared at a hill that was shimmering gold; a few minutes later it was pink, then slate blue, then chocolate brown, while the sky turned hues of crimson and mauve. This was not a place they were entering, she thought; they were walking back in time.

Achmed's aunt welcomed them like a seabird shrieking at the arrival of a school of fish. She flapped and flung her thin arms around Achmed, telling Joe and Lucy, through him, "I'm glad you needed to come here. It means I get to see my nephew."

The aunt gave them her guest house—a pink stone hut on the edge of the plateau. "This is luxury," Joe said. There were blankets to sleep on, a water jug in the corner and a constant stream of food: hot pita, sweet tea, rice cooked in goat's milk, *foul*—delicious fava beans from Cairo—and a whole goat's hide stuffed with dates. The aunt promised to slaughter a sheep, as soon as Lucy and Joe were well.

The camp was buzzing with talk about the flood. Part of the stream bank had been washed out, a camel and two donkeys had been killed but, *Ham du Leilah,* no Bedouin had been hurt.

Achmed told his aunt he would stay in the hut with his charges. He asked for cloth to make a new bandage and sling for Joe. Settled on their blankets, propped against the back wall, Achmed, Joe and Lucy watched the last of the goats being herded into the hut next to theirs. It was like a clown act: the hut was only six feet square, but goats kept disappearing until there were twenty or thirty inside and the door was slammed shut.

"How long do they stay in there?" Lucy said.

"From six at night till six in the morning."

"That's a long time to sleep," Joe said.

"They're not sleeping, they're reading," Achmed said. "They have books."

Lucy laughed, picturing the black goats huddled together with reading glasses.

Soothed by the sounds of lowing animals, tinkling bells and high-voiced children, they fell asleep.

The plan was to rest in the Bedouin camp and let their injuries heal until they could attempt the arduous, three-day climb to Santa. As Lucy lay in the hut with her knee propped up, she was not certain she wanted to complete the journey. She was finding such beauty in the rhythms of the camp. At first light, the goats were taken up to the mountains by the young shepherdesses. There was a whistling of flutes, a throwing of stones—"Esh! Esh!"—a chattering and jingling that grew softer and softer until the camp was quiet.

Most of the men were away, working in El Arish or Eilat, smuggling, trading. The mothers tended the orchards, prepared food and nursed their babies. The babies were not squeaky clean, Gerber babies—this was the hardest aspect for Lucy to accept. They had runny eyes, sores, dust in their hair and torn clothes. They were bathed less frequently than once a week. Lucy's own clothes looked little better now, and her hair was so dirty it stuck to her scalp. Achmed's aunt wanted to dress it Bedouin fashion, and brought a black headpiece and rags to the hut, but Lucy was afraid of the camel urine she had seen them using to mold the horn over the forehead. She kept her hair in tight braids.

As days passed, Joe seemed to be recuperating faster than

Lucy. She felt listless, and her headaches came with greater frequency and severity. Joe wanted her to try to move about each day, and would lead her on walks. Her favorite time was between five and six, the magical hours when the sky would turn fuchsia and the mountains would take fire in the setting sun. The women, in their long black veils, would stop what they were doing and sit on their haunches, watching silently.

Lucy told Joe she yearned to take refuge in this life. Bedouin women were subservient, yes, but there was something appealing in the restrictions they accepted. Born into nature, a closed system, they seemed to attain, within its confines, a cheerfulness, fulfillment and courage.

"That's not a possibility for the likes of us," Joe said.

"I suppose not. We've eaten too freely of the apple."

That night, after Joe had fallen asleep, Lucy lay beside Achmed, watching stars through the chinks in the palm leaves. Achmed said he wanted to hear a typical American song. Lucy gave it some thought, and found herself, ludicrously, singing "Home on the Range."

Achmed sang a Bedouin chant in which the chorus was, "How great it is to say, 'I want.' "

"What does that mean?" Lucy said.

"I want. Happy to feel—I want."

"Want what?"

"Want something. Wanting makes life."

He smiled at her, almost flirting. "I want to make a film. How much does a camera cost?"

"Too much."

"I want to make a film of Bedouin."

"That's not a bad idea. We could make it together." Rusty gears began to creak a little. "Are you serious?"

He shrugged.

"We could make a lot of money."

"And go to Amsterdam."

* * *

Day by day, Lucy grew weaker until there was no possibility of her walking. Just sitting up exhausted her. She had constant pain in her skull, she felt as if she was hanging upside down and blood was rushing to her head, creating such pressure that her head might burst. She was seeing double in her right eye, as she had after the accident. She asked Joe to make her a patch, for it was a strain to keep one eye shut.

She slept long periods, and frequently could not remember what had been said to her a few minutes before. The loss of memory frightened her. It was as if she had walked into the camp, passed through a turnstile and begun to disappear. She heard sounds as if through a flimsy wall. She thought she saw George Washington, a senile man in white fur boots. He said he was living in California, "working on a bathroom novel," and she broke into convulsive laughter.

She was so hot her blankets were clammy and had to be changed, every hour, every day? She did not know who changed them. They came off her body steaming, as from an iron.

The fog would clear for moments, and she would see Joe, leaning over her.

"You look scared. Is it that bad?"

"No, you're going to be fine. We're going home soon. I sent Achmed to Santa Katarina and he's bringing back help."

There was a bolt of pain above her eye.

"Easy." Joe squeezed her hand. "You're strong, Lucy, you can make it. We're going home. Remember your house, the beautiful pink house with the wicker furniture and the oak table and that pale green kitchen? Remember the Jacuzzi in the garden? Think of lying there in the warm water under the stars, smelling the gardenias that bloom outside your door. And the sea is so near, you can almost hear the waves, and you can smell that salty fresh ocean air."

Yes, he was bringing it to her, she could hear the rhythmic breaking of the waves on the beach.

"Remember your bed, with the soft cotton sheets, the kind that have been washed a hundred times, they're so soft, and there's *no sand.*"

Tears were streaming down her cheeks. "Will I ever be there again?"

"Yes, you will."

She wiped her face. "I'm sorry, all the trouble I've caused you."

"No trouble. I feel so close to you. No one in my life has given me more." He put his cheek against hers, and the skin felt cool. "Remember the note I gave you to slip in the Wall, the note in code? What I asked for was courage, and I've found it. If it hadn't been for you, I'd be lying in that plane wreck."

He kissed her eyelids. "Now sleep."

Sometime later she began to vomit. It was violent, projectile vomiting, and after that she could keep nothing down except sips of water. She was not aware of pain or discomfort any longer. She was on the bottom of a pool, and the pains were ripples in the glassy surface. Joe's face was floating on that distant surface. He was calling to her, his voice distorted through the water.

"Hang on, Lucy. They're coming with a helicopter, do you hear me? They're going to take us to Jerusalem, to a hospital."

She struggled to hold his voice.

"Then we're going home, to California, to the peaceful streets by the ocean and we'll get married, do you hear me? We'll get married, I swear, by everything I hold sacred. I've been selfish, I've been spoiled, I've been holding back for stupid, petty reasons but it's going to be different. I love you. Lucy, please!"

She stared in awe. These were the words she had yearned for, waited for and given up hope of ever hearing. She opened her lips but her tongue was dry and cottony.

She could only whisper, "It's too late."

9

In her delirium, Lucy was in the Cessna 402, with the buzzing and vibrating and the beating of propellers.

She became aware of a disturbance in the camp: dust whirling and feet running and a rise in the shrill singsong of the Bedouin. She was being carried on a stretcher by men with beards and dark green clothes. She had a sudden thought, and struggled to sit up. "Joe," she wanted to cry, "don't leave Joe," but she was given an injection and sank down.

Though she was not conscious of it, Joe sat beside her in the helicopter to Santa, in the army plane to Jerusalem and in the ambulance to Hadassah Hospital. The medics questioned him about her injuries, and at the hospital, a neurosurgeon found she had a subdural hematoma. The blows she had suffered in the crash had caused a slow hemorrhaging under the skull. During the days of wandering, the blood had accumulated, pressing on the brain. If she had not been treated, she might have gone into a coma and not recovered.

A burr-hole operation was performed to drain the excess blood, and she was given fluids intravenously. At the end of two weeks, the pain and pressure had gone, her vision was clear and her life signs had returned to normal.

Not long after her release, there was a wedding reception on a terrace on Mount Scopus. Several hundred people had gathered to celebrate the marriage of Zal and Ruthi, the young couple from the moshav who had accompanied Lucy to Mount Sirbal.

It was sunset, and from the terrace, the guests could see the yellow floodlamps beginning to light up the walls of the Old City. People sat in summer clothes, eating cakes and drinking punch. A few Bedouin in *gelabya,* who had come up from the desert, were making brave attempts to eat with forks.

At a corner table, Lucy and Joe were with a group of guides from Santa. Joe's thumb was in a cast. Lucy was wearing an Ace bandage on her knee, and because of the operation, she had tied around her head a bright blue scarf, not unlike those worn by Orthodox women who cover their hair after marriage.

Next to Lucy was Dahlia, in a loose black dress and leather sandals. Her face was pale and calm, but her eyes seemed to have receded, peering out from the back of her head. She was recounting how Santa had been turned over to the Egyptians.

"Losing Uzi and losing Santa were all mixed up," she said. "We couldn't bury Uzi, but we had a ceremony for him the day before Sadat arrived. We all climbed to the top of Mount Sinai, even the children, made a fire and sat around it through the night. We told stories, things we remembered, in those mountains that he knew and loved better than any of us. In the morning, we climbed down and loaded the jeeps with everything they could carry. The last thing we did was pick all the flowers in the garden. Then we closed the doors of the field school and drove away. Just like that." A lone tear ran down her cheek.

"At first," she said, "we felt like pale lost ghosts, who had died abruptly and didn't know how to be in the next world. We needed to stay close together. We drove to Jerusalem and visited Giddi's parents. They're Greek, and his mother cooked a fantastic dinner. We were singing, drinking wine, we just didn't want to go anywhere, so she brought out blankets and we slept on the floor.

"But this couldn't go on," Dahlia said. "The next day a few people left, and then a few more. But we kept meeting for meals and talks. We still want to be together as much as we can. We shared something, and we lost something that no one else understands."

"Where will you go now?" Lucy said.

"To the Galilee. I have family there, and I can't move to the city, the change would be too great. This will be softer."

"I wish you would visit us," Lucy said. "There's room in my house."

"That's a nice idea. We'll see."

Zal and Ruthi, who were walking around the tables in their long, white Bedouin wedding robes, stopped beside Lucy and Joe. "We heard about your experience," Zal said. "We're very glad you met Achmed. We were with him once on a trip to Jebel Bab."

"I loved him," Lucy said.

"Do you know he came to the hospital with us?" Joe said. "He slept on the floor, he wouldn't leave until he saw that Lucy was going to be all right."

"He cried when we said good-bye," Lucy said. "He told us we could write to him through his uncle in Santa. Will that work?"

"Yes," Zal said. "The uncle is like Achmed. Very reliable."

The bride and groom were called to cut the wedding cake, and Joe walked off to the bar for drinks. Left alone, Lucy was savoring the simple things habitually taken for granted: drinking water, wearing clean clothes, seeing clearly out of both eyes. She watched Joe, making his way across the room, carrying cups of punch. His face was attractive, she thought, but it was simply a man's face. His arms, the tanned, muscular arms she had once stared at with longing, were merely arms.

The band began to play "Alleluia," the song that had won first prize for Israel in the Eurovision Song Contest. It was a catchy tune with a chorus that repeated, "Alleluia to the world." The floor soon filled with couples, including Dahlia and her eight-year-old son.

"How about it?" Joe said. Lucy leaned against his shoulder as they danced, and when the song ended, they walked to the edge of the terrace. A warm wind blew gently in their faces, carrying the scent of pine and orange blossoms.

"You know I made a promise," Joe said.

"I bet you're regretting it already, now that we're back in the soft sheets."

He laughed and pointed a finger at her.

"I'm going to let you off the hook."

"I'm not sure I want to be let off," he said. The candles on the tables flickered in a sudden puff of wind. "We made it out of the desert."

"The desert isn't so bad."

"That's what I'm afraid of. The longer you stay, the harder it is to leave."

"The freedom."

"The endless spaces."

He put his arm around her shoulders. "I would do it."

"I know you would. But I made a promise too. If we found our way back, I would appreciate what we have."

She turned to him, her eyes moist and shining. "It's no small thing to have a friend."

10

A Yellow Cab pulled away from the congested exit ramp at Los Angeles International Airport. The late afternoon sun came through the window, warming the backs of the two travelers, who, in twenty hours, had made their transit from one Holy Land to another. They stared in fascination at what seemed an unending stream of large, gleaming cars—Mercedes and Mustangs and Jaguars and Cadillacs and Firebirds and Porsches.

The taxi drove past Marina Del Rey, with its miles and miles of pleasure-boat slips, then along Pacific Avenue, where there was a whirl of people in bathing suits and leotards, jogging and roller skating to music piped in their ears from radio headphones.

Turning onto a narrow lane, the cab stopped before a pink bungalow. The travelers spoke hesitantly.

"You're sure?" Joe said.

"No, I mean, yes, I'll be okay," Lucy said. "There are phones here, if I remember correctly?"

The driver carried her bag through the gate and across the garden to the door. Lucy noticed the Jacuzzi was clogged with dirt and dead leaves. In another time, the sight would have upset her, but she merely thought, in passing, it'll have to be drained.

She slipped her key in the lock and, with a shudder, the door gave way. Silent rooms greeted her. She walked through the living room, then up the stairs to her bedroom, where the light had an unfamiliar ocher cast.

The house looked out of proportion, the rooms were smaller and narrower than she remembered. The chairs seemed too low, the ceiling too high. She did not know how to move about the place. The floors creaked, the colors were strange, even the ferns and cactus plants had different shapes than when she last had seen them.

Her mail, collected by a neighbor, was heaped in confusion on the table. She picked up several pieces and was scanning the return addresses when she started. It was the doorbell; she went to answer it.

"Hi, I'm Joe. Want some company tonight?"

She laughed, feeling a thrill of relief. "My place or yours?"

He took his bags into the living room. "I couldn't go home, I felt like the guides did after leaving Santa."

"I know, I'm totally disoriented."

"Anything to drink here?"

"Haven't looked yet."

Together, they opened the refrigerator and found some shriveled apples, an old bag of carrots and a six-pack of Tab. She poured the Tab into glasses, but it tasted bitter and medicinal. "Let's make some tea."

They switched on lamps, for the sun had gone down, and built a fire from driftwood stacked on the patio. Then they pulled up wicker chairs, propped their feet on the coffee table and sat back, sipping peppermint tea.

"I don't know what to make of this," Lucy said. "Every time my eyes glance at the window, I think I'm going to see red mountains."

"When I was in the cab, I had the impulse to drive right back to the airport."

She laughed softly. "How long do you suppose it will be . . ."

"Before this all seems normal?"

"Before everything glosses over."

"A week."

"No," she said.

"Maybe longer. Soon, though, you'll be telling somebody what happened, and you'll realize, there's no life in the words anymore. It's a story. No matter how close you come to the edge, in time, it's just another story."

In fact, Joe was only partially correct. For what had happened in Sinai—specifically what had happened that night in the cave during the flood—was to have far-reaching effects.

Within a month of their return to California, Lucy would meet the man she was to marry (though she would not know him at first), the man with whom she would move away from the beach, to a neighborhood of ranch homes with basketball hoops over the garages and tricycles in the yards. It was a neighborhood in which she had never imagined she would live, let alone be happy.

Within a month, Joe would sign an agreement to direct his first feature film. Within a month, Achmed would receive a round-trip ticket to Amsterdam.

On this night of their reentry, though, as Lucy and Joe sat in wicker chairs, they could not sense what was to come. They were exhausted and yet tense, like children who are fighting going to bed. They stared into the fire, watching the smooth and sculpted pieces of driftwood burn. They talked softly, and listened to the waves. The fire sputtered and died, and still they did not move, wanting to extend this moment, this crossing, that would not be repeated in their lives.

Finally, when the first light shone through the curtains, they helped each other stand. With the streetlamps winking in the fog, Joe drove away in a taxi and Lucy went to sleep.

FREE!!
BOOKS BY MAIL
CATALOGUE

BOOKS BY MAIL will share with you our current bestselling books as well as hard to find specialty titles in areas that will match your interests. You will be updated on what's new from Pocket Books at no cost to you. Just fill in the coupon below and discover the convenience of having books delivered to your home.